D1799998

Masks

Also by Bishop & Fuller

Available at www.damnedfool.com

Conrad Bishop & Elizabeth Fuller

Masks

— a historical fantasy —

WordWorkers Press
Sebastopol CA

Masks

© 2021 Conrad Bishop & Elizabeth Fuller

All rights reserved.
This work is fully protected under the copyright laws of the United
States of America and all other countries of the Copyright Union.
No part of this publication may be reproduced in any form without
prior consent of the copyright holders, except in the case of brief
quotes embodied in critical articles and reviews.

Printed in the United States of America.

For information:
indepeye@gmail.com

For purchases:
www.damnedfool.com

ISBN: 978-0-9997287-6-5
LCCN: 2020922949

Book design by F. Ackerman

*This story is dedicated to
the actors, bards, and minstrels who've traveled the long road
for millennia.*

Contents

—Dedication—

To Theodoric the Stout, my lord, my liege, my corpulent muse, I offer these words in humble thanks for your nobility, your patronage, and your succulent roast boar. May God patter blessings upon your balding pate and my scribbles brighten these years through which we flounder like ducklings bereft of their mother.

I thank our Holy Virgin for a master to whom I may speak truth without risk of flagellation, a master willing to declare himself *the Stout*. My lord, you are stout indeed: stout of humor, stout of heart. In your cups at midnight, you have opened your soul in friendship transcending rank, and I honor the grace within your impressive bulk.

One tipsy night, at your promptings, I spoke of my boyhood odyssey. You tasked me to set it in writing—for posterity's diversion, I surmise, as my disorderly cat frisks with a ball of yarn. That odd sidewise tilt of your head implied that your whim was command.

And so I approach this task with trepidation. In maturity, I have striven to make my life uneventful. Perhaps I have become too complacent in my daily routine as steward and scribe, allowing my frame to thicken and my soul to crave the wine of late afternoon. Perhaps you felt that I needed to make my bygone journey anew, however I might prefer to stay fixed in quotidian cares. The hero Odysseus risked journeys to Troy and to Hades but not to the scenes of his childhood: riskier far.

Mine is a modest saga. Scant blood is shed. It offers no Cyclops, no Circe, no fall of great cities. At its conclusion I do call forth the end of the world, but as you once said, *We come daily to Armageddon.* Accordingly, I harness up for the journey. From my stool I lift Mia, my querulous cat, swat a persistent bottle fly, and sharpen the tip of my reed. I check that all ghosts are aboard the donkey cart and commence my long night ride into the blazing sun.

—1—
The Road

"Sunlight today!" Papa called outwha as he always did at sunrise unless it was raining frogs. Early spring was wet, and the wind at night off the gulf found every crack in the walls, but the past week had been clear.

"Bragi! Up!" Mama's voice of command. He whined in protest, rolled off his pallet, wrestled into his breeches and tunic, and stumbled out the door to pee in the yard. It came to him, mid-pee, that today was the start.

The rains were done, Gramma was moving better, and it was time to load up. To the boy the tour meant long days of walking or waiting, each night a different place. Last year he got lice the first day and scratched himself raw. He remembered the heat, the sunburn, the drunken muleteers, the howling of wolves, the raucous laughter—and couldn't wait to get started.

"What about lice?" the boy asked Gramma.

"See one, I'll spit in its eye."

The boy was six, they said when anyone asked, but the family never reckoned by Saint's Day. They sometimes attended Mass, but for them one story of gods was as good as another: a story was a story. They reckoned his age by the trips: he was born six tours ago.

The birth, his mother had told him, befell coming home by sea. A pregnant woman aboard made the sailors fearful, and as her water broke a storm blew up. The night hours were fraught with peril of being thrown overboard, but with the babe's crowning at sunrise the winds died sharply, his wails cleared the skies, and the sailors danced.

His infancy was ruled by the wheel of the sun. Spring and summer the family trod the road, and autumn chill brought them home. When absent their haggard neighbor Agnasa tended their plantings, their chickens, the cow, the goat and the annual piglet soon to be salt pork. Returning, they hosted a feast for the villagers, regaling them with travel tales—mostly true—and music of pipes and lute. Then the winter's work: roof repairs, cold-weather crops, butchering the pig, arranging next summer's tour. In those months the boy forgot that much of his short life had been lived on the endless road.

"Bragi, go feed the pig before we go. Look alive!" His mother was sharp today.

He would miss their snug but drafty dwelling, a single room for Papa, Mama, Gramma, with himself in the loft—and he loved the goat he called Goat. He liked milking the cow, though he was never moved to name her, as she ignored his existence. And Gramma forbade him naming the piglet: "No names for a friend you're going to eat."

He liked chasing chickens, but he worried what he'd do if he caught one. Gramma would grab the head and swing it around till the chicken flew off its neck. It did its flop dance and they'd have chicken stew for dinner. He wondered if dead people flopped. He knew people died, but he'd only seen old Demetriou, who was no different dead than alive. Did women die? "Of course we do," said Gramma. She teased him a lot.

"Bragi, don't touch that hamper!" his mother snapped.

"Can I carry it?"

"Just carry your little butt to the cart!"

He was eager to go. His friend Nico had died in the winter, a sennight after they'd had a fight. The hamlet was half a morning away, and some of the boys wouldn't play with him. "Their people don't give us trouble," said Gramma, "but they think we're strange. The kids pick it up." The neighbors would come to their feast and drink their wine, but their family didn't fit in.

His father examined their donkey Truggie—her hooves, her mouth, a chafing on her withers—and hitched up the laden cart. Their costumes were in heavy bags, the reed basket held food and cooking gear, and their bed rolls were bound by rope. Mama carried the wicker hamper out to the cart. She was always the one who carried it, though she didn't look like she liked to.

"What's in it, Mama?"

"Never mind."

As they jostled down the lane the boy felt the thrill of beginnings. He remembered gravestones and an ancient squiggly tree and the statue with its head and its dangle knocked off. It would be a two-day journey along the gulf, a roadway rutted by forevers of feet and wagon wheels. At times a village or a stand of wispy trees would blot the gulf, as smooth as a pond, but he felt secure with the cliffs to his left, the shore to his right, and Truggie's beckoning ears. A stretch of calm before the baffling city's tangle.

They hit a sharp pothole. "Still got all your teeth?" Papa called out. He had lost one baby tooth—the left front chopper, Gramma called it—and the other was loose. Papa always said funny stuff, funny the way he said it, with dumb wonderment at the marvels of life.

Bragi could never sleep on the first night out. They camped in an open field and he heard the familiar chorus of creepy things, but no walls to muffle the din. On the second day, the donkey went surly and weak, balking at every bridge or fording. That night, in their hill camp above the port city that glowed with countless specks, Truggie lay down on her side, gave a mighty shiver and snort, and died.

"Off to a merry start!" Papa's voice was cheery, his brows raised in clownish awe, but his eyes were tired.

Gramma hugged the boy as he cried for Truggie, yet he felt oddly relieved. They had bought the donkey two years before, and in infantile bullheadedness he had demanded to name her Truggie Poop-tail.

But a four-year-old's sins weigh heavily when six: the silliness had haunted him. Papa took most of the night digging a hole, and at dawn they rolled her into it, Bragi tugging on the beast's hind leg.

∾

My liege: lest some high-flown churl charge me with sorcery—*writings from the child of vagabonds?*—I should affirm that we were scions of an ancient line of players who proudly claimed literacy and beat it into each new generation. As a child I fumbled through the few cheap codices we owned—poets ill-spelled by slave copyists—and my father spoke of rare scrolls held in cold stone vaults. Though I have churchly schooling in the proper tongues, I write this in lowly vernacular, being a tale of simple folk. I do heed the sage advice of the ancients to mix wormwood into my inks, dissuading mice from nibbling my hard-wrought prose.

Yet I claim no wisdom in my words. Wisdom has an honored place in human endeavors—like a sacred chapel never entered.

∾

From the seaport they would cross westward by ferry craft. The year before they had gone directly up the coast, but his father heard that the leather-heads were rampant again and it wasn't worth the risk. The boy wished he could see a leather-head. From a safe distance.

In past years the ferry had come midafternoon, so late morning they broke camp above the port and jostled into the city pulling the donkeyless cart—Papa on one shaft, the women on the other, Bragi pushing his father's backside. The first sight was the stretch of reddish tile roofs, then a glare of whitewashed walls and the masts far distant. Patrae, his father called it, was the port for all the western seas to the edge of the world. They pressed their way to the harbor where a dozen ships and barges were docked, a jumble of sail and oar, rope ladders, prows, spider-web nets, tall masts alongside flat crafts that the boy imagined must be the grandmas. The swarm of crewmen and dock hands was as varied as the ships: every sort of tunic, cape and cloak, breeches, a toga, tight-molded leather armor, earrings, tattoos, a breastplate of bronze. The streets above the harbor were scattered with women in gaudy attire, shadowed eyes, crimson lips with the fetchingest smiles.

Yes, the ferry would come, his father was told. They found the shade of an ancient olive tree standing sentinel in the harbor. Mama went off to buy a new donkey. Husbands ruled over wives, the boy knew, so Papa was boss, but Mama ran the show. "You have to be really smart to know you're dumb," his father said cheerfully. Not dumb when he leapt to the trestle stage and sparked waves of laughter, but dumb in making deals. "The way she bargains," he told his son, "she could stand at the gates of Troy and they'd give up the haggle."

The wait was endless. Leaning against his drowsing grandma, Bragi watched the world. A fruit-seller passed with grapes, and a red-faced woman who could barely waddle waddled past. Cargo was unloaded and brought new smells. Warm browns, a whir of sharp yellows, the tang of civet. But the plague, Bragi knew, came from breathing bad air. Could he smell the smells without dying? Would he breathe too much? Fear was a brother who slept beside him, unspeaking and blind.

The sun bore down. Two tall men, sailors they must be, squatted by a line of barrels, playing dice. Their faces and hands were black as pitch. How could they be so black? Were they black all over? Bragi saw them buy almonds from a nut-seller, and they munched like real people did.

Mama returning, Bragi blinked awake and rose from the shade. He saw the new donkey tethered to a post and started to cry, though he'd never forgiven Truggie for that stupid name. "What's wrong now?" Mama hugged him impatiently. The new creature was taller by a hand. Papa surveyed him as Mama pointed out its features. Its rear legs bowed, its middle sagged, but it had strength in the withers. "He might not last the journey," she said. "Four months, I don't know. But he still has some roadway in him."

Bragi hated the beast on sight. His brown coat shagged off in patches—an old rag donkey, thought the boy. His mother explained that he was shedding, having come from the mountain chill, and a curry would make him good as new. "And look," she said, "the tip of his muzzle is white, and white just under his eyes!" Bragi hated his mother's talking the way she'd talk to a six-year-old.

She recounted the bargaining, the price, the donkey-seller's bluster, his huge nose and ravening mustache. "Some day his whiskers will eat his nose."

Gramma hugged her. "Thanks be to the gods that gave my dummy son a smart wife."

"Thanks be the smart wife was dumb enough to marry me," said Papa—his mouth like a duck bill aslant—and hugged them both.

The donkey had a twitch in his eye, but he seemed content. Bragi tried to keep hating him, but he liked the white muzzle tip and the donkey-seller's mustache. To please his mother, he patted the beast.

"So now you can name him. He's a jack so he wants a boy's name." Bragi's heart sank. Always, names.

Names were another fuddle in a world of befuddlements. I was Bragi, and at times I cringed at its oddity. My father Mikolaus, Mik for short, my grandma (his mother) Edra, and my own mother Asta. But why call them Mama and Papa when everyone knew them as Asta and Mik? Gramma I called Gramma, but Papa called her Ma and Mama called her Mother. And Mama said that if I'd been born a girl they'd have named me Mia.

"What happened to Mia?" I asked.

"There isn't any Mia. You were a boy."

"But where is she?"

"It's a name, Bragi. It's just a name."

"Whose is it?"

Very early I learned that thinking could drive you crazy. I asked my questions over and over again. They explained with diminishing patience. And Mia my cat lies drowsing, her tail a-twitch.

They awaited the ferry. The afternoon sun was fierce for early spring, though the wind off the harbor was chill. The kelp beneath the surface sheen danced a soft dance and gave off a shadowy stench.

Bragi noticed a little girl—black hair, thin as a fisher-bird—wandering along the dock as if from that undersea world, but he'd sooner play with boys. He looked away, then back. She was gone.

Papa and Mama were running lines. They would set the words, but in the show they often changed it. "You know where you want it to go," Papa told him once, "but you follow where it leads." They played the main roles, and Gramma played crones and witches and anything else.

"You'll be in the shows when you're older," Gramma would say, though he was older every day. Not that he wanted to be a player: he'd be a soldier. Soldiers clanked, clattered and growled, and people got out of their way. Whereas being a player was just yelling your lines and walking the road. "Long road," said Gramma, "but that's life." He didn't want to hear that. He loved Gramma, but she had never been a child.

Nowhere to escape the sun or the sea stink. Bragi wriggled his toes in the dust, patted the donkey, picked at its shaggy hair. He spotted a scrawny brindle cat and gave chase. Feral cats could be mean, though he'd luckily never caught one. He went behind the tree and peed—one thing he could always count on.

The ferry did not arrive. "It'll come when it does," his father said. Mik knew of an inn where they once stayed, so he hitched the new donkey to the cart and they went to search it out. Like many seaports, there was one street harborside and steep narrow lanes branching into the hills. Up one lane, down another, persuading the cranky donkey to turn the cart around corners. "Like the first time I ever got drunk," said Mik, and staggered his comical stagger. They asked directions, but to no avail.

"Good part is, folks try to be helpful," Gramma groused to Bragi. "Bad part is, they're stupid." She ached from the climb, Asta was stalwart, Bragi bored. Mik called to a tall shabby man, who froze as they approached. His face in the flat light of sunset was as steep and bony as the twisted streets, with a tangled mat of hair, a wide flat nose like a mushroom, and a strangeness about one eye. It was Ludd, though they didn't know it yet.

"Three Sirens Inn?"

"Right there."

They were standing in front of it. Mik thanked the bony man, who raised a questioning finger. "You know of work?"

"Work?"

"I need work."

"Sorry, we're waiting for the ferry."

"There's pirates, they said." He had an odd whine to his voice, like a baby in a barrel.

Mik stared at the stranger. "Need something to eat?" Asta made a curt grunt: Bragi knew Mama hated beggars. Mik offered a coin.

"Thank you, noble sir," the man said, escaping around the corner.

Mik turned to Bragi, went cross-eyed, and stood on his toes, mimicking nobility. "Call me Your Grace." Tired as he was, Bragi tried to laugh.

A wispy husk of an innkeeper answered the bell. He had a room, so they jostled through a gate to the stables, unhitched the donkey, and lugged their baggage upstairs. Asta carried the wickerwork hamper—hers alone to touch. The innkeeper led them up steep steps. Bragi felt shaky, teetering on the stairs: he couldn't remember sleeping on an upper floor. What if the room fell off? There were two narrow beds, one for Mik and Asta, one for Gramma, and a floor mat for Bragi. Gramma scanned the bedding: no sign of bugs, so they might have a good night's sleep.

The wickerwork hamper sat inside the door. *Hamper* or *casket*, they said, though they rarely spoke of it. As big as might hold a half-grown pig, a brass clasp to its leather strap, and its color changed with the light—dark brown, yellowish tan, or a leprous white. It wasn't a basket: you put parsnips in a basket. He had touched it once and his mother slapped his hand. A light slap, but she'd meant it.

"There's word of pirates," the innkeeper said, forcing a toothless smile. He disappeared.

They poured oil in the lamp and lit the wick. "Go out and play," Mama said, adding, "Don't get lost." He crept down the steep steps and through a room where men were drinking and reeling and yelling bad words. A drunken man bared his broken yellow teeth as he groped a painted woman's titties. She didn't seem to notice.

Squatting in the stony street was the little girl from the dock—barefoot, elbows gawky, her dress a rough-woven sack. Digging a cobble, she stared up at him. All one side of her face was an angry bruise, lent a purple glow by torchlight from the tavern. Her slitted cat eyes met his. Bragi gasped, startled. "What's your name?"

The girl stared a long time, answered with a guttural "Dunno."

At least she could talk. "What you here for?"

"Poppy."

"Where's he?"

"Drunk."

Maybe the yellow-tooth groper in the inn. "How come?"

"Likes to."

He couldn't think more to say. He squatted beside her and ran his hand on the paving stones. He spotted an orangish cat and tried to coax it to come, but the cat knew better than trust small humans. Again, he asked her name. She spat.

"Whatcha doing?"

"Spit."

"How come?"

She bared her tiny needle teeth and spat again. She must have seen a grown up do it and thought it was fun. He tried it: it was. They started to play who could spit farthest, but Bragi was never good at games. She was the champion spitter.

"How'd you learn to?"

"Uncle."

"Who's he?"

"Sails ships."

"Sailor?"

"I gotta suck his peter."

"How come?" He didn't know what she meant, but it sounded grown-up.

Her voice was rough in the throat. "He buys us food. Then I gotta spit." Her cat eyes burned, then dulled. She dug harder at the stone.

He groped to say something grown-up. "A man said there's pirates."

She began to nod her head up and down like the beggar he'd seen who banged his skull on a wall. Gramma said that he must have a drum in his head. The girl had a drum in her head.

"Night. Poppy hide. They fuck Mum. All blood." Over and over, then she stopped. She held a stone.

"What's your name?" he asked again.

"Mum named Rona."

"But what's yours?"

Her face curdled up and she muttered a terrible curse in a tongue he didn't know. He spat at the little girl. She spat back, flung the stone at him, missed, and ran up the alley. Mama called from the upper window. He climbed the stairs stomping. He hadn't meant to spit at the little girl. He only wanted to know her.

Papa was asleep. Gramma sat up in her bed, staring into shadows. Mama poured the boy's porridge into his wooden bowl. "Tell me a story," he said. She ignored him. He spat on the floor.

"What are you doing, Bragi? Don't do that!"

"The little girl did."

"Who?"

"Rona." He knew her name was Rona.

"Nice people don't do that."

"She's nice!"

But he wasn't nice. He was a sleepy querulous little boy. He whined and stomped his foot. Gramma looked up and fixed him with her clouded left eye.

"Boy! You'll turn bright green." She could make her voice go gravelly as a gizzard. He'd seen Mama chop up a chicken and turn out the grit in its gizzard. Gramma ground him in her gizzard. "You want a story? I'll tell you about the little boy that spit."

"No!" But he said it in a whisper. She motioned him to curl down by her. He could never not do what Gramma said. Nobody could.

His eyes went to her face, lined like the map of the world he'd seen at a nobleman's once. "Look at this, it's our world," the great man said. One of Gramma's eyes was cloudy—cataract, she called it—and she had a wart on her chin.

"Oh yes. A little boy, a good little boy most times, but he wanted to be big. Big boys spit, so he thought that would make him big. But one day, you know what?"

He tried to stay silent, but he couldn't not say it. "What?"

"He spit on the toes of the goddess Edra." Gramma was Edra. She wasn't a goddess, and he never spit on her toes, but he couldn't not hear the story. "So she looked down at the little boy. She said, *Oh so you want to spit! I'll let you spit.*" Gramma's eyes bugged out like they did in the play with the burping witch. "And the little boy started to grow. He thought, *Hey, I'll be a big boy now!* But no!" Her mouth gaped like it did when she played the snake-haired monster.

"He grew bigger than his papa, bigger than a house, big as a mountain, and then *Boom!* A volcano blew out his red-hot guts. The poor little boy spewed into a million spittings over the sky." Her countenance took on a beatific air. "And when he woke, he was a weeny pile of cinders."

When Gramma told stories, they gave him dreams that scared him, but he liked the stories that gave him the dreams. Her stories, even with silly turtles or talking pigs, were the first he knew of the letting of blood, the crying of mothers, the death of sons, the rape of daughters, the screech of ravens over the vast red seepage, or the payback for spitting on floors. Stories taught what had to be learned: reality.

He whimpered in faint protest. It had been a long long day: breaking camp, new donkey, the bony man's mushroom nose, the spitting girl. Then he must have fallen asleep. He woke to the flash of the pirates' fire.

—11—
Pirates

Black night. Flicker. Crackle. Screams. His mother's voice filtered in from afar, then close, her grip wrenching him awake. "Bragi! Wake up! Fire!"

"Mama?"

"Up! Up now! Mik, you there? Mother?"

Fists banging a wall, then a frantic clatter. Mic was on his feet, Asta at the window slamming the shutters.

"Pirates!"

Naked against the chill, the boy scrambled into his clothes. What the girl said: pirates rowed in from ships in the night, plundered, fled with the dawn. They'd stick you like a pig, bleed you, leave you to rot.

Screech of a horse, stink of pitch, a clank of steel on stone. A babble of tongues from the innyard, a yawp of surprise, a cry and a laugh and a bark of pain. In the slivers of light through shutter cracks the boy groped for his parents. The pirates swarmed into his head, fierce as rats. He could see their teeth, their scars, their merciless eyes. All because he'd spat on the floor.

"Ma? You awake?" Mik whispered.

"Damn, I was sleeping for once." Edra scrambled to her feet, pulled her clothes straight. At once she was stumbling, floundering, lurching across the room. Somehow the boy knew what she sought. By the door was the wickerwork hamper. For a moment she stood stock still, then knelt and fumbled the clasp.

Asta grasped her wrists. "Mother, no!"

"Girl, shut up. Help me here."

"It's curst!"

"Hands off."

"Curst!"

"Lots of curses, Asta. Choose which." Her hiss cut the acrid air. "Girl, you'll be raped by a dozen men. I survived it, maybe you will. But they won't cut your throat till you see your boy—"

"Mother!"

"See your boy hoist on a pike up his little ass." Silence fell like a fist. "Your choice, girl."

The boy saw them kneeling at the hamper, both clutching the lid. A slash of light joined them. He saw the wickerwork hamper open, faces staring up. Next thing he knew, the family clattered down the steep stairs, Edra clasping his arm. "Don't be scared." They each held a sculpted face, leather by feel. "It's a mask," his grandma whispered, "Put it on when I tell you."

They groped their way toward the tumult. At the foot of the stairs, Edra clumped them facing the barred front door. Shouts, rattles, curses, grunts, the thwack of an ax.

"*Who comes?*" Edra's guttural bellow. Silence from the ax.

"Help . . ." A faint yodel of fear. The boy saw a shadow crouched inside the door: the tall bony man with the mushroom nose. "The door was— I just—"

Edra grabbed him, heaved him to his feet. No gentle granny now. "Here! Stand up! Put this on!" She thrust him a mask with one open eye, the other scarred shut. "No fear! Stand up, you ninny! No fear!" He whined. She slapped him hard. An ax split a plank of the door. "I'll bite off your balls, you baby! No fear!" A thwack. Splinters flew.

"It's a mask, it's leather," she whispered to the boy. "Pull the wig down over your head. Pretend." She motioned them to don their masks. They did. "Face the door. You're made of stone. You're gods."

Together, they stood stock still. The boy faced the door, eyes tight shut. He heard his grandmother's words—*your boy on a pike up his ass*—and wondered if she meant him.

The door shattered. Torches, axes, gleaming steel blades, and yellow blood eyes, a clutch of round-bellied boars clogged the entry, grunting, slavering, heavy with bloodlust, snorting to root their tusks. The players stood carved in stone. The pirates stopped dead. The dancing torchlight froze and the distant screams went mute. Players, pirates, flames stood benumbed. Time held its breath.

A faint harmony rose, high and sweet in a dissonance of quarter-tones and a sprinkle of gizzard grit. The boy shivered, hearing his family's voice like the sirens in the tale, and a deeper cold surged through him. A rasping whisper pronounced it: *Death*. Picking up the impulse, the masks inhaled the torches' blaze, and voices swelled up from the bowels—

Thanatos. Muerte. Mort. Umerta. Tod—

The players flashed bottomless eyes. The goddess who had been Gramma—face seamed by centuries—stepped one shudder forward. The killers edged back. Her hands began to rise, slow as the incoming tide, massive as stone. One out-breath: the pirates were gone.

The players stood ensorcelled, then roused by a flurry of wings. A dead-white raven swooped in at the door, fluttered, and perched on the bony man's shoulder. He tugged at his one-eyed mask, a terrified wriggle to free himself, but the bird held firm. The masked beings looked out to the night. The innyard was calm but for tiny jerks. The boy saw a thick-bearded man with his bare rear end sprawled atop a woman, both dead but twitching. A fur-clad burgher staggered along a wall, homeward perhaps, holding his guts as he might nurse a pet. A legless beggar writhed on the stones, a string of ears draped over his head. A mule lay comatose. A hat shop had been looted, and hats blew down the lane. A shaggy dog, set afire as the pirates fled, reeled in circles chasing its tail. The albino raven flew as the fire-stricken dog fell dead.

By fire reflected in a pool of blood, Bragi saw a ragged lump on the stones: the little girl who spat. Her crude dress was pulled up to the neck, her head askew. She was bloody from crotch to heart. Was she dead? He had never seen violent death, except last year's pig. Her face was wide with surprise, and her eyes found his.

The boy's veins were the ice of a god. At last his blood seeped back and he breathed. One by one, they removed their faces. Edra took the leather mask from the bony man, who waved a vague good-bye, rubbed at the talons' sting in his shoulder, and vanished into the shadows.

They climbed the stairs to their room. Asta fumbled for the striker and relit the oil lamp. Bragi examined the mask he held: molded leather, rims reinforced with reed, rounding up over the forehead and held by a mop of hair down the back. The face was long and thin with wide eyes, pug nose, and its half-open lips curled into an awestricken smile. The eyes were glittery stones, tiny slits beneath for sight, though he felt he had peered through the gems. It was only a mask, nothing scary except for knowing that he had become a god. He ran his fingers across the face before his grandma took it.

~

My grandmother Edra was schooled in survival by the player's life. Facing a mob of drunken hecklers, she might play the distressed young virgin mincing down to the edge of the stage to cut them a resonant fart. Once encountering roadway brigands, she bargained to tell their fortunes and sent them off with visions of wealth. Confronting yellow blood eyes, she summoned the means to foil Sir Flop.

Sir Flop was known to every bard, tumbler, or player—as my grandma taught my father and my father taught me. You sniffed him from far away, and abruptly this huge reeking knight in greasy black armor rode upon you. His quest was to make you fail, so the moment you smelled him, you threw yourself into a song or a juggle, you spouted a sure-fire speech from another play, you mimicked a seizure, or you did what you'd never done: stick a mask on your face and pretend you're a god. Whatever you could—then a roll of the dice decided. "Like throw yourself off a cliff and grow wings as you fall," my grandmother said.

And later I heard her tell Asta that, no, she wasn't raped by a dozen men, it was only five, and despite the burning pain, she had whispered to the last one, "You're the best." In gratitude he refrained from cutting her throat.

All tales are tales of survival, even those leading, as mine, to the death of Nine Realms. Our sole imperative is that of the slug on the stem of a weed: to survive. With luck the slug lives to tell it.

〜

Edra said the pirates might return but thought not, and they did not. She gathered the masks, handed them to Asta, who nested them into the hamper, shut the lid, and snapped the clasp.

The wicker showed patches of worn dull red. A leather strap encircled it. Were there other gods within? The boy couldn't risk asking. Asta opened the shutters, shut them again, though she must have known that her child could never shut the shutters in his mind. Mik embraced her from behind. She stood motionless. At last she turned, placed her hand on her husband's heart, then leaned away and blew out the oil lamp.

Bragi was sleepless. He saw the dead who littered the stones and heard the living slink back to bury the dead. The silence made too much noise. He heard whispering. Mama and Gramma—

"Wrong, wrong, wrong."

"Had to."

"Not ever."

"Go to sleep."

He listened, trying to grab a clue. The hamper was opened. Was it the story Gramma told of plagues set loose from some lady's jar? Nightmares unleashed?

"Girl, hear me. Players wore masks in the old days. Way back a dozen granddads ago. It's just masks."

"It's gods."

"It's leather. No gods in a cow."

The boy imagined a cow full of gods and giggled.

"Bragi, go to sleep!"

"I got a flea bite." No bedbugs, but they'd brought their own fleas.

"We've all got flea bites. Go to sleep."

He heard a rustle, and his mother was kneeling beside him. She stroked his brow. "Sleep, sleep now." He wanted her touch, but there was a tenseness in it, forcing a comfort she couldn't feel. He started to cry but turned away, ashamed to cry at the age of six. He was seeing the little girl.

"Go to sleep, honey."

"Is the little girl dead?"

"What little girl?"

"The one that spit."

"That happens."

"She was all blood."

"Well then she's dead." Cold, flat.

He wanted Mama to hold him hard or hit him, or maybe he wanted to nurse. He remembered nursing or thought he did. But now he was six, almost grown, and grown-ups had no mothers. Gramma was Papa's mother but not really any more, and the little girl's mother was dead and maybe the little girl. He couldn't stop thinking, thinking, thinking.

His mother squinted to see him, and he tried to make his eyes as deep as the donkey's so she couldn't see to the bottom. It wasn't only the little girl or the bloody men or the dog on fire: it was other worlds. Her eyes caught a glint of light, and he saw her terror of seeing that he could see.

∼

Much later, when I was a boy no longer, she confided to me that from girlhood she saw the Nine Realms. She was born of the cold, and her father brought her southward. She was the strange one, she knew. A priest of the Cristers once told her, "You see what the dead can see. Don't ever let anyone know." She wanted to ask her father, a warrior who knew death, but he was dead by then. And a father's words were water off a duck. She had heard a man say *water off a duck*, and that suited so many things.

In her girlhood, her father would make long voyages. She tended the sheep with her sister, and once as a tiny girl she climbed the ridge behind their farmstead, under the glacier's fingers, found a hole in the lava rock, and did the most magical thing she could think to do: she pooped in it. (I heard her once, giggling, tell Gramma.) When the men returned, they would feast, and a bard sang their exploits—slaying, pillaging, gathering gold and slaves. She thrilled to the song of the bard but tasted the blood of the plunder. Her mother said he did what had always been done: earning their living and the gods' applause, and that was the way of it. She smelled the worlds.

~

Now, in the glint of the dying fires, the boy saw that she feared his seeing. He felt a tremor between them, and then he was asleep. Someone's crying woke him. It took him a moment to know that the crying was his.

"I'll take him, Asta."

His grandmother curled down by him, and he snuggled to her. She wasn't as jumpy as Mama—more like a snoozing dog who lay flat in the sun. Not a goddess, just a saggy old pillow—she was Gramma again.

"Who were we?" he asked.

"Honey?"

"When we stood there?"

"Go to sleep now."

"Can't."

"We were pretending then. Just to fool'em. That's all done with." She put soft hands around him and took a deep breath. "It's over now, sweetheart. It was just masks, your mama's old masks that we cart along cause they belonged to her daddy. And they were good, weren't they? They scared the bad men."

"The one-eye . . ."

"And wasn't that funny when the raven landed? Right on the skinny man's shoulder. That was so funny."

He tried to keep asking questions, but she hummed a shush and he slipped into sleep. The dreams came in flashes. He watched his father butcher last winter's pig. He had cried for the pig but then he ate it. He dreamt other dreams that fled.

He woke. The moon was full, shining through open shutters. Gramma was back in her bed with a gentle snore. Bragi wanted to go to the window to see if the little girl was still dead, but he couldn't. He tried to go back to sleep, but the fleas were biting, eating him up like the winter pig. He felt for Gramma again, but she wasn't there. If he looked out the window now, the moon might have washed it all clean. He groped his way to the moonlight.

The gods were there. He saw a one-eyed god, a flutter, the raven. He saw a shining god. He saw gods eating apples, gods with the faces of vultures flying into the wind. He saw a great serpent, a snarling wolf, and a god pulling off his face to reveal a face with a sunless grin. He saw mountains catch fire.

The boy ran back from the window but woke as he flopped on his mat. He had only been dreaming. He scratched a bite. Fleas could be fierce in the moonlight.

Voices. He wasn't the only one awake. He listened as children listen to grown-ups, trying to grab a clue.

"What happens now?" Asta whispered to Mik. The boy heard a little girl's whimper from his mother. He had never heard her that way.

"Now? We wait for the ferry. What's done is done, my love."

"I hope it's done." She made a long sniffle as if she'd been crying. Her nose was stuffed.

"We had to. I could have put up a fight, but we'd all been pretty much dead by now. But, hey, we survived and we're in bed and you got a good price on the donkey."

The boy knew her silence. When talk was pointless, his mother kept silent. At last she spoke, just to finish the day. "We think we see the worst, but how do we know the worst is the worst till all that happens happens?"

"We should use that line for a play."

～

I was six. How many times, over the next forty years, would I be six again? That age when bafflement clouds the skies? When the front teeth uproot? When conundrums swarm like blowflies? When the legs and the arms can't stay still? When every word is *Why?* Over the course of years, there were many days when I felt I was six again.

—III—
New Donkey

My liege, I am deeply honored that you have read my scatterings, even more that you commend them. Yet I must resist your counsel that I make explicit the year and the route of our expedition. A reader's expectations, surely, but untrue to my childhood confusion.

In hindsight, I might chart the locales or name the kinglings and popelets who have fallen about us like figs in the tempest. But at that age I awoke in daily bewilderment, knowing not when nor whence nor wherefore, utterly subject to the movement of history's bowels. I must therefore see with my boyhood's blurred vision.

～

He woke to bright sun splashing over the ceiling, and at first he thought it was all a dream—the bloody eyes, the little girl, the dead-white raven. But his flea bites itched, and the others moved about the room etched in the morning glare. It was real. He was still six but older by ages.

"Sunlight!" Mik cried, as if for the first time ever, seeing his son awake. The stubby clown father grabbed his own ear and stretched his neck to pull himself tall. He shuddered as if freezing, then smiled broadly. Bragi held back a laugh.

His mother stood gazing at the wickerwork hamper. She was taller than Papa, thin and sharp like a reed. Asta: the name had a bite of lemon. The boy had seen a goddess in a temple—slender, face to the world, cold stone. Was it she?

A fly buzz, a doggy sea smell, rattles and creaks and an ox driver's curse from the innyard—another day. Edra hobbled to him with a limp. Had he never noticed her limp? She knelt on his mat, stroked his brow, placed her hands on the sides of his head as if hefting a melon, surveying his eyes for scars. "Get up, hon. Food."

The family had their own supplies, but today they descended the narrow stairs to the tavern. They sat at a heavy trestle table. The innkeeper appeared, the wispy old man with palsy, his hands like quivering leaves, his upper teeth gone. He had seen death at his door and distrusted the morning light. He set bread and a hunk of cheese before them, and a flagon of stinking wine. Mik went to check on the donkey.

Bragi tore off a hunk of bread and moved to a bench by the smoldering hearth. He curled against the wall, munched his bread, ignored his mother's summons to the table. Edra rose and sat on the bench beside him, sipping her wine. Her taste was failing, she claimed, so she drank it unwatered.

"Well, you're old enough now," she said, "so I'll tell you about the masks." He wasn't sure he wanted to be old enough, but if grownups had things to tell you, they would. "Masks. They've been with your ma since girlhood." He knew that. "You know that, yes, but stories start from the start." This was going to be long. "So your ma was born in the North. They raised sheep, but her dad sailed out summers to bring back silver, cattle, slaves, all that."

"Was he a pirate?" Bragi had never thought to ask.

Gramma turned to the hearth and poked the coals. From the table came Asta's curt voice. "Don't say fool things. He and the men, they did what was needed. They never killed folks unless they fought back. That wasn't like a pirate. Pirates even kill girls they could sell for whores. He was making ends meet. Understand?"

"Yes." He didn't.

"My father's name was Bragi. That's your name. We named you after him. Are you a pirate?"

"No."

"Then neither was he."

Asta finished her food. The shivery innkeeper brought them a basket of figs, and Bragi took a fat one, then another. The man's squint pulled his mouth into a smile.

"My name is Torr. What's yours?"

"Bragi."

"The poet!" He ruffled Bragi's hair, turned to Asta and spoke a strange tongue of whoops and wheedles, the way sheep would speak if they spoke. She stared as she might at a dog, uncertain whether it would wag or snap. The innkeeper stood like a little lost boy awaiting a word in his native tongue. Asta was mum.

Edra leaned close to the boy. "He's talking the tongue of your ma when she was a little girl. Now don't eat more figs: you'll get a thunder gut." She took the last fig and ate it. The innkeeper nodded and disappeared to the back. "You'll be a poet," Gramma said, and pinched the boy's nose as if to make it poet-shaped. He wondered what a poet was and if they carried swords.

Mik returned to report that the donkey was safe but no word of the ferry. Bragi finished his bread and nudged his grandma to tell about the masks, but she pointed to her mouth: the bread was tough. If he kept nudging, she might grin wide and show her dog teeth and make a scary face, so he did and she did and he laughed—his first laugh since before Truggie died. "All right then," she said.

She began with traders making their way to the south and lodging a night at the farmstead. They drove three pack mules with loads of amber, and they showed little Asta a piece of the luminous stone. "Like honey that's froze," said the child, and they laughed. They spoke of the great southern city—people by thousands, trees dripping with fruit, streets of gold, a building up to the sky. The kings, they informed her father, hired soldiers to fight their battles and knew of the Northmen's skills. The pay was twice what he made from his summer raids. When he ran his fingers over a trader's tempered blade, his warrior spirit leapt. "No more fuckin' sheep," he said. He hated sheep and he hated snow, so when Asta was eight years old, he sold their land to kinsmen and journeyed southward.

"And he brought along the hamper of masks—"

Bragi had heard all that before. "I know."

"Who's telling this?" She made her old-witch face, long lip and droopy tongue. Bragi shrugged. "I'm telling you why your mother's the way that she is."

"What way?" He knew better than to ask. Now she would take twice as long to get to the new part.

She picked a while at the wart on her chin, then continued. "So the journey took moons, and your ma's mother Birgid and sister Mia caught the fever and died. I told you that, I know. That's what Asta told me. They came to the city, and her father was took for a soldier. And all that way, he had brought the wickerwork. Let's go outdoors. It stinks in here."

They went out to an innyard bench under a low tree with broad curly leaves whose shadows dappled the cobbles. The debris had been cleared away. The boy saw a tiny gecko poised in the sun. He looked up to see a hawk and thought of the little girl—hawks would be good spitters. A broken gate swung crazily on its hinges as Mik trotted down to the harbor to check for a boat. What would he do, thought Bragi, if they had to stay longer? Could he play with the little girl if she wasn't dead?

Edra continued the tale. "Remember, your mother was a little girl, curious like you, and the hamper, she asked, *What's in it? Why carry it place to place?* So before he went off to war, he told her." Bragi waited as she picked her lower teeth.

"No danger in soldiering, he told her. Not like raiding a village where a peasant might brain you with a rock. The army was disciplined, rank on rank, with the very best weapons—the battles more like harvesting barley. But he got killed. I know I told you that." She shifted her buttocks on the splintery bench.

"Course this is what Asta told me, and stories change in the telling. The hamper was full of gods." Now the story was new. The

Northmen raided a seacoast town and were swarmed by a rabble with pikes and sickles. They scattered the brutes and ravaged the town, as they'd warned if not offered respect. "And Gerd came into a swineherd's shack, burst through the door—"

"You said his name was Bragi."

Edra glared at him till he lowered his eyes. "People's names change. They get named the way donkeys do, but they change. He was Gerd to start with, but then he was Bragi. Someday they might call you Truggie."

"No."

"Or Bugsie or Fleabite?"

"No!"

Edra sat mute. Bragi watched a fly buzz at a bloodstain on the cobbles. "Then what?" He watched the gecko who basked in the sun and showed no fear of Gramma.

Her old eyes narrowed and her voice went back in time. "So this little shack, he breaks in—this is Asta's father, your granddad on your mother's side—he breaks in. There's an old geezer, sorcerer most like. He's waving a stubble of mistletoe, dead mistletoe, but then the mistletoe's changed. It's a cudgel. *Peace, old man*, says Gerd—later he's Bragi but now he's Gerd—and the old fool comes charging straight at him—"

She broke off. Mik returned through the broken gate. The boat might come at dusk, but nobody knew. "I'll get Asta. We need to work on the donkey play." He went into the inn.

"What then?" Bragi pleaded.

"I need a nap." Gramma blew her nose on her fingers, flicked snot at the tree trunk, closed her eyes, and dropped off to sleep sitting up. He huddled against her. He would have to wait till she woke, a thousand flea bites hence. He couldn't hurry Gramma. She sensed his thirst, and now she would draw out the torment, feeding him in sips. She loved the child and he knew it, but she teased him to fury. Perhaps she thought it would help him survive. Perhaps it did.

It was early afternoon. Bragi saw an older boy tossing a ball in the air and catching it, a blown-up pig's bladder or maybe a goat's.

He must have come from the hills where they herded goats. He wore threadbare leggings and a cracked leather cloak, a pointy wool cap with the tip bent forward, and the dark pinched face of a weasel. Bragi approached from a distance. The boy spoke in a freakish dialect.

"Name?"

"Bragi."

"Funny."

"It's mine." They might have got in a fight, but the sun was growing fierce, so they tossed the bladder back and forth. Bragi was proud to play with an older boy. "It'll be hot today," he ventured.

"God make sun."

"What god?"

"God."

Bragi knew that lots of people, the Cristers they were called, believed in a god named God and ate bread and wine and thought they were eating their god. Maybe God tasted good.

"You pray Lord Yesu?" the older boy asked.

"Okay."

They had few words in common. The older boy spoke in a whackety-clackity tongue that Bragi could barely grasp, but too much comprehension might have started a fight. In a flash, Bragi knew that the donkey's name should be Yesu.

Gramma called, and the older boy ran off to his future, if he ever managed to get there. Bragi felt the familiar sinking. He would make a friend and then move on. Once in a strange land—desert trees, zingy food, baking sun—a huge beast was tied to a post, a camel, his father said later. A boy his own age, tending it, said, "Yitzak." Bragi didn't know if that was a sneeze or the name of the beast. The boy laughed and patted the camel. "Yitzak." Bragi reached out, touched the beast, and the boys were brothers forever. Some day they would ride together to far-off lands and make mighty conquests. Then his mother called him—"We're leaving!"—and he knew: he would never see his brother again. Always, partings.

Gramma's eyes were open. "What about the masks?" he asked.

"Here, let me pick your fleas."

"What happened?"

"Fleas first." She pinched a flea from his ankle. "They're fierce at the ocean."

"Gramma!"

"You can wait."

In the shade of the drooping tree Bragi twisted his torso under and over the rickety bench as Gramma picked his fleas. Nearby, Mik and Asta worked out the play. The early spring sun was scorching, but Asta craved the heat.

The players kept a stock of short farces. When they played a marketplace they did different pieces all day, and word would spread. In a great lord's hall they could play two or three in succession. Now they were making a new play inspired by Truggie's demise. "Use whatever life hands you," Mik told the boy. "You save money that way."

They worked. "So you could be making dinner?" he offered Asta. "Complain about your husband the dummy, then I come in."

"My husband the dummy, he's went off to buy a donkey, cause our old donkey's lame. He oughta be back by now. Probably got drunk."

"Or make it longer. You could do the riff of *He's dumb as a—*" It was a funny speech they'd used in different plays. The boy knew it by heart and sometimes flung out *You're dumb as a turnip* or *You're dumb as flies on fish* at kids he was playing with. They added new lines as inspiration struck.

"Dumb as a bag of beetles," Edra called out.

"That works. So finish with what? *Dumb as a handful of rabbit turds*, and then I'll come in and do a rabbit-turd face."

"You were long enough."

"Great donkey. Great price. You'll love him."

"Where is he?"

"Outside. So we walk in a circle, back to center. *There he is!* We focus down front, see him there."

Bragi whispered to Edra. "Is our donkey in it?"

"No, we pretend he's there. People can see it's pretend. Like you grab a stick and kill the dragon. Don't need a dragon to do it."

Maybe the little girl wasn't dead. She just pretended. "What about the masks?"

"That's a big greedy one." She pinched a flea.

"Gramma!" She would never finish the story. They went on making the play.

"*There he is!*"

"*Well, get him up on his feet.*"

"*Can't.*"

"*Why not?*"

"*He's dead.*"

Mik looked so proud and so dumb. He gestured as if expecting the donkey to take a bow. The boy laughed. His father could capture all the ways that grownups were proud to be dumb.

"*Don't make jokes with me,*" warned Asta, seething.

"*It's true. Three days dead. Can't you smell him?*"

"*Idiot! What good's a dead donkey?*"

"*Well, they wanted twenty. I said, I'll give you ten. I drove a hard bargain. We settled at twelve-two.*"

"*But he's dead.*"

"*I pointed that out.*"

The long-suffering wife went into a frenzy, with wild grimaces: pouring down boiling oil, wringing a chicken's neck, hanging herself, flinging a cat at his head. The marketplace women would empathize.

"And so on." Asta abruptly broke off her murders and suicides. "So where is this going? I carry on a while, but then what's next?" Mik was the one who sired ideas, but Asta thought things through. "So what if I storm off and then Edra— Mother!"

"Here!" Edra called from the shade.

"So you come in, you're the old witch, you tell us you'll resurrect the donkey. Then do your conjuring bit."

"Good," said Edra without getting up. Waving her hand, "*Magic, magic, woo hoo, do stuff.* So I'll go do that a while, then we all take a look at the donkey. I'll lead it, you follow."

"*Why's it just lying there?*" asked dummy husband. "*It's lazy. I'll beat it.*"

"So he beats the dead donkey, then what?" asked Asta. "Maybe the wife beats him?"

"That'd work, but we've got three plays already where I get beat up." They stood perplexed.

"Can I be in it?" Bragi asked his grandma.

"When you're big enough to pick your own fleas."

Same thing he always asked, same thing she answered. He might run in and yell, *Don't beat Papa!* but he knew that wasn't funny. Or give the donkey a carrot and bring it back to life. Or—

"Where's the donkey?"

It was the tall bony man. He had been asleep behind the tree and poked his head around. The actors were used to intrusions, so Mik explained that the donkey was only pretend, that this was a play, and the man could watch if he didn't interrupt.

"So what if he sold some fellow the donkey's brains?" He looked as if he might have need of a donkey's brains. They ignored him, ran through the scene again, then broke for a rest. The bony man wandered off.

Bragi stared hard at his grandma. He didn't dare say it again, he could only think it: *masks, masks, masks*—

"So what was I talking about?"

"Please!" he whispered.

"Masks! You should have reminded me." She rearranged her buttocks, picked at her nose, plunged into the tale. "And here comes the old fart with his cudgel!" She grabbed the boy, protecting him from the geezer. "But Gerd swings his sword, and the sorcerer's head goes splat on the wall. End of story."

The boy waited, then murmured, "Masks?"

"Oh, the masks." She pretended to remember. "So Gerd, he ransacked the old coot's shack but all he found was that hamper. Lid wide open, faces staring up."

Years after, Gerd told his daughter of burying the headless corpse and its head, though a raider's proper role was to loot and to leave the clean-up to crows. He carried his only plunder back to the ships. For days at sea he stared into the multiple eyes and felt them cursing him. As a cloud morphs into a thunderhead, the curse took its toll, on the southward trek, in the loss of his wife and a daughter.

Before his last battle he made Asta swear a blood oath to preserve the casket. He held her right hand over the lid, slit her thumb, and let three drops of blood drip to the wickerwork. She knew not to whimper: she was a Northman's child. She still bore the scar.

"Strange we love our kids and then make'em carry a curse," said Edra.

"Why?" asked Bragi.

"He's the one that knows, except he's dead." She picked off a straggling flea. "And he changed his name to Bragi."

Why indeed? Guilt? He had killed men by the dozens just to make a living. Guilt was a spice you added only if you could afford it. Perhaps, struck by magic, he felt what it was to kill. Perhaps he himself was the wretch whose head he struck off, staring up at himself from the earthen floor. I drew no conclusions.

I have been further perplexed by the source of the masks, and you, my liege, proposed a likely answer. The treasures of your shelves—Libanius, Lucian, others—described the pantomime dancers of the days of empire, changing faces to play all roles. You surmised that some stray dancer came northward, sold his wares for the price of survival, and somehow his masks came to the swineherd, thus to my mother, thus to our donkey cart.

Yet how could masks change? How might a god of southern realms acquire a blind eye? Another, a radiant glow? Another, a singing mouth? I can only intuit that gods—or demons, as we now term them—take new forms from the soil they root in. They shine or go blind as needed. Their natures change with the vegetation.

Near twilight, Mik went down again to check on the ship to Bor. Otherwise, they would stay at the inn and offer a final feast to the fleas.

"Mama?"

"What is it, little poet?"

"Can we name the donkey Yesu?" He didn't know he was going to say it. Some things said themselves.

Edra gave her gizzard chuckle. Mama spoke up. "No, sweetie, we can't do that because Yesu is a god and people might get mad if we named a donkey after their god."

"He's a good donkey."

"End of the ride."

When she said that, it meant no more talk. But that was the donkey's name, so for then he said no more.

At times I shy from this story as our donkey shied from rickety bridges. Yet stories are our breath. We ask not, *Why should I breathe?* We simply feel our lungs cry out like a babe demanding suck. So I string out these words like a merchant caravan, trusting they come to safe harbor before the mules go lame. Our priest scowls on my progenitors, the minstrels and mimes. Yet could Our Savior have endured the dusty roads of Palestine without the rude jokes of the fisherfolk who followed Him?

—IV—
Parsnips

As I craft my story I seek to write truth, yet doubt fills each word. You, my liege, have provided me splendid tools for my task— reed pens, inks, and beeswax candles—as if I were a monk drafting Holy Writ. This vellum is the finest calfskin of stillborn calves, though my epic might be better suited to the hide of a wrinkled pig. I run my fingers across the smooth grain of my new writing desk. *Vanity, all is vanity.*

～

The vessel never docked. Another flea-ridden night at the inn, and at dawn the wispy innkeeper brought the news. "Ten leagues south— Oh terrible— Where you know, no, maybe you don't, where the shore takes a bend— Terrible—"

"Say it! What?"

His hand fluttered like a moth, but he managed to speak. The ship had encountered the pirates. Passengers and crew had been disemboweled or butchered in other creative ways. The bodies were found washed ashore. The ship was sunk.

"They must have hated our play," joked Mik without expression.

Plans had to change. Another vessel might be sailing, so the troupe packed out and hastened to harborside. The innkeeper waved, gave a farewell bleat in his northern tongue, but Asta paid him no mind. Bragi looked back as they left. The wispy man dissolved in the dawn.

The fog had rolled into port, white as a dead fish's belly. The boy always feared it might eat them. He had never heard the word *disemboweled*, but it sounded like cleaning a fish.

"What's that elegant vessel there?" His father pointed to a freight barge with a single square-rigged sail, one of those barnacled crafts that moved as if pulled by a ponderous slug creeping along the sea bed. Mik inquired. Yes, it would crawl up the coast and then make a crossing to Bor, six or eight days, but they would still arrive for the market fair. No passenger berths, but they could sleep on deck with the donkey below, provided they shoveled the dung.

An endless day as cargoes were discharged and loaded. At dusk, that quiet span between the sweaty day's bustle and the revelry and knives of the night, the gaudy stone-eyed women appeared in the dockside street. It was the first time that the boy saw why they looked so friendly. It came to him in a flash. Was it like buying a donkey?

The family hopped onto the boat, but it took more labor to get the donkey and cart aboard. The cart was tied fast and the donkey led below. The family nested on the deck between heavy barrels.

"We'll get squashed if a squall comes up," said Asta.

"Better squashed than swept overboard," Edra replied.

The ship stank of goats and scurvy crew and some vast extravagant rot. The first night a full moon blared and none could sleep. The boy scratched the bites on his legs, flopped over, scratched the bites on his butt, envisioned a gutted fish and flaming dog and the pirates' blood eyes, and stared at the moon.

The dawn wiped softly across the sky, then the rise of the sullen ball of fire. He tried to stay still till the others roused but at last poked Gramma awake. "Where do I go," he asked.

"Go?"

"To poop."

A concern never mentioned in sacred texts. Gramma had told him of palaces with gleaming ceramic bowls, and he imagined nobility spending days in luxurious defecation. But six-year-olds on tour had to ask where to go. Edra pointed him to the rear of the boat. A plank extended out from the deck with three holes side by side. "Go sit there," she told him, giving him a rag to wipe himself. "And don't fall in." The women used a clay pot behind a curtain and emptied it overboard, but he wanted to be a man, which meant sitting out in the open dropping turds like a dog.

A pockmarked sailor with choppy red whiskers sat on the center hole. As Bragi squatted to his right, the man gave a two-toothed grin. The boy tried to ignore him. The sailor began to whistle a tune and waggled his big purple thing. Bragi pretended to finish even though he hadn't begun. The inelegance of memory: all his life he would see the sailor's stiff dangle and hear the toothless whistle. At least he didn't fall in.

Deck passage was cold, but the sun was fierce at midday, and the boy welcomed the shade of the barrels. The days were slow, but wonders came into view. He watched a scatter of islands poking up in the fog like giant seals, the dazzling white cliffs of a distant shore, and one long island with a steepled dwelling at its tip, like a lady he'd seen with a pimple on her nose. He saw schools of dolphins leaping. He saw the sun setting behind an island peak, as if the island had stuck it in the eye. Other peaks rose from the fog, or they might have been slumbering whales. He saw conical rocks reaching upward and heard the terrible whisper of the sea. Was the boat sailing forward or was seawater dawdling past? All was unreal, a world in flux, except his vomiting over the side, which brought him back to reality.

They came into a port with flocks of vendors and beggars crowding the docks and the hard stringy women with their wares thinly veiled. Another late afternoon he was leaning against the rail to watch the change of the clouds, and in the formations he saw eyes and a nose. Camel, raven, innkeeper—maybe the god Yesu? Was he the one they nailed to a tree and ate? The barge rolled this way and that, but he'd puked all he could.

Third day, Bragi was picking Gramma's lice. She had gotten lice in her hair, so she showed him how to pick them out and bite them dead. He felt at last he was pulling his weight. Killing a louse was manly. And out of the blue she said, "So what happened was—" At first he didn't hear that she was picking up the tale from three days before. The story burbled up like porridge. "So they're in the big city, and he marries a baker's widow, Asta's father does. Teodora—Todie they called her. Jolly lady with a huge big butt and bad breath—I met her once—but she was good to Asta, and Asta helped in the bakery. Oh, you got a big one!" Bragi had slain a mighty louse. "Where was I?"

It was the first time that he ever felt his grandma's head was muddled. He looked into her eyes and she wasn't there. A long breath and she came back, speaking flat, distracted. "Her dad was no killer, except when he had to be. He'd tuck her in, tell her stories about the Northmen's gods. And Todie was a Crister. They had a god that got nailed to a tree, and the Northmen had one of those too. Lots of gods get nailed to trees, I guess."

Edra rambled on. The father was killed in battle, and the wickerwork hamper lay in a room behind the ovens under old woolen blankets with a cat perched atop. "You hold onto what's there, even a curse." Edra hugged the boy. "But you'll know how it is when you lose somebody, sweetie, your mama or papa or me—most likely me first, I hope."

"Mama said the barrels might squash us."

"Not if they don't fall over."

He felt the cold fingers up his legs that he'd felt when facing the pirates. He hated his grandma telling him scary things, but Edra did not believe in children remaining children: the sooner you grew up the more likely you'd stay alive.

Her tale meandered as he stared at the barrels' blackened slats. The widow raised Asta like a daughter, took her into the bakery as apprentice and soon as mistress of masterful loaves. The girl had boyfriends but managed not to get pregnant, and then she met Mik. "My younger son, the dumb one. Me and his dad—oh, he had a wonderful voice—we were players going way back. Way far back to grandpas' grandpas, when they did big festivals and gods came out to see the show. But we always played funny stuff." She went into a fit of coughing. Bragi picked off a louse.

"And some years were lean. I turned tricks when I had to." Bragi started to ask what kind of tricks, but she went on. "And then Mik's older brother Alek—he was our tumbler, so graceful—got took for a soldier. Went off, never saw him again." She was a long time silent. Sometimes grownups disappeared, swept in the tide.

When Asta came to live with Mik, Edra told her, "I hope my dummy son told you you're gonna work." The troupe had lost its young actress to a smithy, so Asta learned her roles. Edra had scant faith in the girl's theatrical gifts, but by degrees Asta the baker became Asta the player, and the duo of Mik and Asta found their groove. Whether they swore passion, vowed to kill each other, or haggled over the price of a pig—whatever the plot, they mesmerized the watchers. "You go out there, work every day, you learn your trade. And she did," Edra told the boy. "And then, third season she was with us, she got pregnant. You just couldn't wait, little devil." She ruffled his hair, and he pulled away.

From first suck at the tit, Bragi knew family. Not that he was always happy about it, yet he had food and cuddling and laughter, even amidst the fleas. On their summer tours the family played market fairs and festivals, for nobles in banqueting halls or for muleteers in the innyard. Papa mostly played the dummy, and they loved him. Mama was all sharp edges or distant beauty. Gramma was scary. Whether a witch or a bawd or a daft old crone, she became another creature, no longer Gramma.

"You listening?" she asked with a murderous frown. He nodded, watching a roach scuttle up the slat of a barrel. He had asked about the masks, but once the sorcerer's head hit the wall, that was enough. He tried not to listen, but no stopping Gramma.

"My man died, your grandpa, his voice was so beautiful, he played kings—" Strange what memory did. He died in Bragi's second year, so he couldn't have remembered him, though the man had bright dark eyes and wrinkles all over his face, brown fingers, so gentle . . .

"So after he died I was head of the troupe, business, all that. And stuff changes fast—the money, the roads. Think you're doing fine, but then comes the plague or the wars or the weather, or hit a town where the Cristers got a bug up their butt. You ride the waves."

"When can I be in a play?"

"You were already in a play."

That was new. She told him a story she hadn't told. When he was a baby, some odd bunch of Cristers asked them to play the Nativity—the night their god was born. "And that was you. You played the baby god."

"What'd I do?"

"You just laid there. Very believable," she said. "Fact, it's a beautiful story. Course we had to put in funny stuff. Asta's the mother, she bitches about the smelly stable, pigs and sheep, and Mik trying to work out who the real daddy was. Then I hobble in as a creaky old angel with wings, tell'im the real daddy is God. Mik's pretty funny working that out—*Who? What? How?* He always had the gift. And you were a perfect little baby god. You did just fine."

"Can I be in another?"

"When you're bigger. You never know."

"Never know what?"

"Well that's the point: you never know what you never know."

The days passed. His mother would make a low charcoal fire on a sheet of tin. The pottage was the same but it tasted special at sea. Early morning, he sneaked back to the three-holed toilet, pulling his father's cap low on his brow so no one would see him. Fourth morning, he spotted Ludd.

Just at daybreak through the fog he saw the tall bony man pissing over the rail, or someone who looked like the tall bony man. The figure shambled across the deck and down the stairs to the cargo hold. The boy saw his father rise, pull his tunic straight, hitch up his leggings, take a waterskin and half a loaf from their food sack, and follow. Soon he returned to crawl under the blanket.

"Papa?"

"It's early, Bragi. Back to sleep."

"Who was the man?"

"Just one of the sailors. Go to sleep."

"It's the bony man with the raven."

"You were dreaming."

"I saw him."

He felt Gramma's hand stroking his hair. That meant to be still. "It's a secret, hon. We'll tell you in the morning, all right?" No arguing with that hand.

Bragi bent his will to push the sun up faster, but every time he peeked it lay dead flat on the horizon. He was learning a vital survival skill: waiting. When at last they were up, gathered around the food—the last of the yogurt, though still honey for the bread—Edra told him the secret.

"His name is Ludd. He's a stowaway." Before Bragi formed the question she answered. "A stowaway hasn't paid the fare, and if the crew finds him he might get flogged or thrown to the sharks."

Ludd had come out of hiding the second night and begged for water. Bragi had heard their whispers. Like most families, nothing could be kept secret though much was incomprehensible. The man made his appeal to Mik, Mik was agreeable, but the storm broke with Asta.

"We are not going to help that man. If they catch us—"

"We can't let him die of thirst."

"They'll see him—"

"He's under a tarp down there."

"He's asking for water, next he'll be asking for food—"

"We have food. We'll get more food at the ports—"

"With our bagfuls of gold!"

"He's not with us, he's with barrels of salt pork. I go down, feed the donkey. Simple."

Asta was silent. She would do that. When there was nothing more to be said she didn't say it. More often she changed the subject.

"We'd better name that damn donkey."

"Let Bragi do it."

"He named Truggie and hated the name he gave her."

She was struggling against herself. Even then Bragi knew vaguely how her life had shaped her, how she hated the role she played: the nag, the bargainer, the Northman's child.

Edra spoke up. "He stood with us."

"Well, he stood there. So?"

"We will help this man."

When the old woman spoke in that hollow reptilian voice—with the authority of an empress or simply a creature who had survived—she could still a crowd of carnival drunks. The matter was settled.

"Mother—"

"I hear my magical chin wart speaking," she said in her old-witch chortle to lighten the mood.

"It's a matter of survival—"

"It says, *Mortals, pay heed!*"

"I have a son—"

"I have a son as well! Once I had two!"

You have known that moment, my liege, when years pass in a breath. Each time that we think of our lost ones they die again. Your beloved son, whose youthful friendship raised me far above my station—I relive the day the messenger came with the terrible words. Even in your pain, you saw my own—my wife, daughter too, gone far too soon—and we shared a communion of tears. Their eyes are shut to us, all, yet we hear their voices.

"I am no conjuror," whispered Edra, "but I hear a voice when it speaks loud and clear. Even if I don't like it."

"I don't like it," said Asta.

"You don't have to."

The father's stage fool voice came up. "Well, but I like parsnips!" Edra cackled. Asta gave her harried-wife sigh that always got a laugh. She seemed relieved to lose the quarrel. Mik waved hello to a bald leather-colored crewman swaying past.

Bragi dared to whisper: "The bony man lost part of his ear." Silence gripped them. Everyone knew the mark of a runaway slave.

Edra had a knack for jumping into the fray before the fray heated up. "Good thing you noticed, Bragi. They do that to slaves that've run away once. Cause if we helped him, they'd punish us. Helping a fugitive slave is wrong, wrong, wrong. That's like somebody stealing our donkey. But we don't know for sure." The more common mark was a brand, a tattoo, or an iron collar with the master's name and locality. "He might've lost the lobe in a fight or a turtle snapped it off. Not our business. He's just one of the crew." Bragi understood: strategic ignorance.

Three more days till they came to the port of Bor. Each day the boy would go down with Mik to the cargo hold. His charge was to watch the passage. If a sailor appeared, he should make a commotion till Ludd got covered and Mik got clear.

"What do I do?" Fear tasted like when he'd licked a pewter pot.

"Pretend it's a play," Asta told him, "and make up something. That's what you do in a play."

Next day, as Mik waited for Ludd to drink from the waterskin, a shadow came into the passage. Bragi froze. A shaft of light caught the face of the red-whiskered sailor. He saw Bragi, grinned at the child's numb terror, waggled his fingers, and approached.

Bragi screamed. "Rat! There's a rat!"

"Shut up, kid. "

"I saw a rat! Big rat with teeth!"

"Fuck rats. C'mere."

"I need parsnips!"

Rats were all over the ship. But parsnips? "Parsnips!" Bragi yelled again. "Parsnips!" The whiskery sailor halted, backed off, bonked his head on a rafter, and beat a retreat.

He had done what Gramma once told him. "You get in a jam and can't run away, just shout out anything crazy. *I lost my fish! My dog poops bees! The plague is fun!* With luck they'll think you're nuts and let you be." His father crept down the passageway and rumpled his hair. For once he didn't mind. He was an actor now. "Can I be in the play?" Mik didn't reply, but he knew he could pester him into it. And the donkey would be named Yesu.

By next morning, that day was a blur. He peed over the side of the boat, watched the slow march of the sun, felt like the caterpillar in its cocoon waiting for wings. At dusk the sun plunged again beneath the rim of the world to light the backside of life—none of the spittings, devourings, disembowelings, but life as seen in the donkey's deep eyes. The night song of rats' teeth crackled. Below the horizon lived the future: it trickled out day by day.

～

Foiling the pocky sailor, I was a player now. It opened a vast casket of fear. I was a fledgling, set to take flight, and my days were rife with signs. At midday my eyes were drawn upward to a bird far above, a bird the size of a man. "Albatross," my grandmother said, "a seabird." But I knew otherwise. She had told me the tale of the boy who flew too close to the sun, and I dreamed it time and again. On the rise behind our cottage, feeling the wind at my back and the indrawn breath of the sun—O to be high aloft, looking down on the yammer and babble and stir! Yet being six I was ill-prepared for the wind-borne flight to come.

—V—
New Players

My father's laughter was sweet and wild, my grandmother's gristle and grit. They were so unalike, though their wit shared the same knife edge: it could carve a ham or cut a throat. My mother could draw raucous guffaws from the stage, but in the course of the day she made few jests. I am my mother's child.

They were skilled musicians, but their hearts were in the plays. Whatever woes infected this world of donkeys and doom were spice for the pottage of farce. In the last days even, blown like uprooted weeds, we lived the farces we played.

～

On the eighth day they docked at the port of Bor. The boy patted the donkey as his father harnessed it. "Where's the bony man?"

"He got scared," said Mik. "He thought he'd get caught when we came into port, so last night he jumped overboard. Long way to swim, I told him, but he said no matter, he couldn't swim. I tried to tell him how, paddle paddle, so on, but he said if he knew how to swim then he might drown because it was too far to swim. So he jumped."

They disembarked, Mik leading the donkey down the plank, Bragi grasping its tail. Today he had to name Yesu. He had told Papa, who didn't say no, but it was harder with Mama. As they came ashore he spotted the red-whiskered sailor on deck and waggled his fingers at him.

"Papa?"

"Yes?"

He forgot what he wanted to say.

The dock was busy with men unloading cargo, bringing barrels aboard, pallets of bricks and cages of geese, or men watching other men work. He looked around for the bony man. "The ocean laps with a hungry tongue," his grandma said once. It gave him dreams.

By Asta's account they couldn't afford an inn, so they made their way to the edge of town. The land stretching out from the seacoast was barren, stripped of trees, a flat stubble face pimpled with rocks. They made camp in an olive grove near a shallow brook. Mik caught a big slow fish with his hands.

"Is the water good?" asked Asta.

"Good enough for the fish," said Mik. He made a sucking fish-face.

"Sorry I asked."

She made fish soup. "If we only had parsnips," Papa joked. Bragi laughed. He loved that Mama and Gramma didn't get the joke.

Over soup, they made plans. Market day in Bor was two days hence, so Mik would go into town and see the entertainers' stage and check the planks' stability and pay the fee. Sometimes they were paid by the town, a nobleman or confraternity, or they would split the gate at an innyard, but with market days you paid to be on the trestle stage between the jugglers and dancing bears. You made your pitch for coins and ran about with outstretched hat, but doing three shows a day you could make good money.

Then Ludd appeared. The darkness coughed him out. Dark bramble, firelight flicker, and his chiseled face came into the glow, lips parted in wonder. The boy caught his first clear sight of the man's left eye, which slanted out to the left as if gazing over his shoulder. The man was a softly warbling question mark.

"Can I sit here? Warm up?"

He was staring at the soup pot. Mik and the boy moved apart on a fallen log, and he sat between them. Bragi had emptied his bowl, so Asta ladled it full and shoved it at the supplicant.

"You made it? You swam okay?" asked Mik.

"And followed us here?" said Asta, not in the friendliest tone.

"You got work? I need work."

"No," said Asta.

Edra put a hand on Asta's knee. "We'll see." Asta glared at her.

"Are you play-actors?"

Mik nodded. The man's face lit up. He had seen a play once, he said, where the little tiny wife beat up her big bristly man, but after a while they hugged and went off to bed. "Or if they just pretended, cause they came right back out and sang a song."

"That might have been us you saw, or my dad," said Mik. "My dad was big and bristly."

"Mine too. Fishmonger. That's like an actor, you stand there and yell all day. Gotta sell your fish." And he told of his father gambling, piling up debts, selling off little Ludd as a slave.

"We don't need to know," snapped Asta.

He went on: his escape, his capture, then sold to the salt mines, another escape—

"Don't tell us that stuff!" Asta jerked the bowl from his hand, then grudgingly handed it back. He slurped the dregs.

It was the first that Bragi heard of someone becoming a slave. He thought you were born that way, as you were born a king or player or pig. The pig is a pig and he roots around till he's butchered, and that's what happens to pigs. If the swineherd tried to make him a horse, he'd never be much of a horse.

The women stared into the coals. Mik pointed at Ludd. "He's funny." It was true. Mik was slow in some respects, but he had an eye for talent.

They had to offer Ludd a place to sleep: hospitality was bred in the bone. Asta dug in the costume bag for the fur of the magical bear and spread out bedding at a distance. The bony man lay down and fell asleep in a crash, snoring like a rain of bullfrogs.

Bragi, under his blanket, listened to Edra and Asta whisper together. Mik sat silent by Asta. They could use a worker, Edra argued, and he could be a walk-on in the plays. But Asta recalled Pollo, who claimed that he worked best when drunk—better not risk another mouth to feed, maybe a donkey-thief who'd make off in the night. She was puzzled that hard-headed Edra was promoting this scrawny wall-eyed stranger.

"We can use him."

"We're fine as we are."

"We'll have a need."

"What?"

"What I think you haven't figured out."

"What haven't I figured out?"

"You're pregnant."

The silence was loud enough to wake the dead. Suddenly she knew. Yes, she had missed a bleeding, but that happened. Yes, she'd puked over the rails, but that was the sea. Yes, her nipples were itchy, but— Yes, she was pregnant. Her sharp breath drew in the night.

"Sorry to surprise you. I should've seen it sooner. Now we're out on the road, what do you want to do? Get rid of it?"

"No!" Asta professed practicality, but risk ran in her veins. They counted the months and the dangers.

"She'll be fine. At least till she sees the light of day. Then's the time to worry," said Edra.

"How can you tell it's a girl?"

"I just see it."

Mik put his hand on Asta's knee, leaned his head to her shoulder. Bragi stared wide-eyed at the stars.

At dawn Mik clapped Ludd on the back, "We'll give you a try," and went into town, taking the dumbstruck man to show him the donkey's quirks. They returned mid-afternoon. "Just two shows tomorrow. There's a bunch of other acts."

It was to be Bragi's first role and he was terrified. Mik would beat the dead donkey, then the boy would run in, yell, *Help! I need parsnips!* and run off. Asta was dubious. "There's no sense to it."

"It's like life. Stuff happens. No sense."

The boy went down to the brook to practice his line while they fit Ludd into the play. After Bragi's line Edra would appear as a witch and propose a scheme. "We'll call out, *Donkey brains for sale! Donkey brains!* Whoever's dumb enough to want donkey brains will really need'em. So this lummox appears—Ludd! You! Listen up!—and I promise to conjure'em into his head. So Ludd, you stand there looking goofy while I make signs in the air like this—don't worry, it's all pretend!—and then I'll spin around and make a big fart sound at you. You act it's so stinky it knocks you flat. Then we run off with your money and you chase us yelling, *Hwor-haa! Hwor-haa!* Got it?" Bragg came back to watch. After a while Ludd got it straight: smell the fart *after* she farts, not before.

The boy had a hard time waiting until tomorrow. What if he didn't remember his line? What if they threw rotten fish? What if he flew too close to the sun? Late by the fire, he snuggled up to Mama. "What do we name the baby?"

She inhaled the darkness, then said, "It depends." She didn't say what it depended on.

That night he saw faces. He saw the one-eyed god with his raven, an old frowning queen and a sharp-nosed grinning man with the eyes of a snake. He saw a beautiful shining youth. All stood atop a high cliff, as the family had stood masked against the pirates. Freakish creatures frolicked below, the size of sheep but shaped like frogs with darting tongues, croaking and belching. Bragi laughed. His laughter woke him, and he shook Mama awake to tell her about the frogs. "Go to sleep!" she snapped, cursing Edra for giving him nightmares. But it wasn't a nightmare, he wanted to say. The nightmares were still to come.

They woke at sunrise. The sky was overcast but no rain. They would stay on the site next night, but they had to strike camp for fear of thieves. The distant sea was white with a blanket of fog, burning off as they followed the road into town. They passed a roadside shrine where dwelt a small stone lady the height of a hen. Her hand was raised as if washing a face. Bragi knew she must be a god, but he wondered who. "Depends," said Edra. "Might be Dian, might be Maria. They keep changing the names."

Already there were wagons and pack mules streaming into the town. Ludd led the donkey. Mik and Asta donned the big floppy hats with red and yellow tassels they always wore coming into towns, and Edra wore her old bawd's finery. Mik played his pipes, Asta the tambour. Bragi liked her playing the lute, but the tambour worked better outdoors. Bragi's job was to wave a red and yellow flag on a stick. He waved it with gusto.

~

I waved the flag to pull myself out of the swamp. In my later education, I learned it was excess black bile that drowned me in melancholia, though education provided no spigot to drain it. But I put great store in doing useful work, being part of the troupe, laying my claim to life by waving my colorful flag. Perhaps we lose that love of labor as we become enslaved to the whip of need. Hope of success impels us, whether as player, king or cutpurse, yet I believe we are all of us born with desire to work: to waggle our little flag.

~

Bragi waggled his flag. Coming into the town he saw gulls swarming around women gutting fish at the harbor. An old man muttering streams of invective drove a brindle cow. A squat lady led a mule bearing a crate of chickens in frantic cackle. Two boys herded a dozen baffled sheep through the baffled crowd. Around the square, shopkeepers set out tables and itinerant sellers hoisted curtained booths, casting anxious glances at the sky. Fresh beluga, mullet and tuna were laid out on tables, dried stockfish vended from crates. A hairy bear of a man unloaded sacks of barley, repeatedly fending off a curious goat. Bragi saw baskets of fennel and fava beans, garlic and lettuce, every green or brown or purpleness that popped from a stem or hung from a tree or hid in the earth, and a trestle with wheels of cheese.

"Can we buy some?"

"Look there!" Edra pointed. "There's furs and sacks of wool and hides. And look, oil lamps, candlesticks, and mattocks for farmers.

Rushes, cause people here are just like us, they have to cover their floors. And look at that big naked steer hung up for the butcher? He'll have to work hard to chop that leg. Spices for the rich folks," she said, "but some day you'll be rich, you can eat all that." She rarely lied to the child, but at times she couldn't help it. "And give some to your sweet old granny?"

"Are they fighting?"

"Those two? No no, they're just waving their arms, making a deal. Your mama's good at that. She just stands there like a manure pile and the other fellow gets tired."

"Four!" "Seven!" At last the buyer counted out six coins and held up a seventh in triumph, telling himself he'd won. The boy wondered, when he grew up, if he'd wave his arms or just stand there.

His grandma kept teaching him, or tried to. "See those beautiful loaves of bread? But you gotta be careful. Some bakers bake stones in the bread to bring them up to weight, or butchers might sell meat that's rotten. Only buy meat when you see it in the sun. That butcher there, with the rotten teeth? Would you buy meat from him?" As they shoved through the crowd, swam in the stew, the boy felt adrift in the tumult—all that life offered, the great bags and baskets of desire.

The morning drizzle cleared. Behind the stage they unhitched the cart and led the donkey to a stable. They watched a juggler juggling squashes and lemons and knives, and then in midair he sliced a lemon in half. He was funny, doing his tricks with an amazed expression of *How did I do that?* After him, a strongman whose grumpy attitude was *Look at me!* Bragi loved the juggler.

Their play came after the strongman. They waited behind the rear curtain, what Asta called the attiring place. Bragi went over and over his line: *Help! I need parsnips!*

"You'll do fine," said the trembling Ludd, whose wall eye kept straining to escape.

He had never really talked to the tall bony man. He took comfort that someone else was afraid. "You're funny when you stand there," he told the bony man.

"Oh. Good."

Before going on stage, each player had a ritual. His father bounced quietly, as if ready to dance, whereas his mother stood frozen stiff, save for a tapping finger. His grandma would find anything to do—slapping a fly, scraping a splinter—then burst abruptly into the world of make-believe. Ludd slunk off to be sick.

The crowd had started to drift away from the strongman, so the players leapt straight into the farce. The man comes home with the donkey, his wife calls him nuts for buying a beast that's dead, beats him, storms out. He starts to beat the donkey for being dead, but the witch comes in, scolds him for donkey abuse. "*You bad man!*" was Bragi's cue. He ran across the stage, yelled, "*Help! I need parsnips!*" as loud as he could.

It made no sense and it worked. The farmers, the slaves, the nobleman's knaves, the bakers and fishwives, craftsmen and beggars and drunks—no matter their gods, they knew that the world made no sense, never spared a parsnip when needed. Hearing the truth from the mouth of a babe, they cheered. He would hear that laugh—less a laugh than an acclamation—all through his tangle of years.

The tumult died, and witch plotted with husband to sell the donkey's brains. "*But we have to find the right idiot.*" The cue for Ludd.

No Ludd. Edra improvised. "*No problem,*" she cried. "*Who's the biggest idiot here?*" She scanned the sea of faces. "*There's one! The kid with the ears? Can you flap'em and fly? Or that old coot? Hey dearie, see me after the show.*" She launched into a stock bouquet of simpletons right and left, rich and poor, godless and godly. She knew how to play her audience, building laugh upon laugh. Still no Ludd.

Then he appeared.

Later he confessed to being terrified, paralyzed, sick unto death. He prayed to the gods for deliverance back to the salt mines. At last, driven by desperation, he rooted in their cart, unclasped the hamper, and filched Old One-eye. As it had saved him once, it might again. It fastened itself to his face and flung him onto the stage.

The face was leather, deeply sculpted, its good eye aslant, its blind eye a pit of gore. No voice, just a breath, a sough, a sigh rising off the sheen of a glacier. The air made a shiver and shimmer, a curl and a

crest, more faces, more eyes. *Wadan, Frekka, Loghi, Teorr*—stories
Asta had told the boy and others she never told. Bragi swatted the
air and squinted to peer through the glare. He had seen statues of
gods in polished nakedness but never these long-headed gods who
reeked with a sickening sweetness like pig dung burning on cold
winter nights. The marketplace dissolved and his family wore the
masks. Words spewed from their lips, words in the warbling tongue,
seabird cries.

Daylight—

Beloved son—

Shining One—

Edra's face was a beautiful girl, hands like flickers of flame. Asta
wore a razor's grin, Mik the frown of a bulgy plum. The sorcerer's
head went flying, splatted the wall, and the raven hovered and vanished. A murmur rose from the crowd. The play was going wrong.
Sir Flop galloped apace. Bragi choked on the stench of the gods, felt
words welling up, a tempest within, as when he ate too many figs, out
both ends, no stopping it. He found himself flying to center stage,
stomping a six-year-old's tantrum—

"*I still need parsnips!*"

—And again the throng went wild. He ran down the steps, the
bony man disappeared, and the barefaced Mik and Asta swung into
a song of springtime lovers. To the purist, it might seem confusing
to flit from dead donkeys to gods to springtime cavorts, but purists
were rare in Bor. The rabble cheered as the players grabbed hats to
dance through the crowd shouting, "Feed our dead donkey! Feed
our little boy!" They did well, though someone dropped a parsnip
in Bragi's jittery pot.

As they waited for the juggler and strong man to repeat their
acts, they ate chunks of meat on a skewer, no telling what, and some
nameless yellow root. The boy was a player now, so they didn't water
his wine as much. It tasted bitter. "It's supposed to be like that,"
said Edra. "That's what makes it good." All that day—and onward
through life—he tried to fathom why bitter was good.

∿

To grownups, the wine tasted good. I longed to be older, as do we all until we attain that equivocal condition. We gain and lose. I recall my grandmother teaching me bladder control. "Save up your pee," she said, "and then go pee on the cat." So I chased the cat across the yard and let fly, with mixed results. But once we learn bladder control, they tell us we're too old to pee on the cat.

〰

Ludd surrendered the mask to Mik and begged for another chance. "I just tried to think what to do, so I did."

"No more with the masks."

"No I won't. No. Aw!"

Edra gave the man's upper arm a vicious lobster pinch, then smiled him a sunny smile. Mik handed the mask to Asta, who returned it to the nest. She held her peace: no argument with the generous clank of coins. Bragi refrained from asking what had happened. From where had the faces come? Who spoke the warbling words? He hoped for no gods in the second show, and there were none.

But nothing went so well in the afternoon. The juggler fumbled his lemon and cut his hand on the knife. The strong man strained his back and hobbled off. A dog act failed till the dog began to poop, and then the audience cheered. They did the donkey play as they'd practiced it, and his parsnips line got a laugh, but when Ludd came out—without a mask—he just stood as if waiting to be crucified. Sir Flop loomed, so Bragi did the first thing that flew into his head. He ran up the steps and yelled—

"Mama, I need to pee!"

A tumultuous laugh, Ludd came unstuck, and the act went on. As they burst into song, Asta brought out the boy, who got a huge whoop from the crowd. It was his happiest, scariest day.

In the flurry after the show, Bragi announced that the donkey's name was Yesu. Gramma nodded and his mother was mute. Mayhap the story was true: the boy with wings had flown into the sun, and somehow he survived.

—VI—
The Norns

My liege, you have tasked me with a labor never posed to Heracles: to journey forth to a treacherous land called the Past. We traverse that savage domain but once, gathering scars as souvenirs, yet now you compel me to return in search of a long-lost relative: myself. I knew he had lived there as a child, but I had presumed him dead or changed beyond recognition. Yet now, as I look for my own pinched face in a waterless stream, my heart opens to all the old terrors. As with our timeworn hamper, I dread releasing the clasp.

It would surely give me greater pain to revisit the deathbed of my wife or look again on the face of our dying child. Yet by that stage of my journey I had mastered a prime skill of adulthood: to find a heart chamber where I might crouch, numb to the claws of the night. I was better prepared for being unprepared.

I recall that season when I groped through the fog to catch a glimpse of the road ahead and impressions chiseled into my soul like epitaphs. I had learned to say please and to seek a safe place to defecate, and now my gaze turned from chasing the cat to seeing the shadows quake. My soul pressed toward its next crowning.

Back to camp in the clearing, scant talk on the way. Wisps of cloud skittered over the sky. Some farmer must be asking a god for rain and crops had to have rain, Bragi knew, but he didn't want to wake up wet. Why didn't the gods just make it rain on the barley shoots? He asked Gramma. "Don't depend on the gods," she said. "We believe in gods so we have some sonsabitches to blame. Not to say we shouldn't show respect." He dared not ask about the gods in the wickerwork.

At times Ludd would murmur, "Sorry," the way the donkey farted meaningless farts. Edra kept her hand on the money pouch beneath her cloak. Hers was the task to hold coin from the shows. A thief who made a grab would never foresee a crone's ferocity till she handed him his manhood.

Bragi worried that when he yelled his pee line people might think he really needed to pee. How could an actor sound real but show that he didn't mean it? "You need to believe what you say," his father said, but if he believed he needed to pee, then wouldn't he need to pee? Acting had its perplexities. Yet he whispered to the plodding Yesu that he'd gotten big laughs. The donkey's ears pricked up.

At the camp, all waited for Asta to say that Ludd had to go—donning a mask, missing a cue, dumb as a bucket of slugs—but she was mute. That was her way when she had too much to say to say it. If Bragi lagged in gathering firewood or cleaning the cooking pot, she would look at him with a hush louder than thunder. Perhaps she saw that the masks were out and the curse would come. Unstoppable.

That night, under his blanket a short crying distance from the fire, Bragi drowsed. He would rise to the surface of sleep for a gulp, then sink into a chowder of dreams. The squiggles and motes on his lids formed a face—a long straight nose like the stretch of a tree to the sun, a forehead the gold of sky. He shook it away. Drop guard and the gods would blow through the cracks like a winter chill. Even trying to sleep with his eyes wide open, the masks might be suddenly—

Absent. He dreamt no faces. That night the masks were mute, nested like clamshells. He dreamt only the donkey's hooves plodding, plodding, plodding . . .

Next morning, they broke camp and came into town for the fair. Two shows again, one early afternoon, one just before dusk. Mik spoke quietly to Ludd. "So you're backstage and you're scared shitless, that happens. So what you do, just let yourself be scared, just say *I'm scared shitless, scared shitless, scared shitless.* Make a scared-shitless face. Open your head and let the jitters out. It works." Bragi heard and took it to heart.

More waiting. He had a new role and whispered his line repeatedly. He scanned the crowd for the little spitting girl, though she was far away and probably dead. He wanted her to see him onstage, and he wanted her to laugh.

The first show was a farce they had played many times. The wife complains that her man doesn't earn enough, and he bemoans his wife's fat ass. They pay the old witch Edra to conjure up a demon to make them rich. She waves her arms and Ludd appears with a bag on his head. "*He's too ugly to look at.*" She pokes him, he flaps his arms. "*These folks want three wishes, okay?*" Poke, flap.

Mik dances with joy. "*I want a flagon of wine, right now!*" Ludd flaps, the flagon appears, Mik chugs it, and Asta flies into a rage.

"*You loony! You could have wished for—*" And she launches a litany: "*A pile of coins, an army, a castle with tile toilets, a pig on a spit, a gold crown, a pure silk shit-wipe*" and on and on till Mik can stand it no more.

"*I wish you'd just shut up!*"

Ludd flaps and she goes mute though gesticulating wildly, mouthing horrible oaths, purple with rage, steam shooting out of her nose. "*What?*" asks Mik, exploding. "*Well I wish you'd say what you feel!*" Ludd flaps.

"*—Or a cow!*" Finishing her list.

Then the terrible moment as they mutter in unison: "*Three wishes. One. Two. Three . . .*"

Earlier, they would end with the wife beating the husband. This time, as they realize the disaster, the boy pops in, yells, "*The pigs are eating the porridge!*" The couple run off as the old witch pockets her fee, and they all come back for a song.

They reaped good coin, and one weather-worn farm wife gave them a scrawny rooster, feet tied together and raising a squabble. She couldn't stop laughing at the porridge line, all too familiar with disaster begetting disaster. "One little devil calls another!" she crowed. Bragi grinned. It felt good to make people laugh. It wasn't only for coins or roosters: you did it for the laughter. Yet how strange that people laughed at terrible things: poverty, desperation, pigs eating the porridge. How could disasters raise laughter?

∽

I have read of the ancient poets, though few of their words remain, and at times I dreamt of the ancient festivals my grandmother spoke of: thousands gathered on hillsides to witness the gods descending, the music and dancing, the madness. Now we are done with the gods and the celebrations, though we still nurture the madness.

I knew not then, nor do I now, whether other players like us were on the road. I cannot imagine otherwise. What else would the children of players do when the festivals were banned? Would they all revert to hawking fish? Must there not always be humble comedians beating dead donkeys and crying out fruitless desires? Will there not always be a thirst for laughter?

My story may be true or the droppings of a donkey. A story takes root in the heart, stretches up to embrace the sun and come to seed. The hero dies or finds his way home or marries the princess, kills the wolf, wins the war. Whatever is planted presses through hard-packed clay to come to flower. My father once told of a traveler from a distant land where they made a magic dust. The dust could burn and fling boulders like arrows through the air. Only a story, but one day it might come true and tear whole armies apart. Stories do that.

Still, all human souls love a story—except the one we are caught in.

∽

For the second show, they played the dead-donkey play. This time Ludd did it right, and Bragi scored with his *parsnips* line. The sword-swallower told him that he was the best of all. "I say truth. Stick

sword down throat where truth is sleep, poke it wake. You best." Back
to the stony clearing, making camp again, Mik and Ludd pitched the
old sailcloth in case of rain. Bragi went down to the thicket where
the donkey was tethered. "Your name's Yesu." The beast flared his
nostrils, either feeling godly or fearing crucifixion.

The boy wandered back to the fire, swamped with fatigue. He still
had chores to do—gather firewood, curry the donkey—but Asta saw
that he was a tattered rag. "Sleepy boy. Never mind the chores. Lie
down, I'll wake you for dinner."

"When?"

"Quite a while. It's a tough old bird." She picked up the hatchet
to chop off the rooster's head. The boy was too tired even to watch
it doing its chicken-flop, but he liked her saying *tough old bird*. He
mulled the long journey from being an egg to being a tough old bird,
and what good did it do you? You still got your head chopped off.

Resisting his mother's kindness, he sat on a log by the fire, trying to stay awake, but the wind blew smoke in his face and sleep
squeezed his head in its fist. Like surf on the shore, at last he heard
the bubbling of rooster stew. At length his father tickled him awake,
and he joined the others in eating the stringy goulash. Stringy, but
he had earned it.

The meal done, he stumbled to his bedding and collapsed—
wide-eyed, he thought, until his sleeping eyes blinked open. Dark
many-armed creatures loomed—*trees* they were called. He waggled
his head to stay awake, drifted off, snagged on a fallen branch in a
swirling eddy, again drifted off. The dream floated in like sea fog, a
dream he had dreamt before, or else he was dreaming he dreamt it,
or else it was dreaming him.

〜

Dreams: learned and sainted souls debate whether these odd
night visions are divine revelation, prophecy, or descents to the realm
of the beggared insane who jabber in circles beshitting themselves.
But no stopping the faces that seep into tight-shut eyes. Dreams were
never my friends. To me they were only the leftover dregs of porridge, the rooster bits at the bottom of the pot. Why let them crawl

over me like spiders? Yet under the sounds of the camp—the chatter, the chink of coins, the crackle of fire—the gods came calling.

Bragi's dreams blew in, wet and cold, through the open sides of the tent. The night shuddered under the beat of the rain, chilling him from his feet on up. When the wet blanket woke him, he tried to pull free, but the night visions dug in their claws. He felt Gramma's firm hand. "You're dreaming, hon."

"Faces . . ." he murmured.

"No faces. Forget the faces. That's just pretend."

The faces were blurred. He smelled a rank sea scum—the reek of gods. "There's no silly gods," said Gramma as if in reply, but the stench held the air, and he saw the old god's gouged eye. He clambered into its socket to find dryness, and the dream pulled him down in its suck. He grappled the whirling surf, fighting the undertow.

Gunnlod's theft . . .

Eyes of Thiazi spawned in stars . . .

Hyndia girdled by fire . . .

He heard the babble of gods: the rumble of rocks, the croak of ravens, the crick of shifting ice. Words in the warbling tongue, calls of forest and sea. Words as piercing as fishmongers' cries.

We three!

Sopping wet!

In rain!

Far deep he saw the vultures. Three vultures were perched on a rickety fence, old women with chicken necks, smirking beaks and coats of shabby plumage. Their heads were bald with side shoots of weedy red hair. Their yellow bug eyes bore into the hollow where he tried to hide himself. They cackled, cavorted, clacking their beaks, then froze stone still. He heard the echoes of stories his mother told, tales from before the birth of Time. Were these the gods who didn't exist?

Erd!

Skuld!

Verdandi!

We are Norns!

He knew that story—one of the long-ago bedtime tales his mother told him when he snuggled close. The stories were funny, bloody, scary, but she spoke the residue of her girlhood, as if it were all she could offer him. At times without knowing it she fell into the warbling tongue, but somehow he grasped every word.

The sky was pitched from an ancient god's skull, the story went, and humans were only stray thoughts that rattled its hollows. The Norns shaped each life—what was past, what was now, whatever might come. They patched lives together the way players made up a play: an old song, scenes from another show, a comical fart, a stringy rooster's chicken-flop—lives of snippets and shards, braided into loose strands of years.

The dream dawned in black air. Old One-eye strode forth, and the boy fell out of his blinded eye and hid behind his sinewy leg. The vultures perked up. The god pried open his toothless mouth. His voice was a glacial wind in the firs, a moonrise between each word.

What do the Shining One's dreams portend?

The vultures aped Mik's comic faces, twisting their beaks into grimaces of *Who farted?* Bald brows knitted in deep thought, the gaunt fowls hooted—

Hot spell.

Clearing off.

Chance of showers.

Or not.

They set up another clatter, gullets spewing carrion. Wadan's fists flexed to wring their necks, but he was powerless before them.

Trumpet blares—

Serpent squirms—

Gnash of fangs—

Or not.

They waggled their wings, hopped in circles, pissing down their legs. One vulture waddled up to One-eye, hissed spittle—

We weave the story. You make it be.

The others joined their sister, all smiles, in unison chortle—

For deeper knowledge ask Wadan.
He sees the Nine Realms.
He reads the Runes.
He knows.

The old god wiped the spittle from his brow, pursed his leathery lips, and croaked out a resonant croak—

I am Wadan, I.

Their mandibles gaped. They tilted their heads aslant. They shrugged their wings. They mustered a feeble cackle and slunk away.

Oh dear . . .

Bragi saw the old god's visage clot into a prune, then dissolve in a flash of tatters, rags in the wind. The boy struggled to rouse but couldn't work the clasp. Then the wickerwork lid flapped shut and he woke. The sun was as bright in his face as ice. His first thought was to change his line to *The Norns are eating the porridge.* They'd be funnier than pigs, but only if people could see the Norns.

At breakfast he said nothing of his dream.

～

Forgive me, my liege, if at times I add literary flourish to my six-year-old fancies. Those days were as strange to me then as now, though surely my childhood knowledge of life—formed entirely of questions—surpassed what I know at present.

And from that time—after the pirates, the travel, the masks, the terrors to come—I was never the same. I had glimpsed the dark reddened sewers of life, its waggling man-things, its guttings, putrescence. One day I was child, next day adult, then child again, but never the same. We mature the way a donkey balks and brays. It occurred to me, as the dawning crept forth that day, that I had never yet heard Yesu bray. Did he fear to speak what he saw on the road ahead?

Years later, when my mother was old and I was attempting to be a man, she spoke of that time when we were uprooted weeds—the masks, the voices within, the risk of unleashing the fires. She was always fearful of what she called the Sight, that I might have it. But she must have known that our story was already laid out by the curse we carried with us: our inheritance.

—VII—
Saint's Play

Each year my father paid factotums to arrange the shows, and it was exciting to receive a missive. A rider rode up to our cottage, called out Papa's name, "Mikolaus!" and neighbors would traipse across the fields to marvel: a mere folded scrap of parchment but from worlds away. From a prince we had one we always kept: a scroll of fine vellum inviting our presentation. My sister keeps it now.

~

Next morning they struck camp. Edra said what she always said. "Clean up or some god will yell, *Who made this mess?*"

It was two days' travel to Pavia, Padia, something. Ludd led the donkey, who seemed to feel a kinship. Edra marched at the rear with measured stride even though she complained of achy knees. Bragi had nagged to ride the jouncing cart, but after they hit a deep rut that shook loose a baby tooth, he chose to walk at the side. The two big wooden wheels had thin strips of iron on the rims, and he wondered who ever thought up a wheel. He lost himself in the turning.

The sky was clear. Mik and Asta walked ahead, singing snatches of song. "*On the road to the end of the road—*" They spoke in low voices about a saint's play. Bragi caught a few words but didn't know what a saint's play was. He lagged back to the rear of the cart.

"Gramma, what's a saint?"

"A saint's a dead man that did something good for God."

"What god?"

"Whatever. In Pavia we're hired by the Cristers. They've just got one god, or three, whatever, I don't know how that works, maybe they do." She pondered for a moment. "But lots of their saints got killed."

"Why?"

"They got uppity." Edra was a forgiving soul except to those who got uppity. It was one of her favorite words.

Saints remained a mystery. He trotted forward to walk behind Mama, watching her hips, her long skirt and stride. She would get fat with the baby, Gramma said, but she wouldn't stay that way.

At Pavia, Padia, whatever, they would do their farces in the marketplace, and next night, paid by the merchants, play in the great hall to celebrate the town saint Eleora—not a goddess exactly, though you gave her gifts for favors, same as a god. She liked candles.

"Cristers hate plays." Asta stared at the road.

"Lot of 'em do," said Mik, "but this was Dmitri's idea. He loves us and pays for the feast. They like the feast."

The old plays had ended ages ago, but the little troupe's farces had no whiff of demonic gods, and people liked to laugh. Still, travel was hard, no way to predict the war or plague that lurked around the next bend. On the same route last year, a priest denounced them for having women on stage. The watchers shouted him down: they wanted to see the play. But one never knew. Would someone froth at the mouth if a woman played Eleora?

"She was female, wasn't she? Don't I have the attributes?"

"Maybe with a mask?"

"No masks!"

They trekked in silence as Bragi picked botfly eggs off Yesu. Not even Edra knew of saints' plays, but they had to produce something holy and fun in three days. "Fact is, she never did much," Mik grumbled. "Some saints got tortured or burnt alive, but she only started a nunnery. How do we act out a nunnery?"

It was their working pattern. Mik catalogued the conundrums, and when he ran out of breath Asta proposed the answers. But Bragi knew that a seed didn't sprout without hoeing and spreading manure. Papa was spreading manure.

"Don't their saints have favorite trades?" asked Asta. "The saint of carpenters or the saint of thieves?"

"Eleora's the patron saint of fish."

"Fish?"

"Or fishermen. A fisherman drowned and she raised him from the dead."

"So that's one scene. Ludd can play that. He was a fishmonger once."

"This was a fisherman, not a monger."

"Fish are fish."

As they wended through an endless stretch of olive trees, backing and filling, they formed the play. Bragi had seen a silversmith beating silver tappety-tap, and every tap brought it closer to form. What sounded like babble was craft.

Three scenes, they decided. The first, a praise of the saint. They knew a goddess song that, a few words changed, would work for Eleora. Then she makes a vow of chastity, which brings on a torrent of suitors: scenes from the farce where Mik played a lusty knight, a pedant and an ancient tanner. Founding a nunnery? Maybe after the suitors, she simply sighs, *I'd better found a nunnery!* And the third scene would be the dead fisherman.

Bragi couldn't hold back. "Can I be in it?"

"We'll see." His mother's patience was growing thin, so he didn't pursue it. They plodded on.

"How long should it be? The play?"

"Short. They want to be inspired, but not for long. When they start the third round of wine, we should be done. They'll still have lots of drinking and wenching to do."

"What's wenching?" asked the boy. No answer. The donkey plodded on, unmindful of saints. Bragi watched the tail flick flies away and wondered how Yesu could dump without mucking the strap at his butt. Edra sat at the back of the cart, knees grumpy from a lifetime of roads, looking back at the path she'd traversed. It must be like hearing voices through walls.

The sun was lower. Tree shadows stretched away to the sea. Bragi wondered if gulls slept at night in the trees or in the water. Always more questions, a looming cluster of hydra heads: cut off one and two more sprout up with needle teeth. That tale scared him whenever he thought about it.

They traveled till dusk and camped on a knoll that rose up from the flats like the wart on Gramma's chin. They pitched under a tree with roots writhing up from the earth. Another bedtime tale: the snakes that enwrapped the father and sons. And the moon rising over the sea always frightened him, a dull terror the way a cow would sink in quicksand straining and mooing. He had imagined the cow when his grandma told of it once, but the tale was almost worse than being the cow.

Next day they arrived in Pavia, Padia, whatever. Their host Dmitri was a squat red-nosed merchant with thin fuzzy hair and a bush of black whiskers dragging down his chin. He always paid well, Mik said, though he rarely smiled.

"He's got money," Gramma said. "He buys and sells."

"Sells what?" asked Bragi.

"That's not our concern."

He greeted them distractedly. "Very good, very good. Glad to have you. You'll stay back here. Cute little boy." He instructed his steward and hurried on to whatever he bought and sold. The villa was a cluster of rooms around an atrium, with quarters behind for the servants and slaves. Bragi was too young to know what distinguished servants from slaves. Later he learned the distinction. Still later he learned there wasn't that much distinction.

Ludd would sleep in the stables, while the family squeezed into a tiny room in the servant quarters with pallets on the floor. At the entry, Bragi hesitated. Mik tapped him on the head.

"What's the matter? Go in."

"The floor."

"What about it?"

"It's funny." He could see his toes reflected in the polish.

"It's wood. Rich people have wood floors, like the upstairs room at the inn, only this is shiny. You've been on lots of wood floors."

"Where's the ground?"

"It's under the planks. You won't fall in."

The boy stepped in, wary of the upside-down Bragi beneath him. He saw why Yesu balked at a rickety bridge. But when he sat on his pallet, away from the rattle of cart and clatter of beaks, he felt safer somehow. Maybe Saint Eleora would protect them. They ought to cook her a fish.

He went with his father down to the square to check the stage. Like all the others: a platform the height of a man, a curtain behind, steps front and back. Traversing the stage was learning to walk all over again. You crossed the stage in a curve—a stronger move, his father said. You stood facing halfway out so everyone could see you. You started a move with the foot away from the front except if your character was clumsy. You always crossed in front of others, and when someone entered, you stepped back to let them be seen. And then you forgot all that when you had to say your line. Acting was hard.

Next day in the marketplace they played the dead-donkey play and the three-wishes play, and the boy did his pee and parsnips lines. This time Ludd got some laughs. Over supper Bragi brooded, barely tasting his porridge. His parsnips got a laugh, but the pee line fell flat.

"They couldn't hear you," Mik explained. "You just came up and mumbled it to your mother."

"But that's how I'd say it."

"You have to say it so people can hear."

"I don't want'em to hear that I need to pee."

"Well imagine this is the worst you've ever needed to go, like you're God and God needs to pee out a whole thunderstorm."

"Which god?"

"Any god."

"Why?"

"End of the ride," said Asta.

That night his sleep was a scatter. Hearing the clattering beaks he blinked open his eyes, but he was under a roof. He practiced his pee line, but nobody laughed. He saw the little girl with her eyes fixed on his.

In the morning he resisted breakfast. Mama said the day would be long and he'd be hungry, but he didn't know how to give in without giving in. "All right," she said, and then he was stuck: he would starve all day and his mother didn't care. She set out a piece of bread and a hunk of cheese. "Well, they're here if you change your mind." Relief: he could change his mind, which wasn't the same as giving in to your mother.

He ate, then tagged along with his father to visit Yesu, who nuzzled his hand as the boy scratched his muzzle. *Muzzle, nuzzle*: that could be a song. He could make up songs, travel the lands, and kings would applaud. But what if that was the best song he ever made? There had to be more words than *Muzzle nuzzle*.

The saint's play would be in a church. Mik and Asta had performed in churches before, she on the lute, he the pipes, but they had never played a play there. That afternoon they went there to rehearse. It was a big stone room with heavy ceiling rafters, a floor of packed earth strewn with rushes, and at one end a table holding a wooden cross with a little wooden man dangling off it. The little man looked unhappy.

Mik saw his fascination. "That's their god, Bragi. He's like the god your mama talked about that hung himself on a tree."

"Why?"

"To learn wisdom. I guess he learned it hurts to dangle off a tree. But this one, he dies and comes back to life."

"Like the fisherman?"

"Like the fisherman. But the Cristers think we all come back to life."

"Truggie didn't."

"She didn't know how."

"How do you?"

"End of the ride," said Asta.

A wizened bald-headed priest emerged. His smile was wide, and he ruffled Bragi's hair with a *whee-whee-whee*. The only Cristers the child had met—the ones that he knew were Cristers—were tall and dour and never went *whee-whee-whee*. Gramma once said there were more things under the sun . . . something like that.

No stage, only a curtain on poles. They would play at floor level in front of it, with guests at trestle tables—three dozen of the better people, as termed by the whee-whee priest.

"They will enjoy the repast and imbibe refreshment in keeping with the spirit of the day."

"Meaning they'll all be drunk," Edra whispered to the boy. "Never tell what to expect from Cristers. Used to not be so uppity, but now they're all over the place. Chopping off each other's heads." Bragi wondered if the whee-whee priest had chopped off somebody's head. Not likely: he looked like a chicken himself.

That afternoon they walked through the play several times, saying their lines without acting it. Ludd would come in hawking fish and then drop dead. Bragi would be a cherub with palm-leaf wings, and when Edra called out for help the cherub would circle around the dead man, arms flapping, yelling, "*Help from Saint Eleora!*" and then fly off.

"Can I say I need to pee?"

"Angels don't pee," said Edra. "You're a little angel and you want to help poor Ludd, so you're calling the saint. What would you do if he really dropped dead?"

He thought he'd be so scared that he'd need to pee, but he didn't say it. Gramma would say that an actor pretends, but the *pretend* must be true—something like that. As she adjusted his wings he traced the long line of her nose down to the wart. Her eyes were glazed with cataract, but they pierced through the fog. Her eyebrows, pitched wide of the eyes, were thinned by time. He loved her as much as he feared her, and the fear was as strong as the love.

Help from Saint Eleora! That was his line. The red-nosed rich man gave them supper in the servants' common room, dried fish in a soup they sopped up with bread milled finer than their usual fare. It must be nice to be rich, and Bragi wondered how to do it. From the other table, a world away, the servants watched them warily.

They came into the church. The tables were full and the celebrants loud. The players had envisioned a sober assemblage, kneeling perhaps, hands in prayer, but found three dozen men and a sprinkle of women drinking toast after toast to St. Eleora. The whee-whee priest rose to introduce the play, but no one paid him heed, so he sat down and left the players the task of attracting attention.

That happened often. Part of the players' trade was surviving the unforeseen: a drunken heckler, a rampant cow, a pickpocket stir, or simply general chaos. Mik began a jig on the pipes, Asta on the tambour, and the players came dancing forth, halted, threw their hands in the air and bellowed in unison—

"*The Sacred Play of the Good Saint Eleora!*"

A sudden hush. Their voices blended in rising harmony, words of a poet praising some ancient god, but what worked for one god sufficed for another.

"*Let us praise the Lord of lightning
Hailing his Son with winged words—*"

Men looked up from their goblets, heard something in praise of a Lord and Son that induced a drunken sanctity.

"*Bear witness, Earth and Heaven,
The birth of the Archer Prince
Whose lips breathed nectar—*"

The Archer Prince must be the Savior. Like the old gods, he could fry you with a lightning bolt.

The congregation was silent. Men gnawed their bones and women sipped their oysters, but a reverent hush descended. Edra came forward with the measured stride of authority, despite her knees, and none could shift their eyes. Asta, faded back as she sang, then re-entered through the curtain flap: a woman near forty, pregnant, worn from the journey, but now with the spring and bounce of a teenage girl. Bragi was unsettled by the change that came over his mother.

"*Grandmother!*"

"*Sweet girl!*"

Their scene painted Eleora as the carefree daughter of a carpenter. When the crone mentioned her eager suitors, the girl grew pensive.

"*Grandmother, I feel a higher calling.*"

But soon the congregation of the faithful regained their festive mood. When the granny left and Eleora knelt in prayer, the catcalls began.

"Hey, sweetie, over here!"

"Do a dance!"

"Keep kneeling, babe, I'm on my way!"

The burghers whooped. Torches blazed. The rumble grew. Asta began a prayer. Mik entered, striking a lascivious pose.

"*Ah cutie-pie! I'm here!*"

His perfect mimicry of the catcall earned a raucous laugh, and his lecher was a hit. The players were no strangers to these challenges, though they hadn't expected it in a church. The saint knelt in prayer as her suitor circled her, writhing amorously, tongue lapping imagined flesh, humping his walking stick. They cut most of the dialogue: this audience wasn't receptive to jokes but loved Mik's agonized moans. At last the climax: he clapped greedy hands on her shoulders, and she rose to beat him with his walking stick. He turned tail to boisterous cheers.

Eleora stretched her hands to Heaven but knelt instantly as another suitor entered: the pedant. Opulent gestures, a tide of bloated pomposity and fractured Latin surged forth to conquer her chastity: "*Suculorium fuckuloricus sunt, uxorblueballis cuntorium prixit!*" The celebrants guffawed—they hated priests and scholars and all pretenders to wisdom, and they loved to wallow in smut. But it was a one-joke scene. As soon as the laughter peaked, Asta cut it short, beating him with his own erectile scroll.

Again, she went to her knees. The crowd set up a rhythmic clapping: good things came in threes. Mik donned a tattered white wig, emerged as a doddering coot barely able to breathe, stretched his lewd fingers toward her, further, further, and fell flat on his face. Asta dragged him offstage to a torrent of cheers.

The next scenes were less successful: more singing, more praying, a murky mime recruiting a cloister of nuns. Under one table, a scurvy dog began to howl. Restiveness turned to abuse.

"More funny stuff!"

"Hey, sweetie-pie!"

"Cut it short!"

From backstage, the boy saw his father give the bony man a shove, and Ludd staggered out to the wolves. He stood frozen, then remembered what he was there to do.

"*I got shrimp-sees, I got crab-sees, I got fish-ees, These from the seas! Fry my fish in your ovens, miladies!*"

He was getting into it, and for a moment he held the stage. Then the boy heard his father's loud whisper: "Die!"

What killed him no one knew, but Ludd withered and fell flat. Edra appeared, saw the corpse, and set up a howl. "Oh *help us, Saint Thomas! Help us, Saint Agatha! Help us, Saint Jude!*"

Bragi's cue: he ran onstage, flapping his palm-leaf wings and piping his line loud and clear. "*Help us, Saint Eleora!*"

And off. Applause, but a loud mocking call from the same persistent heckler. "Help us, Saint Ele-o-ora!"

An instant shift of mood, as mobs are prey to. One moment they love you, the next they rip you to shreds. Perhaps the drink, perhaps the bald absurdity of any belief, any hope or salvation, least of all from a local saint. A chunk of bread flung itself at the stage. The dog went into spasms. A drinking mug hit the curtain. A rhythmic table-top pounding arose. A deacon made a lip-fart and a squeeze-faced man drummed on the back of his wife. The hoots and whistles leapt through the church like wildfire. Mockery turned to ferocity like a trained bear turned on its keeper. Bragi shrank in horror.

Amid the storm, Saint Eleora appeared.

The face was the goddess Iduna, afire with spirit. The mob gasped as if slapped by a fish. Some froze, clutching their hearts, others slid to their knees. The air shivered with miracle. It was Asta, masked.

"*Heal. Rise. Live.*"

The saint spoke shrill thunder. Ludd popped up, his face crying wonderment, a baby crowning, eyes agoggle, amazed. The moment he knew himself free from slavery, the moment he got his first laugh, the moment he escaped the suck of the demon sea—in Pavia, Padia, whatever, for the first time ever, visible to all, a dead man was resurrected.

Without losing a beat, Asta stripped off the mask, the cast came forward in song—

"*All praise dear Saint Eleora*
Clad in virtue shining—"

—And the cheers rose in the night. The play was a wonder, causing drunken men to rise, cheer and weep, and then go on swilling as long as they could hold a mug. Behind the curtain, Mik sighed a deep sigh: he knew the performance was mediocre, cobbled together, accidental, flat—yet magical. Edra gathered the props as Ludd sat catching his breath. The boy untied his angel wings. He stared at his mother, astonished. She had chosen to wear a mask.

—VIII—
Fear

Late night they sat together in their tiny room at the red-nosed merchant's villa. Ludd would sleep in the stable again, but for now he was admitted to the circle of light. The oil lamp lit as much of their faces as needed to be seen. Their host had sent them a special treat, a pastry of honey and sesame seeds in a crisp baked shell. They savored the sweet crumbly gift, even as silence held them in its jaws.

After the play the merchant's compliments had been terse, but honey was better than plaudits, and the steward had paid their fee in full—not always a certainty. Still, Bragi sensed something amiss. Mik suggested an early morning departure. "Never wear out your welcome," with his lecherous pedant's finger upraised, "Carpe diem!" He could never let his son see a twitch of fear.

Despite scattered efforts to resume festive boozing, the spectators had trickled out soon after the play, draped in deep awe. Was it possible to penetrate too deeply into armored souls? The whee-whee priest approached them gingerly, his face in a tortured smile. He loved the music, the fisherman, the funny suitors, but said nothing of the saint. "Well, you know, we all believe, of course, but at times—" He groped for words. "There are occasions when— Not that we— Though one never knows if what we expect is— I loved your little cherub!" He ruffled Bragi's hair. It might be that grownups ruffled children's hair to make them grow up faster and say *Stop it!*

"All I remember . . ." Asta spoke in a whisper. Her face was pale, her hands trembled, and she took only a nibble of the sweets. She was rarely tender—more like the pointy bird that rat-tatted beetles out of the bark and protected her nest from the teeming cats—and yet under her wing he felt chilly but safe, till now. His mother's confusion filled the boy with a terror as deep as Time. With shadows moving sleepily on the walls, the pastry's sweetness intensified his fear. He tried to ask something but didn't know what to ask. A moth scorched itself crisp in the flame of the oil lamp.

Asta struggled with words. "I remember the tumult," she said, "and a thump on the curtain from something they threw." Disaster loomed, she knew: strong wine, a ramshackle show. "Our own fault," she said. "We didn't take time to think it through. We just stuck scenes together like sticking a swan's head onto a pig. Once we got the big laughs they wanted more of the same. They didn't know how to react."

"Although it felt more like a miracle," Mik said with a *who-can-say* gesture, "when they got all stirred up and then *Wham!*" He bonked himself on the forehead and went cross-eyed as if struck by divine intervention.

"If we want to stir up a hornets' nest. Remember we saw that mob tear a bear to pieces?"

"Though that bear was sick and couldn't raise a claw. Plus it didn't speak Latin." Mik hugged her shoulders. "Love, you did what you had to do. Things get weird, stick a mask on your face and act nutty—"

"I don't think I acted nutty—"

"No, Asta, you scared them half to death. Sir Flop went off in a cloud of dust."

"Is he coming back?" whispered Bragi.

"He tries, but we sniff him a mile away." Mik made his wise-idiot face, but the boy knew that when Papa went into his funny grimaces something was scary. "I know it's nothing to joke about," he once said of some misfortune, "but the only things worth joking about are what's nothing to joke about."

"Can we please drop it!"

Asta's voice cut through the shadow. She had told Bragi of her father's daily drill with his two-handed broadsword, lopping imagined heads with the practiced skill of trimming his beard. Her words could slash like that. Now she commanded silence to speak. Long wait. She might have stayed frozen there till eroded by wind, but she raised a tear-rutted face.

"All the yelling, and Bragi was out on stage, and I couldn't see what— And then I was out there, the song and the cheers. The whole middle of it is gone. The mask, putting it on, but how— The hamper was in the cart outside, and the cart was guarded. I couldn't have—" She made a wild gesture. No one spoke.

Her voice went low, controlled, almost inaudible. "My father killed for the masks. He couldn't help the killing, he said, or the curse. He told me those things in a voice I'd never heard, a little boy's voice in the dark. This huge bull of a man with a ghost inside him. Like hookworm."

Mik put his hand on her thigh. Edra yawned, ready for bed. Ludd nodded, confused. Bragi picked the last crumbs of dessert.

~

My mother had donned the mask. Out of panic, but making that choice of her own free will. That time by the light of the oil lamp was the first time I truly saw her, and I knew I would never know her. I felt thankful that I was a boy and would never be a mother.

In later years I understood more. She was a motherless mother, with only the faintest memories of her own mother's hands. She protected her nest from perils, her child from his childhood and her husband from his folly. On each tour she escaped robbers, rapes, disembowelings, not to mention Sir Flop, by the capricious grace of the Norns. She was heiress to a long-gone beheading and an endless trek.

Others' needs were clear. My father asked only to rouse laughter— what he was gifted to do. My grandma's imperative was surviving her rickety knees and her grandson, Ludd merely to make it through the day. For me these people's faces were open, while my mother was myth carved in runes. She saw the Nine Realms—the blood, the dung, the vulpine shadows—and feared that I saw them too. As I did.

Much later I came to see each human soul as a palimpsest. The true danger of names is to create the delusion that they confirm the existence of what they name. You, my lord, know me as Francellas—Francesco of Hellas—the name I chose at the onset of formal schooling. And yet that soul—his memories, his beliefs, his sparse chin beard—is only a chart of accounts, a fable or frivolous jest written over layers of text that Time has scraped away. Perhaps we should change our names at intervals before they root themselves and cling to our nose like a cyst.

Once in my childhood I peeled an onion to see what it held inside. Of course it held only more layers. That night might have been the first that I felt of the peeling-away of days and a doubt of ever coming to the core. Thinking of the play-acted fisherman, I had no clear concept of death, but I imagined that you just lay there and let the flies land. No wonder we dreaded it.

∼

"I was Iduna." Her voice was a little girl's from the distant past. She sang a fragment of song in another tongue, a melody she might have sung with her sister Mia. She forgot the words, sang *da-da-da*, and stopped. "They saw me as the saint, but the face was Iduna. I felt apples in my hands. The gods ate apples to stay young, and I was the giver of apples."

Unable to follow the thread, Ludd cleared his throat and asked if he'd done all right. Yes, Mik told him, fine, he had a natural talent, growing by leaps and bounds. With that, Ludd perked up, inspired. "And so what if the fishmonger is really the one-eyed god, and I flop on the floor but the saint gives a wave so I pop in a new eye and stand up and yell, *I can see!*" He saw the faces go blank. "Just an idea." Ludd rose, said good-night, and departed to sleep in the stable.

A silence enveloped them. Edra blew her nose, flicked it away. murmured, "Some god is taking a dump." It was a favorite phrase of hers when wordlessness reigned.

"The masks are curst," said Asta.

Edra spoke. "Do tell. It's you that holds onto the things."

"My blood oath—"

"Blood oath!" Edra looked up to the heavens or the ceiling in comic disbelief. Asta held back the invective that surged to her lips. "Well," the old woman ventured, "if there's a curse in a play, it has to come true. We'd feel swindled if it didn't. That's why you keep 'em, I guess."

"That's not real life. That's stories." Asta was lost in the maze.

"Where you think they come from? Who hasn't bought the dead donkey or beat the dead horse?"

The boy saw stories in his grandmother's clouded eyes, those she had told and those that lurked untold. Was she seeing the monsters around the bend, he wondered, or were we the monsters, terrified of ourselves?

Asta's words came ahead of her breath. "Time for bed," she told the boy. He objected but knew it was futile. "Long day tomorrow. That's all for tonight."

"Who's Iduna?"

"It's just a story. Tomorrow."

He flopped on his pallet and stared at the ceiling flickers. Tonight he missed the stars. The grownups' voices came to him in whispers. Edra chuckled, recalling a paunchy burgher who had gone to sleep with his fingers in his trencher, waking abruptly at the fearsome saint's entry and splatting his palm in the stew. They strained to stay lighthearted.

"You have more eyes than Argus," Mik joked, "You see so much."

"I see better now through my cataracts."

Asta was quiet. She poured another cup of wine and forgot to water it. Odd, thought the boy. Usually his mother drank wine only when the water was bad. She said it made the water safe. A chill in the air. Edra retired to her pallet.

Mik and Asta shared the narrow bed. Mik kept on his clothes as he shuffled under the blanket. Asta rose and snuffed out the oil lamp. The boy heard them talking but couldn't make out the words.

Quiet laughter and then a sob. What was said between man and woman at night?

In the cracks of moonlight he saw his mother rise, felt her kneel down and snuggle in beside him. Again her voice was a little girl's.

"I just want to be with my boy a little bit."

"Okay."

After a time she spoke, more to herself than to him. "Sometimes it feels like . . . what? You're somebody else. There's a face that people see, but you're not there, you're hollowed out, you're—"

"Who?"

His voice startled her. She hadn't known he was hearing her speak. She tried to find words. "You can't tell who. Your mother, your sister, your father, all of them gone. They knew you, but they're gone, so who are you? I just want— Sorry, sweetie, I guess— Just a moment where I feel this creature that was part of me for a while. You, little boy."

She was all edge. She desired to be warm and loving but had scant gift for it. They lay staring into the dark of a god's blind eye, and the boy heard fear on her breath. The first that it ever occurred to him that his mother knew fear.

Before he was asleep, he woke. Mama was hugging him. "You were crying in your sleep," she said. He felt ashamed, six years old and needing baby comfort.

He mumbled. "Iduna . . ."

She heard him but couldn't understand, nor could he. Nothing to be understood, not a crack to see the world that flickered its shadow soul in his face. He strained to have a glimpse through the veil—and then in a flash a thousand suns at a bridge from frost to fire. He was seeing something he shouldn't see. In the glare of the moon they opened their eyes to each other, and both grasped the knowledge. She was horrified. He could see the gods. The gods wanted free.

—IX—
The Froggies

Up early to hit the road. The next stretch would take three days. The weather had cleared but the sky was overcast, so they would head in from the seacoast in hopes to find shelter if it blew up a storm. Their sleeping gear, draped over stalls in the merchant's stables, had at last dried out, and their stock of barley, sausages, onions and wine was replenished, so all was readied.

The red-nose appeared. "Morning." He motioned Mik into the stable to confer. Ludd picked himself up from the straw, led out the donkey to harness, and helped the women to load the cart. Bragi and Yesu stared at one another in unspoken brotherhood.

Mik returned. "What did he say?" asked Asta with quiet concern.

"Well, first off, amazing: he gave us more money." He held two gold coins in his palm. The donkey jerked its head, sensing Asta's wonder or else annoyed by a fly. "Which I think means he won't have us here again." He checked Yesu's bridle. "He felt obliged to warn us that some of our audience, though drunk, were fearful of sorcery. That we conjured the dead to rise."

"But they believe in that. That's their whole story."

"You can do it if you're a saint. We're no saints." He hung his head in mock shame, came up cross-eyed, bonked himself in the temple to straighten his gaze—an old, old comic bit. "But he himself was very moved, so he paid us a bonus and urged that we get our asses gone."

The sun rose over the sea at their backs and pushed them toward the hills. Yesu stopped now and then to graze, and Bragi frisked ahead to kill robbers with a stick. The path took an upward slant and their steps became a trudge. And the first night, on a hillside naked to the stars, the boy dreamt.

～

We regard dreams as unreal, though much of our life is spent in that unreality. That night's vision was like nothing I had ever dreamt before, but I was a player now and players would dream in plays. It had begun with my sight of the Norns—the true authors of our folly—and ended only as my childhood ended a few months hence.

My mother must have told me the story before my birth, some distant night when I was still in her womb. She often spoke to the nameless stir within her. Though nothing more than ripening fruit, I felt her voice—then lost it amid the riptide of birth.

～

It was a play. The boy—in his mask as Bragi the singer of songs—was dreaming a play. On the trestle stage he awaited his cue. Onlookers gawking open-mouthed crowded the innyard. He saw the cat-eyed spitting girl and the whee-whee priest in rapt attention. The farm wife held out a rooster. Others were holding out roosters as if to the gods.

The players wore fearsome masks: long concave faces, sharp noses from crown to lip, tumultuous hair. He knew each god from their gemstone eyes. Frekka, ice crystal. Reya, soft coals. Teorr, granite. Wadan with one huge emerald orb, one raw hole. The names came to him through the walls of the womb. Their lips were sealed, but their words were the drumming of blood.

Our son—

An alien tongue in the burr of stinging flies, flickers of flame. One moment they were living stone, then suddenly dream stuff, reflections on water, shadows in air.

Balthur—

Shining One—

Beloved son—

The amber sparkle of Balthur was too bright to be endured. He raised hands to his shimmering face as if to erase his eyes. The boy half-woke in the tumult. He remembered. Balthur the God of Light had dreamt a dark dream of—

Elementals—

Primals—

Strange Ones—

Freaks! The mighty Teorr rumbled thunder. *Squash'em under my thumb!*

A family squabble, perfect for a play. Wrinkle ruts deepened in Wadan's mask. Frekka the careworn mother fumed. Veins bulged on Teorr's brow. Each breath brought a volley of words, flung, spat or hissed in the whirling wind. Bragi's heart knew the tale from infancy. The Primals, Elementals, Strange Ones lived naked, raw, bestial lives. They were said to hate the gods, though the Shining One cried to be heard—

I have crossed the Primals' realm. They turned belly-up to my light. They are no more threat than the tide that drowns only those who defy it. We have nothing to fear.

They hate us! his half-blind father raged.

The dreaming boy woke to the howling of wolves. It was only a play, a dream of a dream. The spitting girl watched, roosters cackled, and Bragi awaited the cue to call out his parsnips line, but the lips of his mask were sealed.

The fearsome silhouettes played out a farcical squabble. The ice-crystal mother embraced the Shining One, thrust a bone finger at One-eye: *Our son dreams of chattering teeth, so you trumpet war?*

Wadan emitted a mighty roar. *Out of my father's flesh I have butchered worlds. I have gouged out an eye for keener sight, hung crucified on the World Tree to learn the runes. My judgment is true.*

Because you speak it?

Bragi's dream ran rampant. He tried to grab the reins, but the cart was jolting and veering off the edge— The echoes of angry gods pattered down in a gentle rain on the sailcloth tenting. He must have been asleep when the tent was pitched. Now it was still, except for the rain. He stared into the night, floating back into the dream that spread over him like honey.

He tried to catch the strange warble and screech of the feud. Ghost words of the mother goddess or only the whistle of wind? *Is blindness vision? Is truth the crafting of better lies to live by? When we suck at the breast, do we suck in shadow?*

The play proceeded implacably. Faced with his queen's invective, One-eye was irresolute. The ham-fisted Teorr offered to spy, perhaps to launch a killing spree, but the sharp-eyed Loghi joined him: *I know the Primals' tongue and share their blood.* They set off circling the stage, a journey between the worlds. Teorr carried his hammer, a maul the length of an arm, in one meaty paw.

Loghi grinned: *On the road again, friend.*

Friend? Teorr's gristle lips grew taut.

Telling the tale long ago, his mother had caught their voices—the acrid burble of Ham-fist, the lemon-sharp slur of the trickster god.

Friend indeed. Did I not steal Iduna from Thiazi's clutch, saving the gods from a withering death?

Having shoved her into his hands.

And spun your wife a golden mane?

After shaving her bald. You do knuckle under to death threats. Ham-fist laughed at his own riposte.

Loghi grinned. *Did I not bring gifts to the gods? Your hammer that never fails?*

Ham-fist held up his paw. *Wait! A mortal!* From far off he heard a plea for revenge and the offer of a goat. He flung his hammer, a distant *Oof!* and the hammer flew back to his grip.

The *Oof!* woke Bragi. He heard a tattle of rain on the tenting that sounded like the skitter of rats. The Primals slipped out of the shadows into his wakeful sleeping eyes: a dozen crabbed creatures hunched like bears, with glacial skin and the gaping faces of frogs.

A hush, then the Froggy Ones spoke, lips moving in unison croak. They waved their knurled hands.

Look! Funny! Ho ho!

Ham-fist demanded translation. The grim grinner obliged. *They say, We greet you, mighty ones.*

Small fry! Come eat! Suck tittie?

They say, Welcome to our feast.

Grim-grin explained to his comrade the Primals' tradition: to challenge honored guests to games, with a drinking bout for a start. The Froggy Ones blatted one mighty *Ho!*

Teorr laughed. *Drinking? We'll drink you under the table, Blubberguts!*

Blubberguts! The Froggies guffawed. They produced drinking horns, sloshed them full, gulped the brew in one gulp, and belched a choral belch.

Teorr upended his vessel, chugging a waterfall. His swig went on and on and on. He gasped, face purple, knuckles white, and collapsed in a geyser of drool. The Froggies chuckled politely.

Whatta they say? demanded Teorr. *Nice try*, his friend replied. Laughter, but where was the audience? Naught but rocks on the mountainside. Now the boy saw that the gods were funny. The troupe could play this play and get rich and buy a big horse—if they found enough Froggies to play it.

Foot race! Fast runner! Hot foot!

Grim-grin grinned. *I fly like the slice of a sword.* As Teorr glared, Loghi's skull stretched to an arrowhead and the length of his spine sprouted fletching.

Their champion runner waddled forth from a wheeze of dust: flushed face, stiff haunches, scarcely able to lug his beer belly a step to the starting line. The gape-mouth goons proclaimed the rules: *Run to forest, pluck holly, run back. Count of three. Go.* Loghi was off like lightning. Beer-belly held up a holly sprig. *The winnah!*

The stones of the mountainside popped in laughter. The Grinner stormed back. Teorr raised his mighty hammer, but the Froggies froze into pillars of salt, no twitch of life, nothing to kill.

Befuddled but undefeated, Teorr snarled. *Wrestling. I'll battle your champ. Bring on your colossus!*

From the froggy megaliths rose a hearty *Wowser!* Through their ranks hobbled a doddering crone, bird thighs, wrists like straws. *She the champ*, quoth the pillars of salt. *Tough cookie.*

The livid Ham-fist lunged at the crone, ran into her withered palm, sprawled flat. He rose, grabbed her wrist to fling her ten thousand leagues, and collapsed beneath the weight of her butterfly thumb. He squeezed her in a bear hug, but a delicate cough sent him reeling. He charged, clutched her neck in an armlock but felt his own forearm crushing out his breath. He sank to his knees, gasped, wheezed. The crone doddered away as the Froggies guffawed, belched, chirped *Bye bye!* They waddled over the crest.

Bragi's eyes blinked open. No spark of light, no moon, no mountainside. No clapping, no cheers, no clink of coins in the pot. The end of the play? Would they sing a song? Panic struck him, though he didn't know what he feared. In his head he started to run, hit a slippery spot, and sprawled back into his dream.

We must face hard truths, said Loghi.

Teorr stumbled to his feet, flexed his spent sinews. *Truth is a bitch*, he moaned.

Do tell. They turned to see a scrawny woman, if woman she was, perched on the low wheeled cart of a legless beggar. Her skin was a sheet of gristle over a skull-bone face, her fingers spines, her eyelids translucent as moth wing.

Spare change?

Piss off! Teorr was in no mood for aught but hammer blows.

The beggar persisted. *Spare change, friends? Plug that hole in your heart?*

We're gods, slut! Gods don't have hearts, we have hammers!

The hag squinted. *It's him!* she crowed. *Him and the Funny Ones! They sure fooled him!* Her laughter came near to shaking her joints apart. His grip on his hammer hardened.

Between chortles and gasps, Skull-face revealed the deceptions. *He thought he was drinking beer: he was drinking the ocean, drank it half up, whole cities up from the sea.*

Teorr foamed at the nose and stomped in rage.

You, Grinner, you ran a race, but the runner was Thought. Thought's there as soon as you think it.

Teorr hooted. Loghi's grin twisted into a Gordian knot.

And big boy wrestled the crone: she was Age. No beating that stiff-arm, not even a god.

They stood like little boys who'd just wet their pants. The beggar hawked phlegm and offered consolation. They had terrified the Froggies: drinking up half the ocean, flying like arrows, surviving the claw of the crone. But Teorr would not suffer humiliation. He flung his hammer. The beggar's brains spattered the stones and set the granite afire.

The flames brought dawn to the eyes of the boy, but he clenched his lids more tightly. He tried to finish the dream, but it kept repeating: same fling of the hammer, the spatter, the fire. Teorr's breath recalled their neighbor's old ox who huffed out its grunts, any weather.

They'll die laughing. Teorr wrestles old ladies and they beat him! Ham-fist was in despair.

Grim-grin ventured to place his smooth hand over Ham-fist's white knuckles. *My friend, be at ease. We may trust in fear.*

Fear? They'll laugh their asses off.

Fear is our friend. Consider. Loghi laid out the plan. *We say only what we have seen. Devious hearts swift as light, whose weakest creature conquers the mighty Teorr. Is this a cause for mockery or for dread? Strange Ones, Funny Ones, no! These are the . . . Fearsome Ones!*

We say what we saw?

We do.

That's honest.

Not even gods—

Are secure.

So then prepare—

For war.

Through the flames of the burning rock the boy watched them swagger away. He saw the brainless beggar drag herself onto her cart and chuckle into the fire. He woke to a fearsome dawn.

No dawn: the dawn was a dream. The grownups were still at the fire. He had dreamt horror, yet he surfed on a joyous tide. He had made up a play, a whole play, and the play was funny. They could play it, make money, and he could be one of the Froggies. He cried out.

His mother tried to restrain herself from heeding his wails, fearing he might grow babyish, but Edra had no such worry. Like the rooster his hide would toughen soon enough. She came to him.

"Can't sleep? Long day?"

"Dream."

"Dreams, yeh. They crawl in your ears and can't find their way out. That's why they get nasty."

He whined at her cajoling him like a child when he'd just dreamt a play that would make them rich.

"Scary?"

He nodded. It was dark so he hoped she wouldn't see his nod, but her wrinkles caught the firelight and he saw the glint of her cloudy eyes. He mumbled about the Froggies.

"Oh, them!" she said. "That was a story your mama told, long time ago. You wanted a story so she told it."

"It was masks."

"Those things. Well, we won't let'em out of their basket now. They're locked up tight."

"No!" They would need them to do his play. They would make money and they'd build a castle with shiny toilet bowls. But already the dream was slipping through his fingers like tiny fish. By morning it might be fishbones.

That night the trees were silver. If they cut down the trees they'd be even more rich, but he could only snuggle into his blanket. He hoped that Mama would tuck him in—she was softer at night—but it was still Gramma beside him.

"Can we put on the faces again?"

"Go to sleep now."

"Can we?"

"Your mama doesn't like the masks. They scare people, like the pirates. Go to sleep."

"Gramma . . ."

"That's me."

"What happens?"

"What happens when?"

"With the mask. Are you somebody else?"

"Well I did it just that once."

She knew more than she was saying. Mostly she told the truth, looking straight into him with sharp clouded eyes, but now she glanced into the tree limbs that flickered with firelight.

"Gramma?"

"I already told you. Now go to sleep, or that moon will come down and gobble you up. It's all big and fat from gobbling up little boys."

"Please!"

She was set to tell him one final time to sleep—and it better be the last! Instead, she laid her hand on his chest. *Hold this to your heart*, she was saying. Her gravelly voice changed color. She was a little girl whispering a secret.

"We never used masks. My man's granddad saw them once when he was a little boy. Scary, he said. A player, it sucks him up and he disappears. Just leather scraps on his face but it taps a river down in the bone. Take it off, it's dead. Put it on, it's resurrected, like the Cristers would say. But stuff get resurrected that had ought to stay dead."

When Edra started talking she rambled on like a goat to the next clump of weeds. She spoke of the long-ago players who played in masks. Horrific plays. A mother killed her babies. A god drove women mad. A hero went crazy and slaughtered sheep. A king tore out his eyes. A sure way to make the boy sleep: tell him terrible things and he'd squeeze his eyes shut from the sight. And so she droned on, her voice growing ever woolier until it covered the sleeping child.

~

The dream of the Froggy Ones surely derived from my mother's tales, but it played like a farce. Nothing but my father's gifted gibberish matched their utterance. Perhaps, as priests might claim, my tender ears were open gates to demons.

Even then the masks puzzled me. The Norsemen had no such things, yet they took shape and speech as my mother's gods. Was the casket a chrysalis sheltering change from grub to butterfly, from Juno to Frekka? Were they seashells possessed by hermit crabs? Did the old sorcerer's gush of blood beget a monstrous pregnancy?

Yet the faces I saw daily—my parents, my grandma, the hireling—those were the greater bewilderments. What blind hopes, illusions, obsessions propelled them? My family might have taken a season's earnings, bought a small shop or tavern, and lived out their lives in peace. Instead we wended northward, driven and pregnant and curst. Yet all would be well, I believed, if I could only recall that singular dream of the Froggies.

—X—
The Wall

The only thing left of the dream was the fear. And the Norns came again to mind, hopping and pissing and making a clatter. I longed to wear the mask of the singing god, to open its lips in praise of the dawn, the olive trees, the salt air, but I feared the fear. I carried the fear in my heart like a sacred stone. I could only hope that some day it would make us rich.

Yet in troubled times, then as now, who could be free of noontide nightmares? Feed on fear, we grow fat with it. We eat ourselves.

~

All the next day, behind the swish of Yesu's tail and the creak of the wheels, Bragi strained to recall his froggy dream. He saw the burly man under the hand of a spindly crone, the grin of the Grinner, the burning rocks, but the rest was a blur. He couldn't stop thinking of coins dropping into the pot.

Midday he was struggling to think of the dream but heard himself ask his mother, "Why can't we eat like we do?"

"You mean at midday? We eat. I give you some cheese then, some bread, but we're on the road. We can't dig out the cookware and make a fire. We have to wait till we stop for the night. You want some cheese?"

"Will we always?"

"Till we get home. You know that. Then we'll be back to normal."

"Couldn't we just—"

"End of the ride."

During the long plodding afternoon he looked into a tangle of vines and suddenly saw the monster with snakes in her hair. Another old bedtime tale, but it had always haunted him, spawning sharp-clawed, fanged, unthinkable dreams, useless for plays: people wanted to laugh. Or maybe a play where they saw that the monster was only a tangle of vines? But who would believe it? Monsters were more credible.

That night by the edge of the fire he stirred coals with a stick, still struggling to remember the froggy dream but seeing only the splatter of brains. His mother came to him, placed her hand on his forehead and gazed into his eyes. "Just checking if there's fever, but you're fine." She mustered a smile, but she wasn't checking for fever. She was looking for what she feared: that he had the curse of Sight. That he could see other realms.

Late night, she came to lie next to him on his pallet. "Just till you're sleeping, little boy." She rarely did that, though he thirsted for it. She was always a Northman's daughter: childhood was weakness, and weakness was fatal. He saw that her eyes were looking through him, past him, into another night. She saw her father telling a story to his girls, to her and her lost sister Mia. Their faces shone in the firelight.

"Mama?"

"What is it?"

"Tell about the wall."

"Not now." She lay silent. "I never said anything about a wall."

"Yes you did."

"I never did." A tense silence. "I thought of it. I never said it." No, she hadn't said it, but he had heard it.

"Please?" He saw her lips go taut, and he couldn't help but push harder. There came a fleeting image: the day when he would be as tall as his mother, when his will met hers, when they flung storms of invective like stones at one another. The image fled. He was still only six but seized by a desperate itch to be consumed by fear.

"Not now, sweetie. It's a funny story, but it brings back my sister Mia. How our daddy told us stories after our mother died, by the campfire at night, and the wolves hushed up to listen. And then Mia died and I don't want to see her right now."

He knew, if he stayed silent, that the blackness would draw it out of her. He tried to match her breath, to breathe as she breathed, and at last she turned toward him, propped herself on an elbow, and began to tell the tale of the wall, though he was never sure if she spoke it or if he dreamt it.

She spoke in a half-sung drone as her father would have told it, as the bard he had heard it from told it, as bards back to the birth of Time had breathed it alive. The tone was flat, matter-of-fact, as her father must have recited the tales of his raids—a kindly man, speaking of his killings as if they were fish he had caught. *This I did*, he would say, *and then this.* Only much later did Bragi recall that she spoke in the alien warbling tongue and that he grasped it.

~

I lost my dream of the Froggies. For your amusement I have retrieved it after forty years, but far too late to make my mother and father rich. Nor have I ever professed belief in magic or in worlds beyond this world. Of course I accept the doctrines of Heaven and Hell, legions of angels and other mystical improbabilities revealed by Divine Revelation—a heretic has no future in this day. And yet I, above most others, have seen, heard, felt the cold breath of the Unreal. It is said that if one has suffered the pox God's mercy may render you immune. Mayhap I am immune to gods because they have possessed me.

~

The gods were slowly dying from doubt, distress, disquietude, she said. Like humans, the gods could die. Iduna's apples sustained them but never dissolved the grinding dread that eroded their bones. Teorr and Loghi reported the deadly threat of the Fearsome Ones, stirring a cloud of stinging flies in every heart. All-father Wadan

ordered a wall to be built surrounding Asgard—a bulwark against
the future. A tremor shook the celestial hills, and out of a whirlwind
the Builder appeared: a flurry of smoke extruding a pair of huge,
heavy-knuckled, callused gray hands.

I'll build you a wall, quoth he.

How do we trust your skills?

No choice. I am your Builder.

Your price?

What price walls that shut out death?

The haggling commenced with deafening tumult. At each gust
the price went higher, and at last the Builder made his final bid—

I claim the Sun, the Moon, and the goddess Reya.

Asta's normal way with stories was to keep it brief, whereas Edra
spun it out with the ripple and squeeze of milking a cow or the breath
of an ancient tree. Yet now Asta spun it out, smoothing the lumpy
dough with her baker's fingers.

"*I build walls that stand forever*, the Builder claimed in his snooty
voice." With a wry grimace Asta interjected, "That was a part I never
believed, nor my sister neither. No wall stands forever." She took a
long breath. "But the Builder's price was terrible: give him the goddess Reya, who brings love to the world?" She shuddered, whether in
pretense or chilled to the bone. "What about that? What if I couldn't
love your father? What if I couldn't love you?"

Bragi clung to her hand. "Imagine a world without love," she said,
and the boy saw the goddess drifting away—green eyes, auburn hair
and her fluttery hands—the way a stream went dry in the drought.
"Love makes new life, even donkeys and sisters and cats. Imagine
long ago that rickety priest and our red-nosed bushy Dmitri were
babies born of love. Like rain: it has to rain for the grain to grow."

Somehow the boy knew that the greater the strength of the gods
the greater would be their fear and the folly born of their fear. Asta
embraced her son more tightly, as if to protect him from the Sight
she awakened in him.

"And Balthur assailed the Builder's blast of demands. *What is
life without light and love? Do we huddle behind our wall eternally*

atremble? And the gods agreed: *Never! Won't do it! Can't!* Yet they glanced at the goddess Reya, asking, *Can we?* And old One-eye stood like deadwood, his blind socket black, his good eye clouding over."

The boy stared at the oaken figure of Wadan. "And Reya asked them, she said, *Would you squander life's renewal for a masonry of dread?*" Then Asta went silent. For a moment the boy feared she was demanding him to reply. Why had he asked for the story? He hadn't known he would have to decide the fate of donkeys and sisters and cats.

"In my father's voice it was fearful," she continued, embracing him. "Not only the words, but his icy blue eyes. My sister whimpered, I held her tight and she held me. But she liked the story. She liked the scary ones."

"What happened to her?"

"I told you that." Her eyes went cold. "Our mother got sick and died, and then Mia got sick and died. I told you that. My father buried them somewhere. Remember what you're told!"

He remembered, but some things had to be told again. Another telling might straighten the tangles. He clung to his mother more tightly.

"Mama?"

"What?"

"Do stories change?"

Asta made no reply. She was sitting by the fire with Mia. Their father had fallen asleep to the howling of wolves. His chanting enflamed them, each deep in the other's eyes. Through the next days of the journey, as the cord frayed and snapped, Asta clung to the sight of those burning eyes. When the father resumed the story, he told it to one living girl.

"So, the gods—" his mother went on. "Are you listening, Bragi?"

"Yes."

"So the gods said no, they would not pay the price. *Then build your own wall*, he said. *Build it with love songs. Build it with soap bubbles, feathers, fluffs of wool on the breeze. But then better sleep with your eyes wide open.* And the Builder sneered a mighty sneer." She looked down at the boy. "So what if you played the Builder? Could you sneer a mighty sneer?" Bragi was too sleepy to try. "No matter. You'll learn to." His mother was joking with him. She never did that. There must be something terribly wrong.

"So the gods were even too scared to pee. But Loghi, remember him? The grinny god?"

"Was he bad?"

"Well, but he could do nothing they didn't allow him to do. Like if our donkey wanted to wade in a swamp and he sank in quicksand, could we say, *Well, not our fault, he wanted to wade*?"

"I don't want him to."

They subsided to a whisper. Bragi didn't want to hear more of the story and Asta didn't want to tell it, but now the story was telling itself. Again the wolves hushed their howling to hear it.

"And he gave the gods gifts, remember? So Loghi told them to make the bargain but set a day to finish that the Builder couldn't meet. He would run out of days and the gods could lay the last stones. Was that a good way to go, you think?"

His mother didn't wait for an answer. She was playing with him. Her voice was lightened of years, freed from her sister's dead eyes. Her words formed snarling lips, sharp smirks, and the Builder's great sinewy hands. She was hearing the story anew.

They commanded the Builder to finish the wall in six months' time. *Agreed.* The love goddess glowered, Grim-grin grinned. The Builder spat to seal the bargain. He harnessed his horse to haul the stones. A mighty stallion, ten times the size of Yesu.

(Mama said *Yesu.* She said the donkey's name.)

The Builder outpaced his promise. Before the first frost of winter the wall was halfway done. By the spring melt he would rob them of love and light. Time lurched to the finish line: last day, last hour, and the mighty horse drew the last massive stone. The gods stood benumbed. Who would save them?

"Loghi!" The boy heard his own dreamy whisper.

His mother's voice. "Loghi was wise to horses. He took the form of a mare. The stallion stopped, sniffed, smelt spring and went after the mare, despite the Builder's whip. *One last stone for the archway!* he cried, but the stallion pursued his desires."

Asta went silent, the boy snuggled close, the dead sister strained to hear, and Gramma snored a delicate snore as the story wended its way to the end. No words from Asta, only images dancing in air. The Builder raged, the horses did what horses will do, the sun came to its zenith, the Builder lost the bargain, and the gods set the final stone.

"My sister laughed at that. She hated the Builder. He was greedy, she said, but I felt sorry. He did all the work and they cheated him."

"But he wanted the moon and stuff."

"That's what Mia said. We fought a lot. Once I found a turtle and wanted to keep it, but she said let it go. We started to yell and Daddy picked up the turtle and flung it into the river."

"What happened?"

"It swam off."

"I mean to the Builder!"

"They killed him, I guess. Teorr, with his hammer. Like my father got killed."

"In a play?"

"No, your grandpa the soldier. The other side won the battle. I told you that. Everyone's got two grandpas."

"Where?"

"They're dead! End of the ride!"

The boy turned his face to his pallet. His mother was silent, scratching an itchy elbow, then wrapped up the tale. "So they were safe. Or felt safer. Who knows? We think stories finish, but they go right on."

She tucked the blanket around him and saw his haunted eyes. "Time to sleep. Long day," she whispered. "It's just a story, sweetie, it didn't really happen. Now you dream you're feeding Yesu an apple, and he says, *Thank you, Bragi.*"

She kissed him, rose from the pallet, felt her way to her bedding. The boy heard his parents embrace. He heard her sob, and he heard his father's murmur under the hoot of the wind or the distant wolves. He saw the Builder's horse and the shapeshifter Loghi, the way he'd

seen horses do it, the stallion clambering up the back of the grinning god, who suddenly lost his grin. That's what made baby horses,
Gramma said, or baby cats, baby fleas, baby people, all the same.

He heard low sounds in the dark. He knew from nights before
that they must be making a baby. But there was already a baby inside
his mother, so would there be room for two? If tomorrow . . . He
slept.

～

Why had my mother told me this story, a tale of prickles and
bristles, schemes and lies, strange story to lull a child to peaceful
sleep? I had asked it, of course, and she was her father's warrior child,
so she likely felt terror was good for me. I loved her as best I could.

That night I threaded my way between the unsettled dreams that
I had called forth. My terrors were those of the gods: that I might die.
I knew the threat of pirates and drunken throngs but I was slower to
know that one day I should stand, gawking and limp, to see my girl
child plucked from my wife's ripped womb. To see the mother's eyes
go dead. To see the tiny prisoner flailing for a hand-hold on life and
her fingers slipping away.

My present dreams put one foot ahead of the other, measuring
out the road. They neither terrify nor gratify, entertain nor inform. I
dream of accounts, the writing of diplomatic letters, recording of tax
liens, the clean-up of droppings from my cat. I float with the waves,
and now the waves are gentle. For me it suffices to hear the wolves
in the distance: I need not invite them to curl at my feet.

—XI—
The May Dance

I would be remiss if I omitted a key feature of this my childhood odyssey: boredom. Many days, nothing happened. Our memories hop over vast passages like the frog-leap game of children. For you, my liege, the hours are filled with the business of your estates, the morning mass, the walk with the hounds, the tedium of supervision, the torpid late afternoons, the bountiful table, the calm of firelight, and minstrel ribaldry when offered. For my journey it was endless plodding. The bard of the ancient sagas glossed over the endless days when the Achaeans merely sat at the gates of Troy staring up at the gulls and being shat upon. Poets of every era ignore the mundane heroics of endurance: harnessing donkeys, boiling pottage, waiting for rain to cease. They extol the clash of armies, but none mark the long night labor of the mothers who birth the soldiers.

I have never fully mastered the art of waiting, so essential to survival. All acts of birth—be it a child or a sacred lyric—involve a seemingly endless wait. For the ferry to come into port, for the wound to heal, for pregnancy coming to term. And for night, for dawn, for the Second Coming of Christ. Our education, whether as priest or chicken-plucker, prepares us for action but not for the epic dormancy of our daily lives.

What do we do while waiting? Let the mind roam? Breathe? Strain to think deep-thinking thoughts? Tap out a rhythm? Scratch a vagrant itch? At the age of six I would pat the donkey, frisk around the cart slaying Huns the size of a horse, and simply trust that this endless quiescence would end.

That was forty years ago and I was very young. All are dead now, except perhaps Ludd, who disappeared when it all came down. He may have thought we blamed him, though we didn't. We all play the role we are given to play—flapping our arms, crying for parsnips, falling dead to be resurrected—and tread the road before us. Our twisted paths weave themselves into burial shrouds, yet we persist on our journey.

I once watched a cat chase its tail. Amazingly it caught it, and then it faced a conundrum.

∼

Early morning the sky was clear. "Let it be so!" cried Mik and it was. They made their way back to the seacoast. It was two more days' travel to Samano, where they would do plays and music for a lord. Bragi recalled that lord's slant eyebrows, tiny pin eyes, persistent sniffle, and they had eaten a pudding there. Lords ate pudding daily.

Mik was eager to get out early, but he had begun instructing Bragi in harnessing the donkey. They led Yesu to the cart. "So now look. We have to do it right or the straps might rub and get him sore—"

"Yesu."

"Yesu. So here's the breast strap, neck strap, that's this, and your mama does it her way, but it runs right across here, not too high. Feel that bone? That's the point of his shoulder. This guy, he's smart—"

"Yesu."

"Yesu. He's smart, he'll help out. So here's the bridle and bit. See, one finger, two of yours, between his lower jaw and here, not too tight." To be an actor, thought the boy, it wasn't enough to learn your lines: you had to harness a donkey. Better to be a soldier on a horse. Horses were big enough to harness themselves.

Yesu stood patiently as Mik continued to strap and buckle, but it all went too fast for the boy—in one ear and out the other, his grandma would say. His father never hit him as other fathers would, but Papa's sad cross-eyes were worse than a blow.

"So the traces go back to here, this is what makes it turn, and the two shafts go either side of the donkey—"

"Yesu."

"Yesu. Which are supported by the saddle." He patted the weathered leather. "That's not to ride on, that's to support it. But watch if it's rubbing. We don't want sores. You follow?" Bragi stared blankly at the impossibility of living life. "If not, you'll get it." His father smiled his goofy lopsided smile, a smile the boy had known ever since letting go the nipple. Yesu raised his deep brown eyes to father and son.

The sun rose up from the sea, dragging the day into view. The morning chill vanished. A long dull journey along the seacoast, and Bragi led Yesu a while, clutching the rope in both hands. The donkey paid him no heed, just put one foot ahead of the other, ahead of the other, ahead of the other, the way grownups did. He wondered how many steps you had to take before you died, and if they were getting near the edge of the world where they might fall off. He couldn't ask, he would sound like a child. Only children asked questions.

Bragi's friend Nico had said that the whole world was flat and that sailors sailed off the edge. "But if there's an edge," Bragi said, "then all the ocean would spill." So they had a fight and he hit Nico in the nose and Nico ran away. The issue remained unresolved when Nico died next week.

He asked Gramma about it. "Wise men believe the world is round, so you'd never come to an edge," she said. "Look how the shadow hits the moon."

"If it's round, couldn't we could roll downhill?"

"You're too smart, little boy."

He agreed. People said he was smart, which they thought would make him feel good, but it only meant that he knew how little he knew. His grandma taught him things, but the more he learned the dumber he felt. He sailed off the edges of questions.

They plodded on. At times the land was as flat as the ocean face. Other times they walked along sea cliffs where gulls floated the updrafts without flitting their wings. The surface would be as smooth as a pond, then a breaker crashed on the rocks, and sea foam topped the dark tangles of kelp. "The sea is our mother," his grandma said—and yes, he saw in his mother the face, the breakers, the tangles, the cold.

For a while his grandmother rode in the cart. Her knees were giving out, she said. What happened if knees gave out, did your legs fall off? Mik held the donkey's bridle, offering guidance. Yesu balked only twice all day—unlike Truggie, who would stop at every clod—but it was tricky to start him up once they'd stopped to rest. Mik would wait to see what the donkey did and then tell him to do it. He would stroke the beast until it began to move and then yell, "Hi!" Explaining to Bragi: "We want him to move his butt when I tell him *Move your butt.* So whenever he feels like moving his butt, I give him the cue. He forgets which came first. It's like learning lines: the gesture makes the words pop out." Bragi didn't follow what was meant, but as long as his father seemed to know, somebody did.

Yesu balked. "Just pat him so he knows he's safe. Gentle tug on the lead, not like you're forcing him, just saying, *Trust me, it's fine.*" The boy tried, but the beast stood immovable. Then he patted him again, giggled, whispered his parsnips line into the big twitching ear, and the creature moved on. A line that never failed. A line that might get the fearful boy through life.

"Oh dammit!" Mik rarely got angry, but he had abrupt eruptions. The cart jerked to a halt. A harness strap had pulled loose. There were leather straps across Yesu's chest, over his withers, around his middle and under his tail—straps to pull the load, to hold the shafts, and straps to hold all the straps in place. More curses. Mik managed to tie the fitting with a leather thong.

Asta inspected it. "No no no no." Bragi couldn't make out their whispered quarrel—something about the chest strap. They both knew donkeys, but their theologies clashed on the harnessing. Should the breast strap be two fingers higher, two fingers lower, or stay where it was? They wound up quarreling about the need for a collar harness, though both knew there was none to be had.

Yesu stood patiently between them. Bragi could only scratch his muzzle. "Hi, hi, hi, look at you!" The words were meaningless, but Yesu knew the muzzle scratch. He blinked away a fly and turned his great eyes to the boy.

~

On these long trudges, as I grew tired of watching the donkey's tail, my gaze went to my assembled family. Gramma was always Gramma—her blunt tongue, her teasing, the wart on her chin and the grab of her hand—and Ludd was an utter puzzlement. Of my parents I began to see more than my mother's angularity and my father's funny faces. I knew the sharp-edged practical Asta and Mik the warm-hearted clown, but now I saw contradictions. In her stride I saw the implacable will but also the rope-dancer's cautious step, setting foot in alien land. I loved my father's vigor, his humor, his hope, yet as the midafternoons wore on, his strut slowed to the grim progress of Sisyphus.

I began to question if each of God's creatures had not one soul but two. Heretical, surely: it might force Divine Judgment to send one soul to Heaven, the other to Hell. Yet I was but six years old. At that age heresies abound.

~

His parents finished their squabble with a few final blurts. "We best get going," called Edra. They got underway. The road was in good repair, no deep ruts, and the seacoast route was flat.

The second day they veered again into the mountains. The path was steep, rutted, descending into valleys, then up, then around. They had to ford a swift stream and Bragi was chilled to the bone. In precipitate ascents Edra climbed down from the cart and walked to lighten the donkey's load.

That night Bragi heard wolves. They sounded hungry. "Where are the wolves?" he asked Gramma at daybreak after a sleepless night.

"What wolves?"

"That howl."

"Nothing to worry, sweetie. They're scared of people. They think we're nasty. And so we are." He looked away gloomily. "Now don't you worry. We'd never take you where it's dangerous." As soon as she said it she knew that he knew what a lie it was. "But if you're out by yourself and you see a wolf and the wolf sees you, don't run. Don't try to stare him down, cause he'll think you want to fight and you don't. Just back away very slow. I did that once, but old Wolfie looked kind of uppity, so I started waving my arms and puffed myself up to three times my size, and Wolfie ran off."

She wanted the boy to ask how she could puff herself up, but he turned and went to curry the donkey.

~

That night it was the same bedding-down, pulling the coverlet this way and that, an itch on the back of the neck, and a knobby root under the matting. I stretched out long, feeling a deep contentment, then a sharp clutch of fear. The world was so incomprehensible, besides being very tall, and sailing near to the edge I spilled over.

In the dream I was stark awake. At a bend in the path the masks came into view like drowned faces under water. A spicy stench of gods. The Shining One stared into a shadow too deep to see what cast it: his brother Hod, wide eyes white, his voice a stir of dry leaves. Hod was blind as a mole. Had he no sight or was there nothing to see?

Brother!

The Shining One reached like the roots of a luminous tree to grasp a thick clog of blackness.

Hod, my brother. I would enter your dark.

Is there room for us both?

They spoke the strange tongue with the upward lilt, the way yogurt tasted. I heard their voices inside the hills, out the hollows of trees, between Yesu's great yellow teeth. I heard what made the present so real and the future so frightful: the present was daytime, the future was murk. The sun rose each day and pulled the future to light.

~

His mother's hand came to his cheek. "You dreaming?" And his grandmother's voice: "Leave him be. Let him have his nightmares."

Shortly past dawn, Bragi sat hunched by the glowering coals, eating his pottage. "We'll miss the May dancing." Asta spoke as if it made no matter, as if she cared not a whit, but then why had she said it? Many times he had heard it spoken of. It was spring, and spring was dancing and drinking and doing the deeds of life. The hardships of winter were lost in exploding greenery. The Cristers celebrated their god's resurrection. Others, a daughter springing out of the underworld. Others, that the sun was bright, the goats were frisky, and they felt a lot like the goats. Some years the troupe was in a town, caught in the music, other times on a rutted path where only the birds and wild boars frolicked. "Well, no, we'll not miss it. We're in it," his mother said. The May frolic was everywhere.

Mid-morning, as the road narrowed to a pass between granite cliffs, they encountered a peasant leading a draft horse, a great mare exuding springtime. Yesu's ears perked forward, his upper lip jutted, and despite the heights to be overcome he strained to pursue his destiny. Mik pulled back on the lead rope, Asta held to the donkey's halter, Ludd to the reins, and Bragi grabbed the tail.

"Get her gone!" shouted Asta. The terrified peasant flogged his mare mercilessly and fled up the road. Yesu, in a crisis of lust, jerked this way and that. Bragi flung his arms around Yesu's neck with a vehement whisper—

"It's Loghi!"

Mik pulled the boy away from the donkey's flailing head, kept hold of the lead rope and laid his hands on the neck, humming him gently back to chastity. Yesu, with snuffles and snorts, regained his composure. The boy drifted back to the rear of the cart where Asta, after the storm, had gone to curl on her side. Her eyes were shut. She had other things on her mind.

"Mama?"

"Yes?"

"Yesu tried to do the May dance."

"Well, because he hadn't been gelded. I knew that'd be a problem, but we needed him and he was cheap. "

"What's *gelded*? "

"You know that. Where they cut off the balls so he doesn't get rambunctious." The rest of the day Bragi tried not to get rambunctious.

Mid-afternoon they came to a wilderness crossroads and paused by a small pitched-roof shrine with the statue of a lady. Someone had placed a bunch of poppies at her feet.

"Who's she?" Bragi asked Gramma.

"That's me in my younger days."

"No!"

"Well, you've seen those before and you asked the same question, so you decide who she is. Gods are always changing their names. Here, give her a fig." He took the dried fig and placed it at the lady's feet. The cart started up with a jounce. The boy and his grandmother walked behind.

"Are there really gods?"

"Ask me something I know, my boy, like playing old witches or cooking rabbit stew. I'm not a god, I'm a grandma. Grandmas exist, that I know."

"But are there?"

"If there are, then maybe that lady's a god and she'll do us a favor. Or maybe eat the fig and forget it. It's only the stories that matter. It's them that has an effect. A story slams harder than any thunderbolt."

The boy knew he would never get a straight answer.

"How you doing?" Edra asked Asta, curled in the cart.

"How far to a village?" Her voice was shaky.

"Likely tomorrow. Don't worry."

Bragi knew that *Don't worry* meant there was something to worry about, but he didn't ask. He was afraid to know.

～

A story slams harder than any thunderbolt. It was in those days I first knew the impact of mortal fear. The pirates, the waggling sailor, the riotous disciples of Saint Eleora, those were unsettling. But when my mother told of the wall, I was truly afraid. We had seen towns with fortifications, but I supposed that when a town got big enough, they simply needed a wall to hold it together. But these gods raised bulwarks against the unseen, like the foul air we blame for the plague. We must breathe, yet one breath and we may never be the same. I heard the howling of wolves in the night and envisioned the Primals, the Strange Ones, the Fierce Ones— They had so many names. Creatures with many names were as dreadful as the one with sprouting heads.

My grandmother saw my new-hatched fear of death: the tie that binds us all, and the font of our absurdity. She was wise enough to offer no consolation.

~

The road flattened, but the forest grew thicker. At times they stopped to clear fallen limbs or guide the cart through straits too narrow to pass. Mik scouted the pathway ahead, Ludd led the donkey, and Bragi picked burrs from Yesu's tail.

Then, approaching a sunny clearing where they might rest, Mik rushed back waving his arms. "Black flies!" Sudden panic. A cloud of dark smoke rose close upon him. "Cover up! Cover over!" He embraced his son and crouched, pulling his cloak over them, then rose to grab the halter as Ludd dived under the cart and the donkey's eyes went wild. "Oh shit! Ow! Shit!"

No defense against the ravenous cloud. The boy heard yelps from the bony man and cries from the back of the cart. He squeezed his eyes shut and tried to disappear. He felt stings on his ankle and calf. He had dreamt of blind Hod but never knew that a blear of blackness could sting. The cloud was a god that smelt blood.

"Hwor-haa! Hwor-haa!" A hoot, a honk, a bugle blast, a Froggie stung in the butt? It was Yesu. Bragi had heard the beast bray but never a full-out eruption to bring whole cities down: a dozen blasts, then abruptly mute. The black whirlwind rose, grew dim, dissolving, gone. The boy emerged with caution from under his father's cloak, scratched his burning ankle and then the donkey's muzzle.

That night they set up camp and Bragi helped unharness Yesu. He led the donkey to graze on a patch of ryegrass and sat watching the gentle munch, lips drawn back, teeth nearly scraping the ground. He glanced to his parents perched at the fire, scratching their itches, preparing food. Yesu scared the black flies, he told his father. No, said Mik, something distracted them. Still, he gave Bragi a clutch of dried apricots to reward the beast.

As Yesu ate from his hand, the boy felt the tremors come again. There was darkness in the May dance. Darkness whirling above him, standing beside him.

—XII—
Bleeding

Next morning, in the shivery span between sleep and wake, the boy dreamt he could see the future. But not directly, just a blur at the edge of his sight. He swung his sword into the blur—a soldier, he had a sword—and turned into six-year-old Bragi waving a stick. He felt someone take his hand and pull him into the day.

He woke with the sun in his face and the smell of wind off the sea. He hadn't known they were close to the sea. He had been scratching fleas all night and now felt a flea on his forehead. He trapped it under his palm, but at that crucial moment Gramma's voice cut through the morning glare. "Up! Bragi! Up!"

"I've got a flea."

"We've all got a flea. Can he do back-flips?"

"No!"

She was always teasing him. He tried to worm a finger under his hand to kill the flea, then rubbed his palm hard on his forehead. What if it ate through the skin and burrowed between the bones and came out to jump in his eye?— Now he was fully awake.

Another day full of impossible choices. Whether to tie on his sandals or go barefoot. Whether to hike on Yesu's right side or left. Whether to throw a rock at a tree or a bird. To scratch the fleabite or let it itch. He pulled on his clothes, rolled up his bedding, and straggled into the day. No wonder old roosters got stringy.

They descended the mountain path to the sea and passed another stone lady in a shrine at the edge of a village. The sky was heavy, struggling out from under a dream. There were burial markers along the road, and a cat crouched to exude its dung on a grave. Bragi rubbed his eyes. They felt like dried figs.

The troupe came into the village, stopped at several doors to ask for a midwife. The boy knew what midwives did, stuff about babies, and wondered if the baby was getting born, but he was afraid to ask. Edra saw his agitation. "Your mother's bleeding and we need to get her some roots to stop the bleeding or else the baby might die. I lost two that way."

"Why?"

"The lady we gave a fig hates figs! Don't ask me why!"

Her voice swelled with an anger he had never heard directed at him. A question welled up, but he swallowed it. He didn't see any blood, and how could the baby die if it hadn't been born?

Directed to a whitewashed hut behind a smithy's shop, Edra led Asta up the path, while Ludd stayed back to tend the donkey cart. The bony man was somehow kin to Yesu, as if they had the same mother though had fathers with different ears. Both were brown-eyed, long-jawed, with a sense of waiting for something vaguely promised. Ludd spent long stretches staring into the unblinking bottomless eyes. They shared a brotherhood of befuddlement.

Mik took Bragi into the nearby tavern, a low dark room with a shelf of jugs, two rough-hewn tables, stools scattered about, rushes on the beaten dirt floor and an open window with its leather curtain tied back. Horseflies buzzed through a stench of garlic, beer, and yesteryear's crusted vomit. One sharp slash of sunlight cut through the tavern's murk.

A bone-thin adolescent girl appeared from the back in jerky limping steps. Her face was yellowish, deformed around the cheek-bones, wavering like the moon on a lake. Her limp had a sleepiness to it, a sense of being forced to move but going nowhere.

"Wine," Mik told her. The girl, thin as willow, stared at him. "Vino? Vinu? Vini?" he ventured. No response. "C'mon, we're not that far north," Mik mumbled. "Krasi? Mir? Sarap?"

Something stirred in the scrawny girl's stare. "Wine?" she murmured. Bragi understood: it wasn't the word that confused her, it was the presence of strangers. He tried to crouch lower at the table, not to be so much *there.*

She went and returned with jugs of wine and water. Mik gave her a coin, drank a cup of watered wine and gave Bragi a slosh in another cup. This was what men did while women had babies, it seemed. The wine was bitter, but Bragi drank what was given him.

"Tastes like piss."

The guttural growl startled them. In a murky corner sat a man. Their eyes adjusted. He was white-haired, deeply bronzed, with a grizzled beard and the angry eyes of a dying wolf. Soldier's dress: knee-length tunic and leather jerkin, short sword at his belt, a gladius—Bragi liked the names of swords his father had told him. The old soldier drank, grimacing at every sip. "It does. We were three days march, no water, all dry. Had to drink our own piss. This is worse."

He gave the newcomers a surly glance, leaned forward, squinted hard. Mik sensed trouble. He was about to grab Bragi and bolt for the door when there came a jovial hoot. "You're the funny guy!" The old soldier's face cracked wide with rabid glee and he shouted to the world, "It's the funny guy!" His countenance took on a beatific glow. He beckoned. "Come on over here, funny guy!"

Mik hesitated, but he had told his son more than once never to cross a soldier. They rose, approached, and at a commanding gesture they sat on the teetering bench. The old soldier slammed down his flagon and waved for another. Bragi saw that the fearsome trooper had only a single arm.

"Funny guy, funny guy . . ." he said to the gimpy lass as she brought him another drink. He pointed to Mik with his one hand and guffawed a phlegmy guffaw, lost in the sumptuous lap of memory. He had seen their show years ago, in a town he didn't remember, on the march to fight an army he couldn't recall. "Next day was the battle, and we knew we were gonna get fucked, we knew we were dead, but we laughed, we laughed . . . You were funny. Make a face!" Mik did his *bee-on-the-nose* grimace. The old soldier split a gut.

Bragi had envisioned his mother—his mother bleeding, his mother crying, his mother dying. The raw acid wine was his terror's taste. Yet now he was deep in the rapids of laughter, a man among men, and he forgot his mother.

The door curtain pulled back. A huge bear of a man—black beard, hogshead chest, the arms of a smithy—appeared. "It's me!" The voice was thunder. All stilled. Even the horseflies went mute. The gimpy young barmaid emerged from the back. She clutched a boning knife in a quivering hand. Time skidded to a stop.

The willowy girl's voice—an odd dialect, but Bragi could grasp it—was the wail of wind through the gaps in stone walls. "Bollus, sorry, but Fatita says, sorry, she said to tell you, said tell him these words, exact . . ." The barmaid shook like the tree with shivering leaves but held the boning knife erect. "She says, *Stay the fu— fuck out of here, you steaming sh— shit, if you don't want both knees broke and your co— cock chewed off.* That's what she said. She said tell you. Give you the message. If you came in. Which you're standing there." Dead silence. "That's what she said to say." She trembled, shivered, quivered, quaked, but the boning knife held firm.

An aeon passed as the volcano sucked in his breath. Then the old soldier rose and placed his one hand on the hilt of his sword. The bristling Bollus stared, backed out, and the leather curtain flopped shut. The willowy girl disappeared, to die soon of her yellowing. The old soldier sprawled back, triumphant, held out his hand—his left hand—to clasp with Mik. "Ruzante. Name's Ruzante."

"Mikolaus. This is Bragi, my son."

The grin of the old soldier froze. "No, you never had any son."

"Sorry?"

"No, you were the knacker that was after the tinker's wife. You came right out at the start and said it. I remember."

"That was in the play, but that was just the character. My wife played the tinker's wife."

"No, she wasn't your wife. The old ugly bitch was your wife."

"That was my mother that played my wife, but my wife was the tinker's wife."

The old soldier's brow knitted, unraveling complications. "Nobody's mother's their wife," he mumbled. "They do that stuff in Afrik, they do anything there, but not us in civilization." He took a swig and missed his mouth, wiped his front, and his frown deepened. Mik was about to concede that, yes, he was the knacker and the tinker's wife was the tinker's and the little boy here was a sacred cherub who needed to pee, but Bragi saved the day.

"What happened to your arm?"

The old soldier jerked back, then grimaced, then smiled. A question from the mouths of babes, a tactless question, but a question he greatly desired. "Hacked off clean. By a Goth the size of a horse. He came at me, charging downhill like a bull, and I gashed open his face, one whack, I gave him a grin ear to ear. But his ax came down and I saw my right arm go sailing over the hedge." He watched it a moment, sailing. "How was she?"

It took a hitch for Mik to grasp that Ruzante was asking how juicy was the tinker's wife. "Pretty hot stuff," he said, returning the old soldier's leer. But he couldn't help explaining again that it was all pretense, that his wife indeed was pretty hot stuff, but the play was only a play.

The old soldier glowered. "When I run a pike through your gut, you're dead. No fake: you lay there. You tell me it's fake if you stick it to her? Women, they know better, the sluts. They know if you've got it up."

Mik would never dispute such logic. He made his *not-me-that-farted* face, and Ruzante grinned in triumph.

Dust settled, and the old soldier regaled them with his deeds. Again, his arm flew off in the breeze, and this time it hit a crow. Again, half his body was blistered with boiling oil. Again, he'd been the only man of his phalanx to survive. He'd hacked off the dongs of a dozen Arians and cut women's throats to save them from being raped. Mik expressed deep admiration. Never cross a soldier.

By this time the old warrior was mumbling-stumbling-falling-down drunk, but Mik took no chances. The boy heard his father slip into the role of lecherous knacker, with a string of dirty jokes in incomprehensible gibberish interspersed with gruntings, spurtles and lip-smacks that brought the old soldier to wheezes of ecstasy. Bragi listened in awe without comprehending a word. When at last there was room for a breath, the soused paladin asked where they were headed, where he could see them again.

"North to Samano."

Sudden silence. The bronzed face clouded. He banged his mug on the table. The girl limped in with a refill, limped out. "Well, that's not— I'd say— If you—" The soldier brooded, at last muttered, "That's not real good."

"Problem?" Mik was no longer the lecherous knacker. He was listening.

"Don't say I said it, but— That's where we're headed. Samano. Two days. Attack it, sack it, clear out. Like you and the tinker's wife." He chuckled, half-rose, clutching the hilt of his gladius as if to launch the slaughter. Then he sat heavily. "You don't want to be there. It gets hairy."

"What are they fighting about?" Mik asked in a plaintive chirp.

"Don't ask me. Not my business. They pay me, straight wage plus whatever I sack. Kill or be killed, that's it. That fucker's trying to kill me, I kill him: nothing personal. You're either damn good or you're dead." He paused to see if the funny guy got it. "It's a job. Just a job. Better than starving."

Mik's eyes went inside himself. The boy saw that their plans might change.

"Ruzzie! Hey!" A silly squeak from a dwarfish youth in the doorway. He looked to be twelve, going on forty if he ever got there. A white slice of scar marked his puckered face from brow to chin, and the face carried a permanent grin of pain. "Cook says get your ass back to camp. There's chickens to pluck."

A sullen rumble: "Tell him suck me!" The fist slammed the table. The table made a crack.

The youth's dwarfish eyes were fixed on the sword near the one good hand, but he couldn't repress a smirk. "Ten chickens or ten lashes, Ruzzie, he says. Your choice."

He giggled and fled. Mik and Bragi sat frozen. Ruzante glared at them, dog teeth glistening, then his eyes dimmed. Finding his balance he rose wearily to his feet. He was no longer the mighty warrior, he was a cook's drunken helper, a chicken-plucker, a scroungy cur who bragged of his days as a wolf.

"Forty years, that's the thanks you get. Pluck the chicken. Pluck the fucking chicken. Fuckers. Tell your kid there: better die young. Don't wait around." His gaze fell on Bragi, who cringed. "Fuckers! I kill better with one arm than— Huns! I killed Huns!"

He meandered to the door with the practiced stagger of a functional drunk. "Think it's a joke . . . Young bucks. We killed Huns. Huns! Never fiends from hell like the Huns! Went up against Huns. Whatever they do you, whatever they can . . ." He stumbled into the doorpost, shook his head to clear it, and staggered out of history.

Mik went to the door to see the old soldier gone, then drank up the last of his wine and motioned Bragi to come. Back at the donkey cart he confided to the boy, "He never fought the Huns. The Huns were way long ago. People still talk about the Huns. *The Huns are coming, look out for the Huns!* But that's the way people do. Don't worry about the Huns. They're pussy-cats now."

Ludd was staring at Yesu. Both appeared lost in thought. Bragi had always been shy of the tall bony man, but he felt compelled to tell of the one-armed chicken-plucker.

"He'd be a good character for a play," said Ludd.

"He'd make people cry," Mik retorted. "People want to laugh."

"Or maybe hide his arm, and then his arm pops out. That'd be pretty funny."

They left it at that, sat waiting for the women's return. Bragi wondered at Yesu's patience, content to stand for hours. Always the waiting.

The women returned. Asta nodded, and Mik took that to mean success. The midwife gave them herbs to stop the bleeding but warned her to stay off her feet till the baby got settled, whatever that meant. Asta could ride the cart but Edra would have to walk, since Yesu tired on the mountain roads. Troubles swarmed like flies. Was it Gramma who talked about one devil calling another or had Bragi dreamt it? He still wondered about the bleeding.

Late afternoon they made camp on a hill above the crossroads, though the weather was good for travel. But travel where? After supper they held council around the fire. If the old soldier spoke true and his army took the town, there would be no town for the playing. If the town held out, they might be in the path of a beaten army's retreat.

"You said he was drunk."

"Probably never not," Mik said, "but he wasn't making a joke."

"We always got good crowds there."

"But we never played under siege."

"Well, we can't go up the coast then." Edra stirred the porridge.

"How far—" Asta was lost in thought, then spoke with deliberation. "We had best turn our path to Sir Paddo."

Mik knew that Asta would say it. He waited and now it was out. It had been, what, three years, four, since their grim reception there? Could they risk it? He gazed at her face through the fire. "Well, that's a possibility."

The boy had never heard of Sir Paddo, but he felt a silence as baleful as the wails of the distant wolves. The gods had raised their wall and still clung to fear. *Better die young*, the old soldier said, before he went off to pluck chickens. The boy went to sleep in shadow.

—XIII—
Kindness

I learned the history of Sir Paddo through my grandmother's double somersault, chronicled in due course. Though she had few reservations in telling me the ways of the world, she would surely have withheld racy tales of my mother. But as her bruises were severe she was given a brew of bitter herbs—the same as your son (may his soul be thrice blest) pressed upon me at the seminary. I sat with him in the cold stone refectory sharing a liquor laced with ergot. One sip and my lips went numb and my head was a tempest of cats. This was the tale my grandmother told while floating on air.

Sir Paddo was of the minor nobility, though wealthy enough to maintain a scribe who kept up correspondence with learned souls, both of Christian and heathen cultures. By his late fifties, he had lost two wives in childbirth, along with the fruits of the womb. He was a gentle, intelligent, intensely lonely man. I see him but vaguely now. Some men even in brightness are hard to visualize, the waver of faces in water.

On their first visit to his demesne the troupe was larger—not only Mik and Asta, Edra and Mik's father, but also a rope dancer, a juggling duo, and a man with a monkey. All played music and took roles in the farces. They had performed for the Emperor's cousin—which emperor mattered not—and that opened doors to a string of noble households.

This was long before I arrived, and the couple fated to be my parents had been together two years. Asta played only small roles, but her flaxen charm was not lost on host aristocrats. With Edra's counsel she learned to fend off advances without giving offense—a vital skill for actresses—but meeting Sir Paddo's sad eyes she wasn't sure she wanted to fend.

Mik was better suited to playing frantic lovers than cuckolded husbands, and Asta informed him of her desire. Had her suitor been another player he might have been jealous, but Sir Paddo was nobility, so it wasn't a matter of competition. She assured Mik that she wouldn't get pregnant.

All went well. Sir Paddo was considerate, asked no more than she offered. She felt she was playing a role, but for the first time she truly grasped the actor's art: to lie truthfully. In those nights she made this broken man feel he was desirable and desired. The troupe stayed three days, and each night, after visiting Sir Paddo, she returned to Mik's bed to make love and sleep content.

Gramma told me this, and perhaps I understood.

~

Over the years the troupe returned to play for Sir Paddo, his household and his villagers. On those occasions they continued their nightly visits. The lord's declining years changed the menu but never diminished the flavor. Yet at their last visit, four years ago, Sir Paddo had a new wife—a gaunt sour-faced aristocrat—who treated them like vagabonds. The tune was discordant, and Asta resisted subsequent invitations to return. Now, in desperate straits, could they trust to an unoffered offer?

Mik was doubtful. "Icy welcome then. Why otherwise now?"

"No choice."

"Maybe just camp here?"

"Till when?"

As one fell into agreement, the other demurred. The murmurs went deep into night, blurred by the howls of wolves, the rumble of gods, the crickets' choral chitter. Next morning, they set out on the rutted mountain road to visit Sir Paddo—

—To their astonishment. The fearsome wife answered the call of a surly servant and came to the service door. She was the same gaunt aristocrat, steel-gray hair pulled back as if under torture into a disciplined bun. Her thin-bladed nose descended from the brow to a thrusting upper lip guarding pallid cheeks. Bragi avoided her eyes, knowing the tale of the witch who turned men into pigs.

"How welcome you are!" Her voice was the taste of honey. Bragi looked up to the harsh ruin of the face and felt her melted heart. "Sir Paddo will receive you with pleasure."

Mik babbled his rehearsed speech for asking hospitality, but the wife waved away the words, repeating her welcome. A groom was summoned to lead Yesu off for a curry and generous feast. Through a maze of hallways they were shown to their quarters—a spacious room for Asta and Mik, another for Edra and Bragi, another for Ludd, as if harbingers of a long-delayed Second Coming.

After a time they were summoned to Sir Paddo's library. They entered, all five, and he rose to greet them. He was as gaunt as his wife, slack-jawed, pale, beardless, with curly white hair fringing a shiny baldness, but his eyes were keen and kind. At the sight of the boy, he brightened.

"Well, look who's here! What a boy! How he's grown!"

"This is Bragi, whom you last saw as a toddler," Asta said. She took the nobleman's offered hand and made a slight curtsey. For a moment she met his eyes.

"Bragi, yes! Do you know, in the Northland they have a god named Bragi? He gives us song. Our religion, of course, denies alien gods, but Our Father surely has the power to make exceptions: I fervently believe that there must be a god of song!"

The boy could not remotely comprehend the man's words. He feared he might have to sing a song, but the eyes that looked down on him were full of laughter. He stared at the nobleman's strange sleeved robe, silken white with embroidered knotwork vines from floor to lapels.

"Strange garment, yes?" Sir Paddo saw the boy's wonder. "From a correspondent far to the East, who sends me yet stranger philosophic perplexities. Quite heterodox, I fear, but no heresies in this delightful gift. We must honor the light in other men, no matter their darkness."

Again the boy was mystified, but he heard the man speaking to him as to an adult. His eyes darted about the room. He had seen a codex before, leather-bound sheets with tiny writing that held deep secrets, his father said. But here were shelves of codices offered out to the touch, and racks of parchment scrolls. Bracketed to a wall were two clay tablets with marks as if crows had danced in the mud: secret writing surely. A table with beeswax taper, a stack of parchments, a stand of reed pens that must hold magical words within them. The dim room breathed light.

The boy knew that for his parents the kindness was unexpected. He saw the old man grasp Asta's hand again. His breath was short, but the words tumbled out as if he had waited years to speak them. "You were good to me once. More than once. I was grateful. You gave me faith in myself. That I might find a wife as kindly as you, that I might—"

He looked to the gaunt woman beside him as if asking permission. She reached to him, touched his baldness then withdrew her hand, content that he spoke.

"And at the outset, she and I— Well, convenience, politics of course, an alliance of— Call it expediency, the obligations of property, rank . . ." He glanced at his wife. The gaunt lady's face took on a curious glow that might have been a smile.

"I speak this knowing you may be puzzled why you are greeted so warmly. But you must be aware of the blessings you offer in your plays on the stage, along with the follies." He was silent for a time.

"The second year of our chill alliance of expediency, we began to . . . see one another. Small things. The shape of an eyebrow, an intelligence in the eyes, our love of peasant music, other moments. The codices on these shelves, each one a lonely struggle for truth. Common desires, common wounds. This was long after your last visit, and when it happened between us, the moment of knowing, the moment of touch . . . I spoke to her of your kindness, and she understood. Understood with her own." He sat back in his chair with difficulty. "Damned hips."

"Knees are worse," said Edra.

He grinned and motioned them to sit. Edra sat at once on an upholstered bench and lifted Bragi into her lap. Asta sat beside them. The two men hesitated: to sit in the presence of nobility violated propriety, and propriety kept them alive. At last Mik chose a side chair near the door, the least comfortable squatting place he could see, and Ludd perched on a stool by the window, set to leap out.

Bragi felt the velvet upholstery, so soft, like stroking the unicorns he'd heard of. The white-curled man chuckled. "Your boy has the best idea: just enjoy it. Or if you might feel better standing, you may."

Ludd stood up abruptly. A moment and he sat. The others ventured no response.

"And this is your colleague? Your name, my fellow?"

Ludd rose, transfixed. At last he remembered his name: "Ludd."

"Ludd. You must be a gifted artist, to share the stage with these players."

He had never thought himself otherwise than a fishmonger or slave. "I guess I try to." He sat abruptly to restrain himself from farting.

The old knight's breath came deeper with the exhilaration of an audience. "I have often thought with astonishment of your travels: what must be involved in the itinerant life. Each night under a different roof or pattern of stars. To see humankind in all its glory and its shame. To wonder whether to bow, stand or sit, prostrate yourself or run for the door. To choose if you should pray to the Christian Mary or to the pagan Dian. To be greeted as celebrants or as pollution. What must you see, on the low road, that we, with our demigod's view from the ramparts, cannot comprehend?"

"Human folly, perhaps, your grace?" The boy heard his father speak words as wise as the nobleman's and felt raised to nobility. Those words encompassed his terrors, the pirates, the spitting girl, his mother's invisible bleeding, the wall. *Human folly*: so simple.

Sir Paddo smiled, rambled on, knew he was rambling on, and tried to draw them into dialogue. He seemed to desire them to speak as equals, comrades, friends, but his rank precluded equality. Even Asta, who had spent hours in his gentle embrace, stroking his forehead, his wounded manhood, gazing into his eyes—even she sat silent. He turned to Bragi. "How old are you, my boy?"

"Six."

"And what will be your trade when you are grown? A player? A soldier? A sailor on the seas? Perhaps a priest or a scribe?" He waved his hand toward the myriad mysteries lurking on his shelves.

The boy knew he was being cajoled. He wanted to say he was already an actor and knew how to harness a donkey, almost. But Sir Paddo was trying to be kind and the boy was trained to be polite. "Actor," he said. He still hoped he could be a soldier too, maybe just in wintertime, if he didn't lose an arm.

"Well, so I welcome your presence, all of you. Players. You have brought great blessing to my life, and God has sent you to me once again. Or the gods, if there be such. And to my wife—" He turned to look at the woman whose heart he shared. "Whom, to be frank, I never expected to love. Imagine that! Nor to be the blessed recipient of love." He smiled, and she smiled a gaunt smile. "And yet for me such a . . ." He lowered his eyes, hiding his nakedness.

At last he dismissed the company, giving his hand to each, turning his wrist slightly upward to ease their anxiety in presuming equality with a lord. To Bragi he gave three fingers for a handshake and made no motion to rumple his hair. Finally with Asta he held the grasp, then slowly lowered his head to touch his brow to her hand, the gesture of a vassal. The wife's soft eyes looked on.

They were lodged three days while the lord sent scouts to surveil the force en route to erase the town—a precaution to assure his own safety. It was Sir Bluffot's army, a youthful friend. "But friendship, in our troubled times, is no guarantor of safety," he observed, "and armies can be fickle." A force deprived of a rich town to sack might seek other prospects, leaving an unwary lord left to breed maggots. And Sir Bluffot had lost his boyish charm amid vast folds of fat.

The white-curled nobleman made them no request to earn their keep, but he welcomed their offer of evening concerts—lute and pipes, tambour and song—to which he invited his servants along with a few local tradesmen, artisans, and an ancient lady reputed to have been the Emperor's courtesan, many emperors past.

During the long afternoons Mik read to Bragi stories of magical changes from a well-thumbed codex. Edra and Asta taught the servants' children comic songs and heard the rotund scribe give them lessons from ancient books. The patrician cautioned his guests not to reveal this sin: his peers would disapprove of corrupting the servant class by education. "It is never politic to make public a violation of societal norms." A sadness in his voice.

Sir Paddo's scouts returned to report all threats averted. Plague had struck the invaders, erasing half their force. The remnants might pillage the countryside, but he would send an armed escort with the players. Bragi wondered if the one armed soldier was dead. Could you catch the plague from plucking chickens?

They would have left next morning, but they had offered to do a play for Sir Paddo, so they planned an early departure the following day. Late morning in the great hall they were set to start rehearsal when Sir Paddo appeared, his visage in deep concern. His wife stood at the door impassively.

"Yes, good morning, beautiful in fact, and the figs this year look to be especially—" He struggled for words. "But I need to ask— My steward had some concerns, which I'm sure that— But nevertheless—" At last he managed to stammer it out. His steward, a pasty-faced man with drooping mustachios, made a routine round of searching guests' luggage. Nothing personal, just common sense given the regrettable custom among the upper classes to murder their kin. "There are those," Sir Paddo explained, "who might find me inconvenient. This is common in families, of course." During his inspection the steward found a hamper, odd in its workmanship. Picking the lock, he was startled to stare into faces staring back.

"And so I felt we should allay misapprehensions, what this might— Nothing serious, I'm sure, but my steward expressed— Of course poor Ulf is hardly an educated man, through no fault of his own, but—" It came down to the lord's fear that if word spread, there might be rumor of sorcery, witchcraft, demons, and one peasant child with a fever could foment a frenzied mob.

Asta explained the masks—the sorcerer, the slaying, the charge. "It was not my choice," she said, "I swore a blood oath."

"Whom do they represent?" he asked.

"I told you the stories once."

"Yes yes, of course, the legends of the North!" he exclaimed. "And the tales from my father's groom. Bloody, horrible tales blown in the frozen wind. Though I was only this child's age for the tales of the groom, so they may not have been so horrific."

"Horrific enough."

"But your stories spurred laughter as well! At a time when that was much needed. The wedding, the war god, I recall—"

"Teorr."

"Teorr, yes. The one who throws his hammer."

"We loved him," said Asta. "He made us feel strong."

"But the story you told me, I remember now. Teorr's wedding! That was it! I laughed so hard I broke wind. I was so embarrassed—" He turned to his wife. "She pretended not to hear." A gaunt smile in response. "Yes, Teorr's wedding!"

Bragi had heard the story but couldn't remember the ending. These days he began to fear stories' endings.

"Yes, Teorr!" The old man turned to Bragi to tell the merry tale. "The gods feared their enemies, whom Teorr killed by the score, by the hundreds, but now he had lost his hammer—"

"Myolnir," Asta murmured.

"Myolnir?"

"The name of the hammer."

"Myolnir, yes! And the gods felt disaster was imminent. As of course it always is." The old man chuckled, then fell silent. He sank into a cushioned arch-back chair, forgetting the steward, the hamper, the threat of rumor—lost in remembrance. "And as well they might in a world of perpetual war."

Asta broke the silence. "We never disturb the masks. My father spoke of a curse."

"A curse? Absurd. There are no curses except those we wreak on ourselves. Peasants' tales."

"My father was no peasant, my lord. He was a warrior."

Sir Paddo tilted his head in apology. "No offense intended, my dear. But then why do you carry it with you? This curse? Why not toss it into the slough?"

"I swore an oath." She held her scarred thumb upward and shivered, feeling the trickle.

"An oath. Ah yes. We do cling to our chains."

～

Sir Paddo is surely long dead, yet he stands before me a puzzlement. So very unlike the one-armed soldier, yet both of those men had lived beyond their allotted years and faced mortality. What pathways led to shelves of ancient texts or to chicken-plucking? Accident of birth? Nothing more?

Out of the blue he said, "My only wisdom consists in this: that I know I know nothing." I felt a kinship. I too was aware of my ignorance. On the road thither, I asked my father when we would turn home but got only a wave of his hand. I asked Ludd what was wrong with his eye, but he simply nodded. I asked my grandmother what it was like to be old. She reached down and pinched my nose. They seemed to be shielding me from knowledge—it never occurred to me that they didn't know. I have never aspired to the lofty peaks of philosophy: the meaning of Evil, the nature of Christ, the motion of the spheres. I would have been overjoyed to attain the level of *Why are there cats?*

Even as I entered your service, my liege, and was granted free run of your priceless shelves, I found little satisfaction. The great authors professed to be searchers but traced only new paths to old destinations, serving up rich truffle-stuffed capons when my true desire was for boiled turnips. The hunger persists.

At six, I knew only that I hated being childish. I had to put up with ruffled hair. I had to spend years knowing my cries were absurd before reaching the age when my cries were ignored. I had to wait years and years, then years and years more. I saw Sir Paddo's eyes fixed on an image in the distance, and I squinted to see what he saw.

~

"How strange that my pesky steward should have brought these stories to mind! A curse or a blessing, who can say? I have one request, sufficiently modest, I hope. Might you play this story tonight?"

"Teorr's wedding?" Asta's voice was a whisper.

"I should welcome both the memory and the laughter."

Their silence told him instantly the magnitude of what he asked. Asta sat like the pillar of salt in the Jewish tale, frozen stiff by the looking-back. Sir Paddo wavered, waved his hand inviting refusal. "No matter, though."

Bragi heard the words before she spoke them. They were not in his mother's voice: they were words afloat in the air, words from his own namesake god, the singer of stories. "Yes, my lord," she said. "Your kindness requires recompense. For you the masks will come alive."

A shudder shook the room. The boy scanned the faces: solemn, a challenge accepted. Then, responding to an unspoken question, Sir Paddo said one word. "Kindness."

—XIV—
Tearr's Wedding

Evening brought an audience of three dozen or so   the old knight and his lady, the droop-whiskered steward, a young priest who served as scribe, friends from nearby manors, servants and local artisans—perched on chairs and stools and benches in the great hall's hollow. A half dozen trestle tables had been lashed together to serve as a rickety stage, with a curtain behind. The guests sat in suspense—no drinking or scattered chat—as if awaiting the Day of Judgment. Only out of respect for their host could these diverse classes be brought to sit in each other's presence. At the rear of the hall stood several peasant families who could not be persuaded nearer. Only Sir Paddo appeared gleeful, greeting all as they arrived, anticipating his visit to younger days.

Over the course of a frantic afternoon, the players had pieced it out. Not the first time had they improvised at short notice, but usually—as with St. Eleora—they could cobble it together from all-purpose songs, stock characters, or sure-fire comic riffs. This required more. The story was funny, but gods were a risk. A bamboozled husband might be ridiculed—no viewer would admit to being one—but there was no safe distance from a god's true believer.

The players had chosen to wear the masks.

They gathered around the hamper, and Asta clicked the clasp. With an tremble, imperceptible except to her son, she handed each one a mask: Wadan to Ludd, Teorr to Mik, a froggy Elemental to Edra, Grim-grin to herself, and a cherubic open-mouthed songster to Bragi.

None wore a mask as they worked out the play. Bragi already knew better than to *act* in rehearsal. You simply established the entrances, exits, the cue for each new scene, and only the presence of the audience brought it to life. You donned your costume, your funny walk, your mask, and then the god took hold. As they sketched through the story, each carried the face of a god in hand.

Bragi had his biggest role to date: his namesake. His Bragi mask was too large for a six-year-old skull, but they padded the crown to let him see through the startled wide eyes. The mouth hung below his chin, but he was told to speak loud and clear, and the resonant nose would add gravitas to his chirp. He had only to deliver a prologue, then depart. "Just say it the way your grandma told you," his father said. At first he feared even to touch the mask, but during the drag of the afternoon it became only a leather patchwork.

Edra offered advice to Bragi and Ludd, the apprentices, but her words were addressed to the veterans as well. "Don't worry what to say. Just say it. Just pretend you know what you're doing. What they said about masks, my grandpa, great-grandpa: the god's in the mask, so do what he wants you to do. The donkey finds water if you let him."

At his first sight of the masks the boy had seen that their features matched the hard statuary he had seen in ruined temples. Now they bore the crags and jowls and burning eyes of the Northland gods. Frozen, yet the torchlight rippled their faces the way the heat rose up from summer roads. Their mouths had been shut, except his, and now their lips were parting to speak.

All were assembled, and Droop-whisker gave them the signal to start. Barefaced, Mik and Asta commenced with pipes and lute, Edra beating the tambour. Suddenly, a violent strum, a squeal, a thwack, and the music skidded to a halt: Bragi's cue. As he entered through the curtain, his mask slipped sideways. He pulled at it but couldn't tell if he spoke through the mouth, nose, or eye.

"*The Play of Teorr's Hammer!*" A riff on the tambour, a shriek of pipes. Sir Paddo clapped, and his guests followed his cue. Then dead silence: Bragi's cue to make the longest speech of his life. "*Teorr had a mighty hammer. He defended the gods from the Fierce Ones.*" He couldn't remember the next. Then it came to his lips. "*Till he lost it . . . The hammer, I mean. He wasn't very smart . . .*" There was more, but he took a bow, and Sir Paddo clapped, the viewers too. The boy groped his way off as his father came charging out as a desperate Teorr.

"*My hammer! Lost! Lost! Lost! My hammer! Lost!*"

Ludd appeared, a majestic shivering One-eye. Behind him, Asta bore the slinky mask of the grinning god, taller than Bragi had ever seen her. He—she—he—challenged Teorr.

"*Think! Where is it lost?*"

"*It's lost. Who knows where? Dammit, if I knew where, it wouldn't be lost!*"

Chuckles. Sir Paddo had promised his guests a comic interlude, so they felt empowered to laugh. Teorr pounded the air in a baby's tantrum. More laughter, and Ludd allowed the laugh to peak, then spoke his line with perfect timing, changing the tone abruptly—

"*We are undefended.*" He was learning fast. The mask imparted hollowness to a voice with the heartbeat rhythm of fear. "*We are defenseless. The Evil Ones come to enslave us, force us to labor in underground mines, breathing a poisonous air, never seeing the light, awakening daily to darkness—*" He was down in the salt mines. All listened transfixed.

The Grinner chastised Teorr for his unrestrained slaughter of Fierce Ones, while Teorr accused Loghi of frivolity. They worked themselves into an old routine, dancing about like fleas, a frenzy of childish insults—"*You pin-brain poopie-head,*" "*You smelly-butt fatso*"—and swatting each other on the pate, the shoulders, the belly on every line. The boy knew this routine by heart: Papa and Mama had played it hundreds of times as husband and wife, brother and sister, soldier and whore—one of a dozen comic bits that defined all humankind, and now the gods, as bubble-brained fools. At last, as the laughter diminished, Loghi addressed the statuesque Ludd.

"*All-Father, we must retrieve Thor's hammer. Without it, no defense.*"

A brass voice rose from Wadan's queen Frekka: "*Our son has a dream. We shiver, we shake. We build walls, we clutch eggshells. Must we dream nothing but horror?*" Only later did the players ask themselves who filled that skeletal role. Edra mayhap, but she was soon to appear in another guise. The masks were playing the play.

Loghi ignored her: "*The hammer is in the grip of the Fierce Ones.*"

Mik's Teorr hopped up and down. He had spent his professional years hopping up and down, making a farce of rage, of grief, of lust, of fear. "*They took it! It had to be them! They're scared I'll kill'em! I will!*" The hilarity rose until—

From the rear of the hall, startling the throng, swaggered the Elemental: a froggy-masked Edra with a wide-kneed waddle, as if hefting a penis the size of a mace and balls like melons. In a deep gargling peasant yodel, she spoke—

"*Hey, whatcha lookin' for?*"

They replied in unison. "*We come from the gods in Asgard.*"

"*The gods in Asgard. Hey, you come from Asgard, I bet. I know that cause you told me.*"

Sir Paddo went into a near-fatal laughing fit. All the absurdity he'd seen in his seven decades of life was crystallized in that moment. The essence of comedy: it yanked you upside-down. His wife laughed at his laughing, and then he laughed at hers.

"*We seek Teorr's hammer.*"

"*And he needs that hammer, I bet. Can't bash out our brains without it. So I swiped it. I'd give it back but I can't unless I do. Pleased to meetcha. I'm Druk.*" A loud fart ripped the air.

The gaunt wife's laughter resounded, a childbirth of glee. The boy knew it was Gramma, but in rehearsal she had plodded about, indicating she'd do wheedles and farts—she was the master craftsman of farts—but Druk's words flowed from an oceanic wellspring.

"*Well, we miss being killed. Squashed like lice. All the funerals, wives and kids and grandpas, see the brains of your sweetie-pie splatting the walls. Cause we're just like the humans: all gooey inside. We cry and we howl and we snot all over the place, and if he didn't kill us we might forget how to die.*"

Bragi felt the sudden hush. Gramma knew—and he was learning—that folks loved surprise. Their lives were so predictable, so bound by the plodding, that they longed for the quake, the avalanche, the lightning flash to shock them free. When laughter peaked, you couldn't go on with the jokes. You had to surprise with a cry from the heart. And then another fart cut the air. The viewers howled.

"*What may we give for the hammer's return?*"

"*How bout some tits'n'ass? Gimme a goddess! A hot one!*"

Mik usually played the lecher, but Edra took it one notch beyond. The froggy Druk's boiling lust evoked a dark terror, comic but more primal. She had been subject to it, seen it, felt it—sometimes welcomed it, sometimes not.

"*Yeh, gimme a girlie to make little Druks. Have fun doin' it. Lotsa little Druks. Make'em faster than he can brain'em. He killed my last ones.*"

The play was playing itself, beyond all that the actors knew. Reya, goddess of love, denounced Teorr: "*Will love be made by hammer? Hammers begetting little hammers, babies from spatters of blood?*" Who was playing Reya? The masks brimmed madness, the viewers gaped, and the steward's limp mustachios went erect.

Loghi cut it short. "*We must give the monster a bride. One who has never known man.*"

Teorr furrowed his brow. His jowls undertook the heavy challenge of thought. "*Who?*" he asked.

"*Teorr.*"

Ham-fist staggered backward, pale with rage. He grasped his hammer, flung it at Grim-grin's head with a roar, then realized: no hammer. He fell to his knees and pounded the stage. Mik played the full repertoire of rage and the audience howled. At last, exhausted, he collapsed, his mask taking on a clownish grimace of impotent grief.

"*Dress Teorr in bridal linen, adorned with Reya's jewels,*" the ice-crystal Loghi directed. "*Bring him as bride to Druk, whose wedding gift shall be Teorr's hammer—*"

"*I the bride?*"

"*And I your lady's maid.*"

Peals of merriment. Bragi felt it: that moment when the story grabs all in its clutch, viewers and players alike. Loghi and Teorr vanished behind the curtain. One-eye stepped forward with an upraised hand commanding silence.

"*Our one hope! Our freedom, supremacy, the heritage of Asgard. Let us conquer fear!*"

Quick change, and Ham-fist stepped forth in bridal veil and virginal fluff. Stunned by the spectacle, Druk cavorted about the stage in hiccups of lust to the viewers' delight. Was this old Edra with her rickety knees or some insane monstrosity? Mik's Teorr minced and pouted like a bull playing Helen of Troy, then gave it all up, stormed offstage, got hauled back by Loghi, and resignedly draped himself in the pose of a beefy nymph.

"*Here she is! I got her! She's mine and nobody else's! Grab her little butt and nobody gets that butt but me! I give her what she wants whether she wants it or not! Druk and Druk and Druk Druk Druk!*"

Loghi restrained Druk from direct assault. "*Let us feast the bride.*"

The bride roared out ravenous hunger. "*Pig! Salmon! Ox! Mead! More!*"

Druk stood aghast. "*That's a big old appetite.*" Guffaws.

Loghi soothed him. "*The bride so madly yearns for her lord's embrace that she has starved herself for eight full days.*"

"*Poor baby! Here's a big fat kiss from her sweetie.*" He raised the bridal veil and reeled back. "*She's got red eyes!*" Huge belly laughs.

Loghi intervened. "*The bride so fiercely lusts for her lord's embrace that she has gone sleepless for eight full nights.*"

"*Poor baby! I'll give her good rooty-toot.*"

The Froggy One clutched the bashful bride and met a thunderous roar that flung him two rear somersaults over the stage. Bragi had never seen his grandmother do such a thing. Snorts and shrieks.

With elegant fussiness Loghi adjusted the bridal garb. "*The bride so fiercely yearns that she cries like a tigress forlorn.*" Druk felt for his manhood to assure it was still at hand. Edra knew all there was to be known about manhood.

The flickering candelabras flared as the nuptial gift—the mighty hammer Myolnir—came borne by the clackety Norns. A throng of Elementals, Fierce Ones, Funny Ones, appeared from the great hall's shadows. Bragi saw the stage teeming with nameless forms summoned from flickering torches.

Druk flung wide his arms. "*Lay the hammer in her lap, and then me.*" The bride clasped the deadly maul, the Norns took flight with a shriek, and the slaughter began.

Bragi had watched from the edge of the stage. In nightmares to come he would see the flash of light, the steel missile, the splatter of Druk, and again feel raw horror at seeing his grandmother slain. As the blood ran cold, Teorr—to honor all creeds— raised his hands to Heaven proclaiming, "*Thanks be to Almighty God for restoring my sacred hammer!*"

And in one mighty gasp, Gramma popped up unmasked and alive, and all came forth joining hands. For a breath, dead silence, then a handclap from Sir Paddo burst the dam. Stomping, merriment, cheers, and the boy, aloft on his father's shoulders, saw the old knight's beaming face and his lady's glittering eyes.

The rest of the night was a jumble. Bragi felt an exhaustion deep in the bone, but his mind was abuzz. Food and drink now, chatter and song, and non-stop jabber from Ludd with new ideas, hushed at last by Asta's "Enough!" He tried to hear if anyone knew from whence came the other players—the goddess, the Norns, the flock of flickery Primals—but none spoke of those mysteries. He may have been only dreaming, or he saw with the Sight that his mother feared he had. He drifted at last from the rapids into a gentle eddy.

Next morning the troupe prepared for departure. Gramma nursed her bruises, regretting her double back somersault. "I haven't done that for how long? Ten years! Fool! If I'd been thinking— That hurts!" Mik laid his hands on his mother's back. "And that Froggie's waddle just about killed my knees. I have to remember: I'm old. *I'm old!*"

Mik made his *you're-hopeless* face. "Well, Ma, I guess you'll never learn."

Sir Paddo appeared with his lady to see them off. He gave Mik a purse that proved to be fulsome payment, went around to offer his hand to each. He struggled to find words, pausing for the squawk of a disrespectful crow, and at last he spoke—

"One never knows what to expect. Of life, that is. A truism, certainly, and we of the Christian faith, of course, feel more secure in what may transpire. Or less, perhaps— Far be it from me to judge. One takes no comfort in the Northmen's tale you tell, though laughter is comfort indeed. I confess myself lax in terms of faith, yet I cling to one vital creed: the concept of Grace. The undeserved gift from God, from the breath of life, freely given to all. The simple touch of a hand to a heart in darkness. Your frantic day of creating a play to please an old man's dotty whim. Your magic."

He broke off abruptly, gave a cordial wave of his hand, and walked away down a garden colonnade. The tall gaunt wife made the rounds of the troupe, a word to each. She came to Asta, embraced her and whispered something in her ear. At Bragi she stopped, took his hands, gazed into his startled eyes. The boy saw the youth in her weary smile.

"You have so many years."

—XV—
Rona

They had been dissuaded from travel to Samano for fear of encountering remnants of the plague-stricken army that might be unpacified. On their many journeys the players had been robbed only twice, both times, miraculously, by respectful miscreants who eschewed rape and recreational murder. Still, disbanded armies were best avoided.

The players turned their sights to their next intended destination, Bavia, and took a steep mountain path—Sir Paddo's scouts advised that the main road was less secure. The old lord sent them an escort, two horsemen who rode ahead, camped at a distance, and never spoke a word.

Mik led the donkey with one hand on the bridle. The boy walked beside him, his hand on his father's hand. Spurred by their triumph, Ludd indulged in a venture new to him: thinking. His brain was finding its legs. "I had some ideas. Stuff we could do."

Mik interrupted. "That trace is tangled, Ludd, Straighten that, okay?"

"What if we're animals, and we're wearing masks so it's like people are animals—"

"Could you straighten that?"

"I mean we act like animals, like this story my father told, this fox, before he died—" He fumbled with the trace. "I mean before my father died—"

"No masks."

"It'd be pretty funny."

"We don't use the masks."

"We did."

"Once. Twice. No more."

Ludd's tide was unstoppable. "Or if we did those old stories, what she was talking about, from way back when? Where the king dresses up like a girl and his mother tears off his head—"

"Great idea, Ludd, but people don't want to see that stuff. They want to laugh." The donkey gave a hiccuping bray.

"But in the play we killed the goony guy."

"It's fun if he's goony, not if he's king."

"But she said they liked it way back when—"

"Back when people were mean and nasty."

"They're pretty nasty now."

"Listen to me!" Mik drew in a deep breath. "When people have money, think they're all kings, then they like to see people die. But right now they see it falling apart—war, starvation—they want to laugh. You've got a lot to learn. I don't tell you how to catch fish—"

"Sell fish."

"Whatever! It's fish. Enough ideas!"

"They just come out."

"Keep it to fish."

Bragi fell back to the back of the cart. His mother rode with her legs dangling off the edge, while Gramma walked. By day the old woman endured, though at night he heard her cursing her aching knees. The baby would be okay, they said, though Asta had to be careful. He wanted to curl up with her, feel her soft parts pressing tight to him, but she was hearing another voice.

Gramma would point to the greenery—towering trees, brambles, creepy mushrooms, bushes with buds coming late to bloom—and urge him to see it all. "It's a gift, but we have to grab it or life goes right past. Look at those squirrels, see'em? Chatter, chatter. We used to fight like that, your grandpa and me, twitching our tails."

He looked. Nothing special, just trees and squirrels. "When does the baby come out?"

"Long time yet. We'll get to Bavia for Midsummer, plenty of time. That means money. Music, dancing, dog fights—remember roast pig? But the baby, she'll be long time yet. We'll be home before then."

"She's inside Mama."

"But she's not ready. She's gotta have a nose. We have to find her a nose. Should we try the butcher shop?" He hated her teasing him. Some day he'd be too big to tease. "But I'll be dead by then." She heard him thinking. He hated when she did that. "All that worry, it dribbles out your ears."

"Does it have to be a sister?"

"Looks like it to me."

"Can she spit?"

"Little boys asking questions! It never ends."

At midday they stopped for food on a ridge overlooking a clouded valley. "Fog on a lake," Edra said. "It should've burnt off by now."

"Little lost sheep, your flock's up there." Mik pointed toward wispy clouds above distant hills and rolled up angelic eyes. Yes, the fog had scattered its siblings.

Asta unpacked the bread and olives. "Nice view," she said. The boy wanted to curl up with his mother, to nestle in, but she was busy. She would give him a hug and tell him to pat the donkey. So he sat on a rock by Gramma, just out of reach, wanting to be close but fearing closeness. He watched the old woman eating. Her jaw worked the food to the side where she still had teeth, and the wart on her chin made a twitch at each chew. Once she told him that he would grow old like her, and he tried to forget it but never knew how to forget.

His mind was a twitching wart. Bragi—his namesake Bragi, Sir Paddo said—was a singer of songs. But what songs would he sing when he was old with a wart on his chin?

Gramma must have heard him think it. "My grandpa told stories he'd heard as a little boy, so far back that even old olive trees couldn't recollect. The world spreads out wide, like an old floppy dog in the sun. Whatever might be apt to happen, it does."

"Like where the mother killed her babies?"

Edra heard her words echoed back, strange in the voice of a child. "Well, that was a play. That didn't really happen." He knew she said never to lie, but she'd also said that sometimes you have to. "But they'd play funny stuff too. One show, these gods go down to where dead people go, and they meet frogs that try to sing. I wish I'd seen that one. Or up in the air with the birds. And there's a war, and all the women, the wives and the sweethearts, they get together, they say, *Hey, stop it! No more love till you stop it. Why we suffer the labor pains and wiping our babies' shit and then you kill'em? You men were all babies once. Grow up!*"

"What happened?"

"They stopped the war. Course I guess they started another." Bragi tried to imagine the play, but it was stuck fast in the way-back-when. Was that when they wore the masks? "Well, I told you that." She was hearing his thoughts again. "Long time ago they used masks, but then they closed down the plays so we had to go on the road. Our grandpas, their grandpas even, they did."

"What happens?"

"What happens when?"

"With the masks." He wasn't sure he wanted to know.

"Well, you saw. Put it on and no knowing. When you had the spider bite and we put the mud on the bite, that white stuff that sucked out the poison, the clay? The masks do that, they grab it and pull out whatever's inside, gods or frogs, they draw it out. That was me with my damn somersault."

She rubbed her shoulder. He felt the sting of the spider bite and the healing mud.

On the early stage of the trek from Sir Paddo's estate to Bavia, the boy ran ahead to scout for lurking Froggies, fell back to walking beside his grandma, and wound up rhythmically patting the donkey, who paid him no mind. He rarely spoke to Ludd—too tall, too strange with his wandering eye—but that day he was drawn to his side. The man was silent for a time, then began to speak as men do when no one is listening.

"What happened, my friend Teo, salt mines, kinda chubby, even what they fed us. But he killed a guard. So they impaled him. All day, and they made us watch." He seemed puzzled to know why he said it.

"He shouldn't have killed the guard," Mik said without glancing at Ludd.

Bragi shooed off Yesu's flies, but questions circled like raptors. "Why did he kill him?"

"The guard? I dunno." They walked a while in silence, then he spoke. "He whipped us, but that was his job, I guess, so it wasn't his fault. Maybe Teo just needed to kill somebody, that was the one. Walked straight up, not a word, swung the shovel, side of the head." Mik frowned at the bony man.

"What's a salt mine?"

"Where you get salt. Kind we use comes from the ocean, that's full of grit. Down there you chop out the salt."

"Why?"

"They sell it. Makes money."

He knew better than ask more questions. Why were they slaves, why were they whipped, why kill the guard for doing his job? Every question was a *Why*, but it was just what was. Imagining mysterious tunnels teeming with Froggies, he said the first thing that came into mind. "Is it fun?" The moment he said it he knew.

Ludd emitted a coughing yawp, a falsetto sneeze with a chuckle to clear it, and his wall eye strained to see his ear. "You're down there all day. You never see the sun. You breathe the dust, the salt dries you out. Fall down, they whip you. Tunnels collapse. Die quick if you're lucky. Tell me if it's fun." It didn't sound like fun.

When Ludd started talking he couldn't stop. "Teo. Funny. What they did, they stuck a stake in the ground, pointed stake. Stuck him on it, point up his butthole, and set him there. Feet off the ground so he sinks down slow and the stake works in. Impaling, they call it."

"What are you telling the boy?" Mik sounded angry.

"He asked."

Ludd paused, but something drew out the words. "So he's perched up there naked on the skewer like he's dancing." He paused to let Teo dance. "Screams all day, jiggles around to stop the pain, but that makes him sink down harder. Just stuck on there like he's dancing. Somebody laughed, and you needed a laugh." The donkey jerked his head to ward off the flies. Ludd brushed at the buzzing and stared hard to see into Yesu's brain.

"But great that we got the day off to watch. Guess we had Teo to thank. Most of the day, and they cut his throat to make him shut up. Then the guards all got drunk, and I snuck off. Lucky for me."

They walked at the donkey's pace. More trees and brambles and boulders, nothing new. Mik guided the donkey to avoid the ruts when the track was wide enough to avoid the ruts. Whenever they got to a bend in the road, they saw more road ahead. Nothing new.

The path was better for one-horse passage or a wild boar's amble than for a cart. It meandered between rock outcrops, under low branches, or along drop-offs that appeared hopeless until necessity prodded someone to say, "I think we can make it," and they did. The boy walked beside Mik, helping to lead Yesu by holding onto his father's belt. He was tired, but his mother had said that walking would make him strong. That inspired him, but he wondered: if he got strong would he have to work in the salt mines?

~

Many times my father told me that in a play things had to happen for a reason. It might be silly, but it had to feel true. We had to believe that he'd buy a dead donkey because it made him feel smart or because he liked the white tip of its nose. It was the magic *Why?*

Why did the pirates kill? What made the gaunt wife kind? What inveigled Gramma into a double somersault? More difficult even to fathom myself. Why was I sometimes a good little boy or a clacky-beak devil? I couldn't help but feel that life was hard to believe.

In maturity, as I studied the Christian catechism, I began to feel that every answer opened another door that led to a passage that led to another door. That perhaps we were created in the image of God to help Him find His way out of the labyrinth.

The boy walked ahead, scanning the roadway for wild boars he could kill and save them all. His gaze fell to the ruts, the juts, the twigs and stickums the mountains offered his bare soles. Edra hobbled along at a steady pace, holding to one slat of the cart. For a time the northward track followed a south-flowing stream. Several times they had to ford, but the fordings were shallow, and even as the stream grew turbulent, its rocks raising great sprays, the cart's jostle stayed steady.

Second day, the two mounted guards departed. No danger from here on, they said, and went trotting up the trail. Bragi was glad to see them go, as they stayed apart from the troupe and rarely spoke. For him they meant only two horses' butts and avoiding an avalanche of turds. Life was on track. No danger, said the guards.

"O Christ!"

The cry ripped a gash in the sky. Yesu balked. A crow squawk echoed. Ludd loped ahead to the bend in the path, stopped and stared. Mik gave the bridle a gentle tug and the donkey edged forward. The cart came to the bend, hit a root, and jerked to a halt.

"O Christ!" A screamed whisper.

I see it before me now. On the same day I saw the chubby man dancing on a stake, this was more real. More real than the spitting girl, even more real than my wife in labor, decades later, dying away from me. From that day I have borne this fiery welt of memory as we once bore the cursed hamper. Our Savior brought the dead to life but never revealed how to wipe a deep scar clear.

A figure sat in the road, rocking forward and back, keening. She was young, naked, fifteen or thereabouts. She rocked compulsively, slapping her knee at every forward rock, with outbursts of counting numbers and calling on Christ. Her face was blank, her eyes the eyeless white of the fog. She looked to be smeared with mud—face, breasts, belly. Edra hobbled forward, unmindful of her bruises, but a half dozen steps away she stopped, moved with caution as one would approach a wounded beast, at last laying hands on the shivering, stinking girl. The mud was her own bloody shit.

"O Christ!" The girl went mute, heartbeats begging release, and her eyes rolled into sight. Asta climbed down from the cart with a blanket to cover the girl. Mik gestured to Ludd to hold the donkey and began to scout a campsite: no more travel that day. The women supported the girl to the stream and washed her. At times she screamed from the water's bite, but they did what had to be done. They dressed her in the long white gown of St. Eleora.

The boy clung to the donkey. The girl mumbled, repeating, at last loud enough to hear. "One two three four five six . . ." Asta brought her water, and after a time she drank.

A long afternoon. He wanted to go to the crouching girl who repeated the dull compulsive count. He might say hello, tell her she looked like his friend the spitting girl—willow thin, black hair, cats' eyes—only bigger. Maybe her name was Rona. Maybe she'd stop the counting. "One two three four five six O Christ . . ." He could only watch from a distance.

Night fell. The troupe sat at the campfire. Edra reported what they already knew. The girl had been raped, multiple onslaughts, likely men from the plague-struck army. "Well, most times they do stuff like this and then get gone," said Edra. Scant comfort. The girl was another burden along with Asta's pregnancy, Edra's knees, the fugitive slave—yet there was no debate. They were the ones who heard the cry. She was in their care. Impossibility was no excuse.

Bedding was dispersed. Mik curled up in the cart with the boy, a show curtain over them, sacks of barley to prop their heads. Bragi stared at the stars. The girl slept soundly with sleep-muffled cries— Toward dawn, they heard her toneless chant. "One two three four five six O Christ . . ." Repeating, repeating, then silence. Her mind was a jar flung at a wall and shattered. "One two three four five six O Christ . . ."

"She's raped by six men," Edra murmured to anyone awake. "She's not counting sheep." The boy had heard the word *rape* but wasn't sure what it meant. Maybe like being knocked over?

On the road next day the girl stumbled along methodically at the rear of the cart. She continued her count as if cut off from herself and the human race. Asta, riding backwards, watched that she stayed with them, heard only—

"One two three four five six O Christ . . ."

Late afternoon, across a valley, they came into sight of Bavia. Perhaps someone there who knew her, someone to take her in, a church of the Cristers or a healer with herbs for rape. They approached a tiny hovel. Goatherds, likely. Mik rapped at the door-frame. A birdlike slattern pulled back the flap. The girl stiffened.

"We have a young woman with us. Do you know her?"

"Bett!" A shriek like the Norns.

The girl spat. The spindly woman cried out, flew to the girl, hugged her, slapped her, shook her, embraced. The girl spat in her face. Slap again, and the spindly woman grabbed her arm and pulled her into the hovel, jerking shut the flap.

The troupe stood bewildered. Moments later, a squat burly man came around the corner, ax in hand, halted and glared. They backed away. They were relieved of their burden.

"Sorry to lose that white gown," said Edra as they continued on the road. "Perfect for virgins or saints."

"I'll soon be too fat to play virgins or saints," said Asta.

They camped for the night outside the town. Few words were spoken except as needed to pitch shelter, tend the donkey, cook food. Somehow they craved silence. After supper Bragi laid his head in his grandmother's lap as she gazed into the crackling fire.

"Long day, honey. You sleepy?"

"What's wrong with her?"

"Oh she got hurt. Who knows?"

"Why did her mama slap her?"

"Well if that was her mama, we don't know. Or maybe like your mama whacked you when you nearly fell in the fire: be more careful."

"What was she counting?"

"Sheep, pigs maybe. Days till Midsummer. She counts good, don't she?"

He felt the flutter of the yellow-eyed Norns, heard a muffled squawk. The girl seemed not to know she was Bett. She knew only the numbers she spoke—*one two three four five six O Christ*—sheep, pigs, men—Gramma forgot that she'd said it was men. Or she was counting all the Betts the rapes had split her into. Or she wasn't Bett.

The boy rose, ran across the rocky field to Yesu, threw his arms around its neck and sobbed. The donkey whiffled its nostrils, lowered its muzzle to graze the sparse grass. The boy stroked the bristly mane.

She wasn't Bett. She was Rona. The naked girl was way older, he knew, she had titties like Mama and hair at her crotch. But he knew it was Rona, though Rona had never said she was Rona, and Rona was dead and wouldn't know how to count. But she was with him. She would always be with him now.

—XVI—
Fart Dance

You have commended me, my liege, on my sunny disposition, albeit overcast whenever I snag on drifting deadfall. Loss inures us to loss. Scar tissue numbs us to the pinpricks, yet numbness holds no joy. We survive the farcical exigencies of life—rapes, plagues, indignities—though never prepared for what lies ahead at the bend. The ancients told horrible tales: a king, blind to himself, who blinds himself. Yet our merry farces held the same madness: pride, burning thirst and the plunge as we fail. As the white mud drew forth the spider's venom from my swollen hand, might this whole swampy world be a great wad of ooze to suck the miasma from our hearts? My sunny mien is beclouded at times.

～

The shows went well in Bavia. The town's Midsummer festivities were nominally blest by the Church as St. John's Day but funded by a great landowner whose pedigree went back to the Western Empire. His intent, Mik surmised, was to lessen religious strife by promoting debauchery. The players could play anything as long as they never spoke of God or gods. Those words would get their ears cut off.

They were lodged at an inn, and the stage was set up in the inn-yard where the troupe had played for many years—two shows a day, one in the afternoon, the second by torchlight. No one wanted to see a play on Midsummer Eve—that was for orgies in the name of St. John—but the days before and after were prime.

For each show they would play three short farces. The first was an old sketch about a man using magic to get an erection, seeing it grow to monstrous dimensions but forgetting the spell to shrink it. The second, two fishwives finding sisterhood as they shared complaints about their men, and then—

"*My man has the funniest prong. It curves.*"

"*To the left?*"

"*With a little wart.*" They look at each other. It dawns: they share the same husband.

The third was a mix of dead-donkey and three-wishes. Over supper Ludd had murmured as if to himself, "So what if the wishes are about the donkey?"

Mik grabbed the idea. "So I say, *I wish he was big and strong,* and we watch him puff up big and strong but still dead. And she's yelling at me, so I say, *I wish you'd just shut up!* Then she goes mute, and I do the tantrum bit and yell, *Stop doing that! Just out with it!*"

"You have to say *I wish*—"

"*I wish you'd just out with it!* And you erupt and we realize, *oops, we've blown it.* Then it goes how we've done it before. That works."

"Thanks, Ludd," said Asta.

"Right. Thanks," Mik added.

"Can I be in it?" He had gotten big laughs, so he shouldn't have to ask. Yesu never asked to do donkey work—they just harnessed him up and he did it. Bragi wished he were a donkey, though he wouldn't like flies in his eyes.

"You're already in it," his father said. "You come in at the end, yell, *The pigs are eating the porridge.*"

Edra spoke up. "Might work better if Ludd did that line. He's funny when he's frantic—"

No! Bragi wailed within.

"—And then Bragi could be the devil that gives the three wishes. Mean little devil."

His grandma saw his delight. Yet for him every blessing was a curse. Here in the low glow of an oil lamp, after porridge with sausage chunks, were the people who loved him. Up on the trestle stage he faced the bloody-eyed world.

The old woman saw him cringe. "So here's how it is. You give'em the wishes but you're mad. Some big smelly devil just ruffled up your hair. So you know these dummies are gonna screw up, and that's great cause you feel really mean. A mean little six-year-old devil. How about that?"

"Can I wear a mask?"

Dead silence, then Asta said, "Why not? You already used the story-singer. That fits, sorta."

"They said no gods," Mik reminded her.

Edra hooted. "They don't like gods, but devils are fine."

Mik was dubious. "That mask doesn't look like a devil."

Ludd piped up. "But devils maybe don't look like devils. They try to look nice."

"Ludd—"

Edra settled it. "Let him use the mask. Who cares how it looks? Our saint scared'em shitless."

The morning before the show he sat staring at the mask. His grandma had told him of actors in the way-back-when who stared at their masks. "To let the spirit come in," she said. So he thought how mad the god Bragi would be if somebody ruffled his hair. He stared as they donned their costumes. He stared as the yard rang with celebrants' howls. He stared as his father called places, and at last he put on the mask. It was smiling, but he felt like a mean little devil.

The first two farces were hits. The crowd was primed to laugh, and with the erection play they guffawed before the punch line landed. Mik froze, looked out at the crowd as if first noticing they were there, startled back, then strode forward scolding them. "No, first I say, *It's big!* and then you're supposed to laugh." He looked down at his crotch. "*And now it's even bigger!*" The laughter broke like thunder. In the second, the women's moment of truth was capped by Ludd's wild-goose frenzy of pigs and porridge—wrong play but it worked.

Time at last for the dead-donkey play. The humid air crackled with the battle of the sexes. The husband exulted that he'd bought the donkey cheap, the wife cursed his stupidity, and the husband asserted his conjugal right to be stupid. It was Bragi's cue. He came through the curtain, a dwarf in a giant's head. "*Surprise. I give you three wishes. Use them wisely.*" He made a wild devil's flourish and disappeared.

"*Three wishes!*" Mik and Asta intoned in unison.

Suddenly, a drunken heckler: "That's stupid! The donkey's dead!"

They dealt with hecklers often, rarely the same way twice. It was usually Mik's initiative. He might thank the fellow, then turn his backside and blow him a juicy fart. He might pretend to swat a blowfly and flick it at the heckler or shout out to hush that squealing pig. Once he'd descended into the pit and kneed the persistent loud-mouth in the balls, then apologized profusely for his clumsiness. It was always a man. It always smelled of neediness. But any taunt was a mosquito that had to be swatted lest a swarm descend. This time he took a direction the boy hadn't seen.

"Omigod! You're right! The donkey's dead! I'm so stupid!" He pounded his skull, ran about the stage chanting, "*The donkey's dead, the donkey's dead!*" He applauded the heckler's insight, bowed to him, led the crowd in a cheer for the stupefied man, then suddenly halted.

"*So whatta we do? We're screwed!*"

He had seized the moment and now he offered the reins. Where would it go? It was Ludd who picked it up, spurred by his pigs-porridge laugh. He appeared through the curtain, cried, "*Yes, you are so stupid. You don't deserve to live. Me neither. Let's kill ourselves.*" Mik embraced him like a long-lost brother, which made no sense, but the crowd was with them now. "*But how?*" Ludd had seen their antics with comical tries at suicide.

Mik struck a *Eureka!* pose. "*We'll fart ourselves to death!*"

And the two men launched an improvised fart dance—blasting gas at each other in pirouettes, prances and rearward assaults. Mik was more flexible and had a wider range of lip-razzles, but Ludd sported a gawky strut that lent a new elegance to flatulence. At last, in perfect unison, the men staggered about the stage, heaved a sigh, and fell into each others' arms. The audience laughed to the edge of death, applauding fiercely—the scrawny young heckler leading the cheers.

Where would it go from there? The wilder the ride the more was expected. With a normal show, they would go into a song, wind it up, take a bow, but attaining an epiphany—

Afterward, Bragi had no memory of his deed. He could only recall its effect. The mean little devil ran to center stage, made wild gyrations of sorcery—whirlwinds, pinches, tickles, lightning zaps, thunderclaps, the repertoire of his grandma—conjuring the invisible donkey to rise. Then he ran off stage, stripped off his mask, and threw up. The others picked up the cue.

"*The donkey's alive! A miracle!*"

"*Incredible!*"

"*Hold it! Wait!*" the wife exclaimed. "*There's no donkey there!*" They froze and stared. "*You dolt! You bought a dead donkey and brought it to life and now we can't even see it!*"

Asta chased Mik off the stage, beating him. The crowd screamed, and without an instant of thought Bragi's mask was back in place. He stepped through the slit in the curtain, a vast hush fell, and in his thin piping voice he proclaimed—

"*Now I get to pee!*"

The laughter was a tempest. They would never forget it, no one, player nor heckler nor feral cat. The troupe came forward to bathe in the plaudits, and Asta motioned Bragi to pull off his mask and take a solo bow. He managed to make a quick bend at the waist, a nod like a pigeon-peck, and beneath the mad acclaim, unheard, a gentle fart.

Backstage they packed their goods, Mik holding open the wickerwork lid as the boy carefully nested his mask between Iduna and Frekka. He felt as happy as when he'd met the little spitting girl whose name he knew was Rona.

"This boy! This boy!"

A wiry figure shoved past the watchman who kept the attiring place clear of intruders. Bragi felt a clutch at his shoulder and turned to face the grizzled one-armed Ruzante, whose face was wide in a rictus of joy. The soldier threw himself into the arms of the dumfounded Mik, then Ludd, then knelt to Bragi. Stuttering, he told his story in snorts, in spasms, in tears, in laughter, all.

"Bad enough I lost an arm. Bad enough pluck the fucking chickens, when I'd gone up against Huns. Huns! And then they all died around me, even the fucking chickens, and my buddy ran off with my sword. A sword that killed fucking Huns. We coulda still took the city if I'd had my fucking sword."

He had tried to join a robber band, but they didn't want a cripple. He escaped to Bavia, found work as a knacker but got fired the first day when an old nag kicked him, hobbled off, and fell in a well. He wanted to cut his throat, but he had no blade. "I was working out how to kill myself when I stopped to watch the show. Thought, I still got the last of my pay, I'll see the show then end it."

He saw himself in every farce: the dummy flummoxed by life, betrayed by circumstance, caught in a fart dance. He felt the laughter's cruelty and its kinship. He heard his boasts and his whimpers, his hopes and his lies. And just when the mirth stirred his wizened bladder, the boy announced his need to pee.

"You gave me a laugh. That's what I needed. I'd forgot how. Sorry to bother. Just had to say it. Luck to all." The old man stood there. He had said his piece, nothing more to say. He gave a wave, backed away, disappeared into the sunlight.

I stood stock still, terrified by the power I held. It felt good to be praised, but what if I'd missed my cue? What if I hadn't been funny? The old chicken-plucker might be dead. And all those souls in the world who needed a laugh . . .

In later days we played that piece with all the new bits: the heckler (arranged in advance), the fart dance, the mean little devil's pee line. Never quite the same, but it worked. Though not always. Once, the response was flat. Afterwards, my father came to sit beside me on a rickety bench—one of countless rickety benches of my boyhood—and I knew what to expect. His fathering was best when he simply made me laugh. When he tried to teach me things he pontificated, too much like the comical pedant he mocked. Still, I heard him.

"Remember this," he said. "You're a player now, and a player has times when you feel like a god, almost. But like the weather: you never know. Sometimes the stuff that works just falls flat, and we're not as great as we think." That offered little comfort: it felt too true. The other thing he said I didn't remotely understand, though I came to see it later. "Next thing you learn is endurance." Then he wheezed a colossal wheeze, fell off the bench in the throes of death, gazed up at me cross-eyed, and smiled.

⁓

The evening show they played as rehearsed, no epiphanies, just a security in the jokes and the story. Late supper at the inn, Ludd had been beaming, but now he gravitated toward isolation, sitting by the hearth with his trencher, back in the salt mines. Mik rose from the table, approached, gave him a stiff shoulder-pat. There was always a distance between the men, more so as Ludd began to find his feet, getting laughs and brimming with ideas. The veteran had an instinctive disdain for the beginner and perhaps a degree of envy: Ludd was in the throes of discovery, while the old pro's life was a holding action.

Mik found words to add to the shoulder-pat. "That was good this afternoon. You picked it up and threw in something new, and we went with that. That's how you do it. We play off each other and it builds. You can't just toss in wild ideas, you have to listen, react—" Was he praising the bony man or berating him? "Anyway, good stuff." He returned to the table.

Ludd nodded at Mik's admonitions, even as the boy saw wild ideas dancing in his eyes. Bragi approached, sat beside him. He meant to say something about the show but heard himself ask, at long last, "What's wrong with your eye?"

The bony man shrugged. "Well, it just goes that way." He fingered the lid as if to tidy it. "It's not much good." They sat there a while, then Ludd added, "Oh hey, you were funny. Good job. Both shows."

"You were good too."

Bragi watched the women by the oil lamp going over accounts. His father picked up his pipes and began to play a weird warbling tune he had learned when they toured the land of camels. Ludd raised his hand as if to speak to the boy, halted, cleared his throat, spoke. "What's it like— I mean— Your dad is— He's pretty funny. You like him, right?

The question made no sense. Grownups never had questions, only words that sounded like questions. Bragi nodded.

"I asked because— Course you and him, you're together. Makes a difference, I guess." He shut both eyes, perhaps to hold them in place. "I had a little boy. Same age, maybe, I guess. How old— I don't know how old before— Before you remember stuff. I just wondered how he'd think about me, or if he would?" Mik's pipes, the soft light of the oil lamp, the clink of coins as the women counted, the muffled hoots of merriment in the streets—all seemed to be asking questions.

Later, from the man's stammerings, Bragi put together a history. Ludd got a girl pregnant and had a son. He sold fish for his father, but his father died, so he left to look for work in the city. But the city fell in the wars. He was lucky to be enslaved instead of being slaughtered, went to the mines, escaped, stowed away, and found himself dancing a fart dance. A different story than he had told before, but Ludd clearly believed whatever story he heard himself telling. He had a talent for that.

But why—he was asking Bragi, who had not a clue—had he not returned to the woman? "Her name was Mara, she had coppery hair— And the boy— Just trying to think what the boy's like now. Can't remember what we named him."

"I dunno."

"Right."

His lids opened wide, his long jaw pulled longer, and his wall-eye bent further askew, as if looking behind himself to see the past catching up. "I ought to play Loghi. The grinny god, is that him? I could do that." He snuffled and sneezed.

The inn had provided one room for the troupe. The stable was filthy, so Ludd was given a pallet on the floor, and they all settled in.

Late night, the boy heard weeping that must have come from the bony man.

—XVII—
Playing for Cats

Three days' travel to Malo. The weather turned warm, then warmer, then hot. Garments worn in layers—the only way to travel—began to be shed. The angry sun toasted rocks and baked the clay hills like bread. Yesu turned balky, and Mik had to jerk and prod. "What's so scary?" whispered Bragi into the twitchy long ear but got no reply. Yesu made his opinions known but offered no explications.

From the hills they descended to a plain of dried rivulets and dust. Far off, Bragi saw the mountains his grandma spoke of. Not mountains as they knew them, but mountains rising white upon white, masses of whiteness piled upward mound over mound to the height of the canopy sky. The boy's blood ran chill. From some lost day of his infancy he felt the sharpness of snow.

Mid-afternoon he looked up from watching his feet tread the dust. The white mountains were gone. Puffy clouds scattered about the sky like sheep wool in wind. How could mountains disappear? He saw only a dark blue line along the horizon, jagged and thin. "See the mountains?" Edra called out. "There they are!" The dark blue nibbled silhouette was mountain, what he had seen were towering piles of cloud. A flash of relief to face no tortuous climb. And a merciless stab of loss.

Two days, and on the third, late morning back in a hilly realm, they came to the outskirts of Malo. Asta had told of its beauty: an old stone bridge dating back to the Empire when roads and city walls were built, and ancient temples now home to the great god Yesu, namesake of their donkey. They had played there many years and had friends who would greet them with joy. Touring was their livelihood, but the true reward was to visit the Verbrucchis, Frato, the mad Cutullo clan, old Kalas—

"Remember old Kalas?" asked Asta.

Yes he did. Old Kalas, with bushy brows and fierce eyes, furry gray stubble, crooked nose and crisp articulation, had bent down to him and croaked, "I will ask you an impossible question." A breath. "Who are you?"

"Bragi."

"Who's that?"

"Me."

The old man prolonged his terrible gaze, then his lips twisted into a grin. "So never forget it."

Now he could tell old Kalas that he was a player and had played a mean little devil and gotten laughs and saved the one-armed soldier. His memory came up with more images of Malo: a patch of red flowers, a shop with toy swords, the ancient bridge, and a tall stone figure of a woman painted in blues and vermilions, nursing a baby—a goddess, a mother, whatever.

The road wound around cliffs and through stands of trees that blocked the view, then smoothed into a pavement of dressed stones. Gramma said it was built long ago, when someone ruled the world. The boy watched for the city walls—a great city, Gramma said, with a thousand people. And through the trees he glimpsed a span of the wall—white stone, tall as a giant—then trees again. "You'll see it," said Gramma. "It's always a big surprise."

They turned a sharp bend and at last got a view of the city. The city was gone.

The cart rolled along the granite walls, then the breaches in the walls. Trenches, mounds of rubble. They came through the splintered gates into streets of litter. What might once have been a bakery was a blackened skull. A spew of muddied rags trailed out from a dress-maker's shop. A charred sign proclaimed the Dragon Inn, but the dragon was long gone. A baby's cradle stood in front of a plundered church. Houses were gutted. Buildings stood like the rotted teeth in a beggar's maw.

Empty sky. The only sign of death was one dried carcass of a dog in a flower-fringed patio, but rot breathed up from the derelict city's corpse. A rat scurried out of a doorway and into a heap of debris—scant pickings left for scavengers. A tree bore a dozen random hacks—some drunken swordsman in combat with anything living. A tangle of ivy enfolded a child's wooden doll. The boy saw reddish brown stains on the stones of the street.

"Where are they?"

"Might've escaped. Or not."

"How long?"

"Months."

"What is it?" asked Bragi.

"War," his mother replied, as if saying *Wash your face.*

He liked to play war with other boys. You tried to not get killed, but it was fun to die. The slain recovered faster than a pig had pigs: you writhed in the throes of death, flattened out, then jumped up alive and charged on. Nobody battered down houses. Nobody killed a dog. He asked his mother when they would see old Kalas. She shook her head. "Where do people live?" asked the boy. She gestured to the rubble.

Cats. The cats began to emerge from the ruin. Always cats in a city, and they always looked hungry, hunted, haunted. Cats had kittens and kittens grew into cats, a fact of life, his grandmother said. "Worse than rats. At least rats have the sense to hide. These, they waggle their butts in the breeze." A cat crept out of a basement window and strutted across the street—a sleek black-smoke tabby with a thick sausage tail. Another followed, a twitching frazzle of panic, its eyes like pinholes, its tail an outburst of hair. Bragi thought he had seen them in Bavia, together, like brothers.

More cats. Cats in the shadows, cats atop waste, cats on the broken tiles. Cats under ancient sewer grates, in crumbling doorways, basking in sunlight. Cats in spasmodic couplings or threading through silent alleys. They barely watched the players lost in the bitter street, or they might be watching sidewise. The boy glanced from cat to cat but saw only their ravenous stares. They sought the barest survival. Their mother had taught as she weaned them: *There's never enough. The strong grab the juiciest nipple, and you'd better bite on tight, cause I'll shed you into the grit.* Now they were dying. They might find food, but only the luckiest would. The rats were too big to kill. Licking their hair they licked up poisonous dust. More cats and more, awaiting death.

"We'll play for the cats!"

Mik shouted it out without a thought. He looked astonished at what he'd said, then struck an intrepid pose and grinned a jaw-splitting grin. The boy knew that his father's humor was marker to his mood, most inspired when his soul was bleakest. His wit sallied forth like a rag-tag crusade against the forces of grief. The boy heard the ragged howl in the frivolous jest.

A jest, but the cats at least were alive, as attentive as any mob. The players were seized with manic frenzy, like tots who'd missed their nap or a mad laughing fool at a funeral or souls who had nothing more to lose because it had all been lost. Mik flourished his arms as he'd seen bull-dancers do and announced in the voice of a stentorian dwarf, "We offer you *The Epic of Idiot Gods!*"

And they played for the cats.

～

Absurd, yet no more so than other puzzlements of our trek. I could never fathom how we had no word of Malo's ruin. My father inquired constantly of the state of the roads, the presence of robbers, the locus of tollgates, the movement of armies or plague. We had often detoured around a rumor.

Nor did I sense how the gods emerged, speaking an alien tongue, as if reciting lines they barely understood. They spoke the way the donkey, quietly grazing, extruded his volley of turds unaware of what emerged. It may have been that under the wrathful sun we only dreamt it.

Ludd asked in a whisper to claim the role of Grim-grin.

~

A squat bouncy Wadan, a bent gray Frekka on wobbly knees, and a pregnant goddess of love stood in the merciless sun. A bony Loghi grinned a needle-sharp grin. Bragi stared through his wide singing mouth, frozen mute. Heat stung their faces under the clinging masks. The myriad cats pressed closer, wailing, purring, hissing, though they may have been only a litter of broken stone.

The albino raven lit on One-eye's shoulder as he turned his clownish majesty to Grim-grin, who bowed as if to scrape the cobbles with his chin. Wadan spoke in hollow sing-song. *Advise me, brother: at least I may trust your deceit.*

The gray goddess spoke to his hollow socket: *My half-blind love, you guzzle his chatter like poisoned mead.*

What would you have me do, dear wife?

Do as always, husband dear. Make your journey, swagger down the starry roadway, seduce some sweetie to nuzzle you at night, leave me to curse.

One-eye mugged bafflement. Gray-nag turned away. The Grinner grinned an opulent slash. Bragi strained to see the bony man through the mask. The cats lay watching, alert.

Grim-grin oozed out his words: *Are wall and hammer sufficient to guard us? Spurn my gifts at your peril.*

What gifts?

My children.

The cats perked up as Gray-nag's words spewed forth: *Your children by Angrboda. Her name is Sorrow-Bearer.*

Every mother's name is Sorrow-Bearer.

No mother bears a snake, a wolf, and a putrescent corpse!

One-eye intervened, commanding, *Show your children.*

Jormungand!

The raven squawked and shat a whitish spume. Wadan brushed at his shoulder. Through a rift in the stone a great iridescent python rose in a graceful bloat, wound an ancient marble column, crushed it and vanished.

Gray-nag: *It will grow.*

—*To infect the seas with venom to fend off the Fierce Ones.* Loghi intoned as if reading Holy Writ.

So be it. Wadan spoke without hearing himself.

Loghi frothed with delight, presenting his second son: *Fenris!* The raven screeched a ragged alarm. A wolf cub burst forth from the keen noon shadows, chasing its thorn-bristle tail, snarling fire, then vanished in a swirl. The cats drew back a whisker-length.

It will grow, murmured Gray-nag.

—*To be chained at our portal to guard us from the Fierce Ones.*
So be it.

The cats edged forward. The Grinner pointed his dagger finger—
Hel!

The raven shrieked and flew. A female rose from an acrid well, sleek as a wolverine. Eggshell face, smooth brow, the slit of a smile, diamond eyes. Gray-nag opened her lips but could only whisper: *She bears another face.* The damsel turned her face to the sun. Her beauty softened, melted, ran into a weeping of slag that oozed down the cheeks and dripped from the chin. The cats froze to stone.

Loghi's glittering words slithered among the gods like a millipede among mastiffs: *Gathering legions in Niflheim to war against the Fierce Ones.*

~

We played out a play not of our own devising, yet all had roles. Each step brought the gods nearer destruction, yet each was taken with forethought. Like the play of the king who blinded himself or the mother killing her sons, it choked on its raw absurdity. No laughter, no plaudits, no clink of coins—only the scuttle of rats in rubble. We carried a curse we never deserved yet carted it jiggety-jostle for leagues and leagues.

~

The cat throngs tensed as one, set to flee. Wadan stared at Frekka, armored against her curses. Astonished, he heard her consent—

So be it. Entrust our fate to serpents, wolves, and rot. But let us not squander the dead. Mortals live out their days in labor and spend their death in fog. Rather let them make war. Let the sons of mortal mothers die singing our glory. I speak as a mother—

Strange words to come from a mother's lips. Loghi was discomfited to hear speech more cruel than his.

The sperm that floods a womb begets the fruit it bears.

The boy saw the cats shrink back another whisker. His grandma was no longer the crone on wobbly knees: she was the ancient mother who murdered her sons. She flung her curse to the wind, a seedpod bursting—

My daughters, who once brought forth spring's fruition, I name you now the Valkyries, Choosers of the Dead. You shall fetch slain heroes to wage perpetual war. By day the men die, by night drink mead, and in the morn stream forth to die and die again to the end of Time.

One-eye faced his savage wife: *No murder in Asgard!*

The killing of mortals is not murder. They expect to die.

Loghi gave a flippant twist of the wrist. *Mothers with fishhooks in their wombs.* The sunlight shivered. A whirlwind of soot danced up from the street, scattering the cats. It settled, and the creatures—dozens now, hundreds—slid back to their perches to see what played out. The Grinner faced the twitchy-tailed throng—

Mortals are Runes. Their corpses spell out the gods' will—we monsters of love and thunder. Myself, the god of maggots, purging rotted flesh. Myself, the water crept into the rocks that, freezing, cracks mountains. Myself, unmaker for what must be unmade.

One-eye flung his arm-ring into the throng. The cats fell upon it as if upon fish guts and tore each other to blood-clogged hairballs. Frekka held her fists to her breasts. Ghost vultures descended to pluck the guts of the ghosts of cats. The sun blazed in the street, a silence spread, and Gray-nag, vanishing, whispered—

Now I mother Death.

⁓

It had not come to pass. My father's call to play for the cats was his fragile jest. My mother, father, grandma, Ludd—all stood silent, faces naked, sweating. I had dreamt a sunstricken dream and now I stared at the ravaged street. No mask, no mouth, no song.

Again the stench of memory: the blood eyes, the dog in flames, the geezer holding his guts, the little girl gored. And then I heard clapping, the way peasants beat their hands to cheer the play, a slap and a slap and a slap. In the shadows, mad eyes, breasts bare, a young woman beat her hands as if to bloody them. Six claps and gone.

I would see her many times. I was in a strange city, adult, lost, alone. My wife had been dead three years. To lose myself further, I bought a woman for the night. We did what was paid for, and then I asked her name. Bella, she said. That wasn't her name. She turned away to wash herself and spat.

~

They camped to the north of the city. The memories of Malo were vivid. The boy saw his mother weeping, and as she cooked supper his father embraced her the way a sob embraces. Ludd sat on a fallen log, not having known their friends, exiled from their grief.

Bragi sat staring into the fire. After a while his mother sat beside him, put her hand on his shoulder. He felt he must have done something wrong.

"What did you see?"

"Nothing!"

It was the wrong thing to say. He knew what she meant—the cats, the performance, the gods—and *Nothing!* told her he saw it. He should have said *What?* or *When?* She was silent. Her hand remained.

"I just saw cats," he said at last.

"Don't be afraid," she whispered. "It's the Sight. It won't hurt us."

So he knew that she knew. She was telling him not to be afraid, but why was it that the more you did to be less afraid, the more afraid you were? You were like the gods, or the gods were like you. He met her eyes. "I just saw cats." She refrained from speaking, rose and went back to her cooking.

Slurping his pottage the boy saw eyes in the shivering dark. The glint coalesced into the brother cats, the muscled one and the frazzle-tail. They had steered clear of his crazed illusion of carnage.

"Look at the cats!" he cried, but no one looked: he may not have said it out loud. He named the one of them Fluffy, the other Sausage-tail, and he knew they would follow him like the bee that always landed on the rim of his cup, no matter where. They flashed into the night.

Before he drifted off, Bragi saw old Kalas' eyes: *So never forget it.* Memories, like ticks, dig deep.

—XVIII—
The Quickening

At intervals I ask myself my purpose in this telling. Compliance with my patron is scant excuse for the sin of authorship. What is the essence of my tale? A farrago of rustic humor? A fable of folly? An epic of bewilderment? My frowsy feline Mia, curled at my backside, would have it the saga of cats.

But the widow offers her mite, the plutocrat his shekels, and I my tattered memories. We strive to serve the Almighty, lest His eyes wander from our daily farce toward more edifying spectacles. Each dawn we frolic or grieve amid the litter of yesterday.

I once imagined that books rewrote themselves, as every newborn does from birth to death through the changing air. So it may well be that this chronicle is writing itself on the wind. The donkey cart jogs onward.

∼

Their journey led northward. In each unpronounceable town they caught a glimpse of the cats, the one whose tail blossomed, the other's a muscular whip. They kept their distance, begged no provender, merely claimed a presence. Asta warned Bragi off petting them: cats were as wild as any beast, and they might have lice or the frothing disease. They might reward a tender hand with a nip that turned your finger black, and you'd have to find a barber to cut off your arm. Kindness was risky.

The next weeks the sky burned even hotter. A breeze came up only to stir the dust of the road. Edra cursed her knees, and Asta took great care climbing into the cart. Mik held the donkey on track, and the wall eye of Ludd kept watch on unknown realms. They followed a route of towns and manors that had served them for years, and their friends made the same old jokes as they rumpled Bragi's hair.

For Asta's pregnancy they changed the stagings as needed, and her dresses concealed her shape. "They want to believe I'm magic," she told Mik one night. "Magical women don't bulge out, they hatch babies from eggs."

"No matter," said Mik, "you're funnier when you're fat." She swatted him. "I'm joking!"

Asta grimaced. "You'll be funnier when you're old and bald and have to push hard to piss!" Instantly he hunched over, doddered in a circle, and mimed a clogged urination. She laughed and hugged him.

The cats had followed. That night at the campsite Bragi watched them slink into the firelight's flicker. Suddenly they began to wrestle, pouncing on one another, one rolling on its back to rip out its brother's belly, then springing straight for the throat.

"Gramma, they're fighting!"

"No no. If they were fighting you'd hear it. Cats tussle for fun. Like your papa and mama, they've got their claws retracted." The boy saw his parents embracing. Their fights didn't always end in jokes, but they could make one another laugh. He might have laughed with the spitting girl, but no way to change it now. Wounds healed but scars remained.

Over the span of the days the boy plodded with his father leading the donkey or with Ludd, who carried a duffel to ease the weight of the cart. At times he rode with his mother or walked behind. He remembered the story his grandmother told: the poor man rolling the boulder uphill. Did he ever get it to stay at the top? Did the road ever end? The more road that rolled under the cart, the more it stretched out.

At times he heard a clapping that could only be the mad girl walking a hidden trail beside them. He heard her in his sleep, counting and counting. He had tried to forget little spitting Rona, tried to hum a tune whenever she came to mind. but the clapping brought her back. "You never get rid of the past," his grandmother told him. "It's like fleas, you carry the eggs."

Ludd was an actor now, and Mik was irked at an apprentice asserting mastery. "Problem with that guy," he told Asta, "he's good, but he doesn't know how much he doesn't know." Yet Mik and the fishmonger blossomed as a team. Another donkey farce, this one Ludd's idea, presented a ferocious, hard-kicking, man-eating donk. The bumpkin Mik watched the beast kick and buck while the smooth-talking Ludd promised a magical chant to render the fierce beast docile. Stock bits: Ludd hissing the chant to Mik, who swabbed spittle out of his ear. Mik with opulent gestures proclaiming the spell. The two men watching in tandem, coordinating focus, as the beast galloped about, turned somersaults, rose like a twister, vaulted over houses, and shook the earth as it landed. Ludd's huckster was so outlandishly sleazy that Mik's bumpkin attained a quintessence of *dolt*. Bragi did his pigs-eating-porridge line, which never failed.

They scored another hit with Ludd's notion of an animal fable— the Grinner a clever fox, the jowly Teorr a thick-headed ox, Frekka a grumpy old granny skunk. Asta raised no objection to using the masks. She was a practical soul and they were making money. The masks induced a heightened diction and formal gesture in ludicrous contrast to beasts picking lice and scratching their butts.

At a town with a name like a cow belch, they met a pudgy Crister priest. He loved the play they made from a girlhood story that Edra recalled. Princess Asta fled the clutches of evil king Mik, and when, in a frenzy, he ordered Ludd to pursue her, the gawky servant ran this way and that, confused by nonsensical commands. Mik was a master of gibberish, and his rant at the hapless stooge—much like his dead-donkey rant, his rant at his profligate wife, his rant at the cheeky child—never failed. Laughter shook the pudgy priest like a jellyfish. He invited them to dinner.

Bragi was fearful of the priest. Though his jolly demeanor was reassuring, the face he turned to the boy was deathly pale. His hair was stark white, even the brows and lashes, and his eyes a sour pink. "He was born that way," Asta whispered to the boy. "Don't stare."

At dinner, the priest—Father Genesius, he called himself—drank his wine unwatered. Before passing out, his forehead to the table, he asked if they wanted a horse. "I want to . . . blessings, oh my, so funny, so . . . give you God's horse . . ." They couldn't refuse. Mik thanked him profusely, knowing the priest would forget it when sober. Yet the next morning he led forth a spindly mare.

"She's on her last legs, but she hefts me, and I'm a tidy fat lump of beatitude. Make sure she says her prayers and she'll last you a while." He made an odd finger sign toward each of the players and at last to the doddering horse. Though hung over, he still shook with spasms of laughter as he embraced first Mik then Ludd. Before the women he hesitated, then offered them his bronze crucifix to kiss. They obliged. He came to Bragi, who couldn't avert a wide-eyed stare.

"So you've never seen a funny man like me?" Bragi tried to breathe. "Know how I got this way?" He shook his head. "Why, I took a trip to Heaven, just to see the sights, and it was so bright that my eyes turned pink, and a cute little angel scrubbed me all white." The albino priest extended the crucifix for the boy to kiss.

Bragi saw the tiny figure on the cross like a worm on a hook. He reached out his finger and petted the wee twisted man as if to comfort him. The priest giggled, sighed, took the cord from his neck and placed it over Bragi's head. The tiny man dangled to below his belly.

They departed, leading the horse behind the cart till it got accustomed to players. Yesu flared his upper lip but made no further comment, and the aged mare showed scant interest in donkeys. After a time Edra climbed aboard the listless beast to rest her knees, braving a timeworn saddle. If the horse could speed up without falling apart, they might send Ludd ahead to check arrangements in upcoming towns. The priest had not told them the horse's name, so the naming was Bragi's privilege and curse: he changed his mind daily.

∼

I still finger the small bronze crucifix and its tiny writhing thing. It hangs from a peg by my writing desk, and my cat sometimes paws it to make it swing. At the time it was only a curiosity like a dead beetle, a rat skull, a seashell. Years later, to save my soul and secure employment, I underwent our Church's sprinkle, but my boyhood soul had already reached out to the little bronze wiggler pinned to the post. I stroked his brow with one finger and felt the yearning that linked us.

~

For the market fair a day south of Jenev they revived what they called the play of the dirty-old-man: the virgin Asta, courted by ardent suitor Ludd, aided by slimy bawd Edra, opposed by wealthy lecher Mik. A less arduous role for Asta: she would simply appear through the curtain looking sweet or panicked as required. Not the best day for a show: a sparse crowd in the square, some cranky mules emitting raucous bleats, and the merciless sun—stage planks too hot to touch, actors sweating through costumes, the onlookers toasted and crisped.

Midway, Asta collapsed. She was backstage with Edra awaiting her second appearance. Out front, the suitor and lecher ranted at one another, quaking with lust, vowing mayhem. At the climax they were to cry in unison, *Teodora! Teodora!* whereupon Asta would stick her head through the curtain, moan, *Oh dear, what shall I do?* and the quarrel would build to a climax. Then both would collapse panting: *It's too hot to fight. Let's go for a beer.*

But at Asta's cue Edra saw her sink listlessly onto a stool and roll gently to the boards. The men cried out again. The old woman—no stranger to emergencies—rushed onstage, cried that Teodora had eloped with a traveling minstrel, and went off in frenzied lament.

Bragi was watching from the side. He was torn between rushing backstage to find his mother or staying to see how they would end the play. He stayed for the play. The men stared at each other, unbelieving. The boy could see the fear in his father's eyes, but the onlookers took it as bafflement. The fighting cocks, robbed of their hen, began to wail, spurring each other to greater heights, and the play caught hold. At last, when the joke had run its course, Mik switched direction:

"*Is that your donkey?*"

"*Sure is. Great donkey?*"

"*Why's he lying down?*"

"*The heat.*"

"*He looks dead.*"

"*Wanna buy him?*"

Mik bought the donkey, and Edra charged out to beat him—for no apparent reason, but it got a laugh. The play ended in triumph, and the men, boy and old bawd made their rounds, holding out hats for coins—a fair revenue, it proved—and then rushed backstage to Asta. She sat on the stool, grim-lipped, brooding. She had never before missed a cue. Never ever. Bragi embraced her knees, Mik brought her water, and Edra felt her pulse. Ludd stood dumfounded, finally spoke. "That worked pretty good."

~

You have known that moment, my liege, when years go by in a breath. Hers was only a fainting spell brought on by the heat, yet I saw my mother as if naked. I saw her mortality. My night-haunt monsters sprang from another world, but this was real.

I never knew why tears came. Sometimes a starving cat, the spitting girl, or the first time I felt the lonely pangs of the dangling god. But tears as I curried the donkey? And yet next day I gave it little thought. The new day is born from yesterday's labor, new seed sprouts from the dung of the past, and we turn our eyes to the birth squall.

~

Edra declared they should end the tour. They had done well, even without Malo, and a loop across to Duburok would get them home sooner. They sent Ludd ahead on the nameless mare to inform their Jenev host they would have to turn back. Two days of waiting, and Ludd returned. His word: their host demanded they come. Their reputation would be tainted if they refused. Moreover, the eastward route was imperiled: hordes of savages menaced Duburok.

Silence at the campfire. Ludd bore a nasty cut above his wall eye, starting to scab up, and one side of his face was a thunderhead of bruises.

"What happened to you?" asked Edra.

"Stopped for a drink. One beer. This nice lady, we talked. Then her friend showed up. He wasn't friendly."

Edra bore in on him. "So who did you talk to besides the juicy whore? You spoke to the Seneschal? To Zbiegniew? Where'd these savages come from? Are you thinking you don't want to go back, make us stay out here forever?" She cut it short. They stared at Ludd. "If we find you're not telling the truth, you will have cause for regret." He was making strides as an actor, but as a liar he still lacked journeyman skills.

A chill breeze stirred the day's heat away but blew the coals into flame. The smell of fresh donkey dung wafted their way, and the nameless horse's whinny. The cats lurked at the edge of the firelight, then crept away.

To ease tension Mik asked Ludd, "Any break to the heat, did they say?"

"Well, some fellow said if the sun burns up it might cool off."

Asta spoke up. "We'd better do Jenev. We said we would. I'll be okay if the weather cools. And the savage hordes, we'll ask about them."

Thankfully the heat broke. They came into a town they intended to bypass, but the sky, like Ludd, had deep bruises over its face. In these hills the weather could turn and snarl like a rabid cur, so they stopped at the Inn of the Bedbug.

Mik named it as soon as they'd checked the bedding. Fleas were just the normal price of existence, but these vermin were ravenous. The troupers spread their show curtain on the floor and stretched out elbow to elbow. Edra cast about pinches of acrid leaves. "They can't stand the smell." Neither could Bragi, but he had learned to survive her medicinals. Once, forcing vile dregs down his throat for an unsettled gut, she said, "Don't you know that grandmas are meant to torment little kids? It's all that gives grannies any fun!" The stink hung thick through the night, like the heavy tattoos on the fat man, but it kept the Huns at bay.

The boy had a hard time sleeping. Would the mites sniff him out? Would the cats find food? Where was the mad-eyed girl? Old Sir Paddo: what if he woke in the night and found himself dead? Bragi clutched the tiny dangling man.

"Mama? I'm hungry."

"No, you're not. We just ate. Go to sleep."

He remembered. That was true.

"Get some rest, girl, you're tossing around." Gramma's voice. She always called his mother *girl*—funny thing to say. Night talk he was never supposed to hear, but it was more edifying than the talk of the day. He had heard his parents' fear of making another baby, and then he heard them doing it. He had heard his granny offer to kill his sister before she was born but Mama saying no. He had heard Gramma quarreling with Grampa, and Grampa stone silent, being dead. He had heard the bony man sobbing. Tonight he heard the women's whispers.

"How does it feel?"

"Different than Bragi."

"Most likely it's a girl."

"Some bleeding again."

"Well I lost two before Mik, and he was never the strongest. Six months and two months."

"You told me that and you don't need to tell me again."

They went on whispering things he didn't understand. One snoring honk from Ludd.

"But we can't go farther north than Jenev. We wouldn't get home in time. I don't want to give birth in a rat hole like this."

"No point to go farther. They don't want to see a gravid lady on stage."

"I just worry."

"You're supposed to worry, girl. You're having a baby."

"Well, after Jenev we have to go back."

"I said yes. Go to sleep."

A chuckle from Asta. "I'm telling Bragi go to sleep, and you're telling me."

"One generation tells another. Not that anyone listens."

Bragi heard his grandma's hand pressed to his mother's hair. Or that's what he thought he heard. He lay listening to their breath and drifted off, having almost thought of a name for the horse. Then he woke with a start, confused. His mother was with him. He must have been crying again. Her hand was soft on his forehead. Long time since he'd felt her softness.

"Come here. Put your hand right there. Right there." She placed his sleepy hand on the bulge of her belly. "Feel that?" Under his fingers, a whisper of a wiggle. "That's your sister. She's squirming around in there."

A tremor passed through him, as if the little bronze man on the cross had twitched. "What's wrong with her?"

"Nothing wrong. You did that too. Babies just do that. She's saying she's alive. but she doesn't have words for it yet, so she kicks. It's called the quickening. She's saying, *I'm here!*"

He could tell his mama thought he would like the wiggle, but it felt like the time he ate an oyster—so unnatural. She tried to be motherly, offering him the wonder of quickening, when a soul squeezed into his tiny sister and set her awiggle. But he felt a surge of dread. He had seen death before, but new life— He had no words for that.

His mother had told him that when her birthing began, he had to be brave and not worry to hear her scream. That was just the way of it: you screamed and grunted, grunted and screamed, and then you birthed a baby. But it came so slowly.

"Well, never mind. Just letting you know she's in there."

He pulled up his blanket. He imagined curling up with the cats in a cave. He glimpsed a cat vision of teeth and swooping birds, then jerked awake. Some day he would have to join the grownups' talk of playing the play and how to steer clear of the savage hordes. He fingered the tiny dangler who quickened on the cross. For a time he feared he might cry himself to sleep, and then he slept.

—XIX—
Fever

In Jenev there was no difficulty in checking the truth of Ludd's reports: they were total fabrication. As he sat by the hearth of their lodging, poking the coals with a poker, Edra approached him. He looked up. She pointed one finger at him and stood there. He cringed beneath the finger.

"Didn't mean to cause trouble."

"But you did."

"Wanted to not go back. I needed work. I like it."

"But we will."

Edra said no more. She left him to stew in his juice. But she understood his desperation. A captured slave might merely be flogged if they thought he could last another year in the mines. But to set an example he might be flayed or impaled. He had seen impalement: his friend had made horrible inhuman bellows like Yesu's bray. Flaying was worse. They skinned you like a rabbit. Alive.

Yet beyond the fear: he had found his calling. All his life he had lived for nothing except hopes of a painless death. He was a grain of sand, a clod of clay, a wind-blown strew of feathers. Now, for a few gawky moments, he was winning applause as knight of the boards, prince of planks, pope of the fart dance.

And Edra had no options. They needed him.

Their host in Jenev was a wealthy linen-draper who called himself Karol of Sturr. Years ago he had become an ardent fan. They played a show in which, as an innocent young wife, a forty-year-old Edra appeared barefoot—no shoes, no sandals, heels and toes shamelessly naked. The linen-draper was awestruck, his curls atingle, his bone marrow surging with lust. Yet despite the reputation of female entertainers his behavior was as respectful as to a goddess. When they returned next year he inquired discreetly whether any plays featured a barefoot lady. His queries were futile, but his devotion to Edra's virginal feet remained. He inquired of the local priest whether angels went barefoot in Heaven. When the priest answered, "Most likely, as heavenly weather is mild," he arranged for prompt baptism and proceeded to live a virtuous life. The chuckling priest recounted the story to Edra with thanks for her saving a soul.

As he grew in wealth, devotion never flagging, Karol became a regular sponsor of their sojourn. For a time, in gratitude, they considered reviving the barefoot play with Asta in Edra's role. But they shelved the notion: Asta was concerned about the planks' slivers, and Edra feared they might move the poor man to apoplexy. Over the years Karol lost his curly chestnut hair, and Bragi was mesmerized by a head like shiny wet stone. But the boy could never see the charms of Gramma's rawboned, knobby, leathery feet.

"Why's your big toe funny?"

"Mule stepped on it. Hurt awful."

The shows in Jenev were mostly uneventful, except the first. They were in a big hall, Mik and Ludd, playing a sob-drenched scene of long-lost brothers reunited, and the two cats ran across the stage. A chained watchdog was roused to frantic outrage, and a guard beat the dog into a whining wad of fang and fur. Whereupon the sobbing brothers picked up the dog's spirit, turning on each other, yapping, snarling, baying, then beating each other until they fell into a wailing embrace.

The linen-draper laughed uncontrollably. He had been in failing health, and when he first greeted them his bright smile glowed a moment, then fell back to dullness. He took sharp gasps of air, the way their first donkey had breathed, and he looked ready, like that donkey, to be rolled into a hole. Yet now he laughed.

Their host had intended to house them through their stay, but on the final day he feared he was coming down with a fever and lodged them at an inn. After the evening's play, they had retired, intending an early start in a loop that would bring them home. Bragi felt a chill as he drew his blanket around him. He heard distant thunder, a grumbling bedtime tale that lulled him over the edge of sleep.

Then the sky split open, lightning spewed, mountains rolled over one another, and the torrent came down in sheets. He woke with a start, grabbed a breath, and plunged back into the rapids. They had to cross a bridge, but Yesu balked and the stark white raven soared up from the brush. The masks, dead leather, hung in the trees, gem eyes aglitter. The one-eyed Wadan loomed. The masks in the trees gaped open their mouths, rasped out a howl. Words erupting, One-eye to Gray-nag—

I go to speak with one long dead whom I knew when her lips were full.

May you suffer no lack of sluts whose lips are full.

I seek to save my son.

You have your yammering raven, your runes, you have your talkative severed head, but when will your sight be sharp enough to see both sides of your nose?

Lines from a farce: Mama and Papa facing off to curse each other, the audience howling like a throng of cats. *One two three . . .* The mad girl was in the play. Bragi clung to the dream by his fingertips. He saw his own raw feet with a funny big toe. He had never noticed feet, but now he saw feet. Feet on splintery planks, feet crushed by mules, feet on endless roadways, and his own feet were far far away. What if they took him where he never wanted to go?

"Bragi!" His grandmother's face. "You were yelling. Loud as the donkey." Her cold hand was on his forehead. "He's got a fever. He's burning up."

~

I felt cold, not hot. Fever was supposed to be hot. Was life always opposite to reality? Could the sun rise cold and the moon burn our faces? If Loghi was the unmaker was he unmaking me?

Of course I should have known that my feverish skin would chill in the colder air and that life offers endless perceptions counter to truth—as any six-year-old should know. But I was not exploring the matter with Aristotelian rigor: I was dying.

From quickening to unmaking: one shiver.

~

Rain beat down. Roused from bed, the surly innkeeper gave Mik directions to a healer. "Blue door under the sign of a squid," he said. "He's old and lame, he'd never come out in the storm." The boy was bundled into a cloak to be carried by his father. "No time to lose. That fever's took lots."

The quest was a blur to Bragi. His father heard the directions, repeated them, ventured out, but the directives were no match for the streets. Not more than two or three furtherings, the innkeeper said, but Mik had no idea the length of a furthering. The alleys were narrow, branching, doubling back like the labyrinth his grandma told of, all corridors leading to the monster at its heart. The rain kept a steady beat, *Four five six one . . .* The mad girl was counting the throb of the rain. She slapped her palms. *Two three four five six . . .*

The narrow streets steepened as the father trudged on. The town's face was knotted into a frown, and they climbed the slippery wrinkles, stone steps that narrowed to alleys and ended in walls. The streets were deserted, not even light from a window, and the father, his son in his arms, made his way by lightning flash. At a corner he saw a V carved into the wall of a house and recalled something said of a V, so he turned the corner into a dead-end wall.

Teorr's thunderheads belched. The boy cried out, shivering. The father tried to trace his way back to the inn. "We'll leave you there, get you dried out while I go find the old fart. If he won't come out I'll pull him by the nose, I'll wad him up in a ball, I'll tickle him to death." But the passageways had shifted. They were lost in the guts of the minotaur.

Bragi clutched air then dug his fingers into his father's arms to make him hug harder. He was going to die. Would he go to the dead land where frogs tried to sing? That might be funny, but he wouldn't be able to hear them over the thunder. He flailed to tear open his eyes.

Broken teeth, ragged sky, clouds swarming the moon— The boy's weight grew heavy as the father struggled to find any dark artery descending, ascending, downward, upward out of the blinding deluge. Thuds, babble, frog belch, clack of beaks, guttural brays. The father squinted to see the sign the innkeeper spoke of: blue door, dancing squid. The boy couldn't tell if the driving torrent was rain or his father's tears.

A lantern flickered, a staggering figure approached, a drunken man with a slur of curses under his breath. Mik called out the healer's name but got no response, tried other dialects, stepped into his path, but the tippler, sobered by fear of assault, turned on his heels and wobbled away.

The boy felt the arms go slack. He had never felt so near his father, sharing one mind. He grieved as his father grieved, together fording a rapids of despair. The boy was Balthur, held to the heart of Old One-eye, hearing the elder god's wordless cry dissolving like spider-web in the rain. Drained of strength, bereft of hope, Mik sobbed, held his son to him with all his clown's grief. He raised his face from the blue door before him, up into the pelting rain, and saw the dancing squid.

~

Fear tastes sour. Once on a dare from a playmate I tasted my urine: a cheap acidic cider. But at the darkest time, when I felt my father's hands begin the letting-go, I was filled with a surge of— I tasted a sweetness. I saw the scene playing out surrounded by throngs of strangers come to witness poor Bragi's demise: breathing my last, crying for parsnips, struggling to name the rickety horse, and needing badly to pee. My body rehearsed its death: I was a good enough actor now to play the corpse.

~

Mik battered the door with one fist as he clutched the boy. He was near collapse when a crack of light appeared and a wrinkled walnut face peeked through the narrow slit. The sunken eyes were fogged by cataract, sullenness pinched the razor lips, and the healer hawked spittle for a curt reply. But at sight of the huddled child his face came alight. His voice was a whistle through cracks in the wall.

"Your boy?"

Mik nodded, unable to speak.

"Yah yah. Fever." He half-turned, nodded as if to ghosts. "Bring him in." The ageless man, his face more bone than skin, made tiny whimpers as he motioned the father to lay the boy on a bench by the hearth. He grasped the child's head in his spidery hands.

"Yah."

The healer hobbled to a cabinet, took a cup from the shelf and a pinch of white dust, signed the boy to stick out his tongue, and fed him the powder. The bitterness twisted his lips. The beat of the rain trailed off and the thunder sounded more distant. Last scraps of the dream: Wadan groped for the Shining One. His son was on his blind side. He groped in vain, but Bragi's flushed face took on a healthier fish-belly hue.

"Healed?" asked Mik.

"Healed before. You healed him. He felt you."

"Then what's the powder?"

"So it sticks. They remember the bitter." The wrinkled man sat a while, touched the boy's forehead, dried his hair with a cloth. "I had one. Boy. Died of it. Thirty years."

"Died at thirty years or thirty years ago?"

"Either way."

"You couldn't heal him?"

No reply. They sat in the after-smell of the storm. A gutter dripped in an odd start-stop, no keeping count. The healer's crinkly leaf of a hand brushed Bragi's face. He instructed Mik next day to purchase a rabbit, find a temple behind a rug merchant's shop, and put it in the hands of a crone with a wen on her eyelid. He made what looked like the pale priest's finger sign, wrong way around.

"Course I worship the Holy Christ, only son, so forth, but— The old gods are more dependable. They do what they're paid to do."

They stood in the blue doorway, the boy beside his father on wobbly legs. The old healer was already half asleep. "The ones that are already healed, they see the squid. Otherwise no." The boy stroked the tiny man on his crucifix.

"What can I offer you?" asked Mik. The healer shook his head and shut the door. The darkness closed around them. No trace of a dancing squid.

〜

I recount this adventure as I recall it, though many such shards of the past are only memories of memory. I had never read the world's literature of misery, so the visions may have come from demonic realms. Memory, like the heart, skips beats yet persists.

The first time I looked through a windowpane of melted sand—a crystalline magic like water suspended midair—I felt that all things were within my range of sight. And yet that portal rippled, wrinkled and warped my view of the distant hills. So much more must we squint to see the future. Even more to see the past.

〜

Next morning Asta went in search of a rabbit. At the market she bargained for a large brown surly thing that crouched awaiting its fate. She knew that if Bragi saw it he would cling to the floppy beast. She bought it, carried it far from the plaza to the fenced garden park of a palace. She shoved it through the grating into the shrubbery. If the gods wanted it they could come get it.

"I found him in the market," she told her son. "His name was Rabbit and he looked very sad. So I carried him to a garden with bushes and flowers, and I let him go. His life is with the gods. Like ours."

Bragi heard her talking as mothers talk to babies, hoping he would believe that all rabbits were blest and no big dogs in the garden. He was glad that the rabbit named Rabbit might have a life. He might have started to weep for not petting the rabbit named Rabbit, for having felt his father's agony, for being a boy like the boy the old healer remembered, but for a knock at their doorpost. Mik drew back the drape.

He faced a grinning, dead-eyed messenger in carmine livery. Behind him stood five burly soldiers, their bewhiskered faces blank. A new rumble of thunder.

"Yes," said the dead-eyed messenger. "Oh yes."

—XX—
Prince Helmut

"Yes. Well. So." The messenger's dead-fish eyes gazed past them, unseeing. His most noteworthy feature, besides the beefy soldiers looming behind him, was his tremor. Speaking or silent, his chin seemed detached from his face, shivering through each word or phrase along with the twitch of an eyelid. Bragi wondered if it traveled with him the way the cats followed the cart.

"Yes. I convey a request from my lord Prince Helmut, Kingdom of Southeast Dumarik, to the renowned artists of your band." Despite his tremor the message was clear. They were invited to a castle two days to the north. They would be royally hosted, well paid, and have the honor of amusing the illustrious Prince. As a child he had viewed their work with joy, and now, grown to man's estate, he longed for the merry play he recalled from boyhood.

Mik thanked the messenger warmly and recounted the reasons compelling them to decline the honor: the journey's rigors, the pregnancy, their son's recent illness. Next year certainly they would be pleased to present the requested play to perfection.

"Yes. Understandable. To be sure. We shall assist you in packing all necessities for the journey. We can discuss the terms en route." He spoke as if reciting a schoolboy poem, required to be word-perfect.

Mik was no fool. He understood *request* to mean *command*. There was no contradicting the sightless dead-fish stare, and the soldiers had been selected for their bull-neck bulk. Asta made another attempt. They were past due to start home, she said, and travel was a risk to her unborn child. She soon gave it up. "He seemed to have no idea that women bore babies," she grumbled later. "How presumptuous of them!"

Edra sensed Mik's temper rising. Clearly the messenger was a brainless dolt, but trouble could spring from a dolt. She intervened: "We are grateful for the honor," adding, "Yes."

Soon the caravan proceeded northward. A horse-drawn wagon was provided for the women and the child. Riding a borrowed horse, Mik led Yesu, who pulled a lighter cart, and Ludd rode the hobbling nag. The envoy kept his tremor in check as he negotiated terms with Mik. Edra watched from the rear of the wagon. "If anyone calls you an artist," she mumbled to Bragi, "best hold onto your money-pouch."

At the castle's majestic entry, a columned portico with a wide flight of marble steps, the Prince greeted them ardently. A surprise: Prince Helmut was a plumpish blond adolescent not much past his sixteenth year—not fat, precisely, but as if stuffed like sausage into his silken finery. He smiled an apology for his youth. "I practice aging daily, but as an adult I am only in my apprenticeship." He enjoyed his own wit. "My uncle Boris is regent until I come of age, so my authority extends solely to the strategic task of arranging entertainments."

He offered them each his hand and ruffled Bragi's hair. Patting Yesu, he beamed. "Though they call me Prince, I am only the ass of the court. Princes abound in these troubled times, not to mention emperors and popes. A prince for every dunghill." He addressed Yesu sternly: "Are you too ruled by a higher power, my hairy cousin? Are we not all bridled and hitched, though we think we run free?" Unschooled in court etiquette, Yesu gave a slight rise to his tail and shat. The Prince laughed. "Socrates himself could not have offered a riposte more apt. *Quod erat demonstrandum.*" A servant scrambled to scoop up Yesu's replies.

Bragi took a great liking to the young aristocrat. Except for kind old Sir Paddo, his impression of the upper classes was of stiff porcine men and snooty ladies whose stench cut through a mist of civet. He felt kinship with both Prince and donkey—led by the nose up the mountains and down the valleys, blind to the journey's goal, bound by the crawl of Time.

"I saw your play a dozen years ago. No, perhaps eight or ten. I was likely this boy's age. What's your name, child?"

"Bragi."

"Bragi! A god of the Northland. Of course we're all Christians here, or so we tell ourselves. Perhaps I should christen you, say, Benyamin, a fine young man from Scripture."

"No! Bragi!"

Bragi looked up anxiously at his mother. Never talk back to nobility, he knew, but he had done it. Asta grabbed his arm, but the young Prince smiled. "Let you be Bragi then. Noble name, nobly defended." Bragi returned his smile. *Don't forget who you are*, old Kalas spoke in his ear.

The Prince recalled the old play in more detail than the players did. "Of course at that age I couldn't make sense of the bawdry, and yet I grasped the yearning, even the joy in life's absurdity." Mik made bold to interrupt, warning that, like life, plays change and are never the same from one time to another. "No matter," said the Prince, "I like surprises."

He stood for a moment in thought. Nobility, Bragi knew, meant that people would wait for your words. Princes could take their time. Even Gramma stood waiting for the anointed youth to speak.

"You are practitioners of a dying art, if I read the times aright. My tutor has shown me the ancient texts which describe great festivals devoted to the gods—demons, we call them now. But the stones of the stages where those tales were played have long since been repurposed into our churches and city walls. Yet you persist. How is that? What impels you to cling to this singular pursuit?"

Mik shrugged. He might have answered that it was what he knew. That some were born to wealth while players had to work. That God surely loved fools if He had made so many. That Christ himself was a storyteller— But he played the safer role of simpleton. He shrugged.

"Well, no matter, but I mourn the demise of the player. You give us a glimpse of worlds that would otherwise go unseen. Discomfiting at times: things we would sooner hide. Might that be the source of laughter? A surprise at secrets revealed? My peasants' children at slaughter time blow up pigs' bladders, toss them about. They laugh and laugh, despite the screech of the pigs. You play your plays and we laugh like those lowly children. You show us ourselves, and of course we pretend, *No, that's not I, that's my uncle, my tutor, my foe.*" He took a distracted pause, too long for comfort. "But we cannot dodge the finger of truth."

The youth liked to talk and must have had little chance of it. He accepted his natural superiority, felt himself generous in giving his listeners the benefit of his presence, yet he appeared to yearn for their approval. His loneliness colored his words. Again he mentioned the farce he recalled with such glee, asking if they might add a speech he had penned—

"Being no poet, but we must nourish aspirations beyond our capabilities. Otherwise our brains might shrivel like worms in the sweltering sun." He giggled. "That in itself being my crude attempt at poetic metaphor!" Again he ruffled Bragi's hair, but the boy didn't mind: it was like a big brother's caress.

"We would be honored to include your words," said Mik. Anything to please their host enough to buy a viable horse.

The youth explained that his text was a joke that only the household would find amusing, so the players need not worry out its meaning. He gestured toward the dead-fish attendant who stood at a distance, chin a-tremble. "Ah well, my steward tires of our colloquy. I should let you retire. You shall dine with the servants. I would much prefer your company at table, but we must comply with custom. When I succeed to the reins of power, I shall make radical change, decreeing roast boar for every peasant and truffles on Sunday!" With a nod to Fish-eye, he turned and climbed the steps to the carved oaken door of kingship.

Bragi had never seen guest quarters so sumptuous. Mik whispered that he hoped it augured the fat kid's generosity. Spacious accommodations: three rooms, stone walls warmed by broad tapestries depicting merry scenes of long-bearded men being tortured, beheaded, and rising to Heaven. Their cow eyes stared out as if in a play they had played countless times but had to endure again. Below flashed tongues of fire, above a frothy sunrise, but in the world of the living an unending scream.

Fish-eye ventured to explain. "Yes, you are amazed by the weavings. No other realm boasts these inspiring wonders of craft. The king, rest his soul, acquired them at the cost of a thousand men." He absented himself.

It was noon, and the players had work to do. Two days of steady travel, and now they had one afternoon to come up with a play they hadn't performed for ten years. No great worry: the play fixed in the Prince's mind was one of their dozen variations on the old-lecher theme, and the audience would be drunk, they could be sure of that. The engagement would offer a final shake of the money tree—not to mention the fact that they had no choice in the matter.

They briefed a stable boy on Yesu's feed, detailed construction of the stage where they were to play, devised a dress to conceal Asta's virginal pregnancy, and rehearsed a play they vaguely recalled from a decade past. Nobility had scant concept of Time, and the dozen lines that the Prince desired them to incorporate were a puzzlement. Prince Helmut, however precocious, was no poet.

Except for the aristocratic scribbles, the dialogue would be improvised, but they still had to set the cues, the gist of each scene, the entrances and exits. Their movements on stage—the way they configured themselves, threw focus one to another, played fights— were the craft of centuries, bred into the bone. Whenever Ludd blundered they elbowed him into place.

Bragi was dead tired. His mother feared a recurrence of his fever, so he was put to bed for a nap. He had nothing to do in the play, and for once he was grateful. From the next room he heard them rehearsing. "So I grab you and say *Finders keepers*, then Ludd comes in and startles— So, Ludd, give a big startle, rock back on your foot, hands in the air, mouth open wide— No, bigger— And back there to the left, okay? You shove me away, and I'll do a roll—" Bragi drifted off.

～

Once my dreams were hirsute and brash, sharp-clawed and fanged. Now they slink in, gelded. My present dreams are of mundane cares, trite quests, quotidian monstrosities, and they neither enlighten nor terrify. They put one foot ahead of the other, measuring out the road. I value many aspects of maturity, but I miss the fierce torrent of nightmare.

As a child I would feel a shadow behind me, matching stride for stride. Or down the roadway a dream would be lurking beneath a fallen log, and as I came close it leapt to confront me, gaped wide and swallowed me whole. Frightening, yes, but the deeper dread was the loneliness. I could be surrounded by family, playmates or ghouls, but I was forever alone. That much is true to this day. That may have been what drew me to Prince Helmut: the loneliness I heard in his witty chatter.

That evening we played the play and fled for our lives.

～

The chapel was roomy, large enough for a hundred to stand, but benches and chairs had been placed for only a score: the family, clergy, neighboring nobility, and other significant others. A third cousin to the Emperor—some emperor somewhere, sometime, hard to keep track—was a special guest. Servants watched from the shadows. Bragi had no part in the play, so he stood at the rear.

Prince Helmut was an exuberant host. He greeted each guest upon arrival as if to prepare them for an astounding experience. No drink was offered, which puzzled the guests. The Regent and Queen sat front and center as the Prince rose to address the seated assemblage. Bragi admired the way he commanded attention, even without a mask. Or perhaps he wore his mask within.

"Welcome to a night I have long envisioned. As a child, I had the privilege to see this play. It has remained an inspiration, though in our time, it pains me to say, players are not as highly esteemed as in

pagan days. Yet like the words of Plato and Virgil they offer us blessings. Simple laughter indeed, yet laughter as a gift from Heaven to
assuage our mortal pains. Behind each trivial jest we may hear the
cry of our Savior on the Cross: *Why hast Thou forsaken me?* In this
vein, then, let us attend the words of these heralds as we might hear
the voices of saints."

The players had never heard such fulsome praise—nor more
calamitous. The Prince's words prepared the viewers for the Passion
of Christ but not for Mik's entrance nursing his boner, cursing
death, taxes and unrequited erections. They had never pondered the
Messiah bemoaning his dick. Some ladies went into coughing jags to
suppress their laughter. Facing a dour crowd the players' instinct was
to lay back and play it for deeper meaning, but this farce—despite the
Prince's panegyric—was nothing more than a bawdy romp. It raised
not a laugh, only repeated coughing jags.

Bragi had seen shows fail. Once, an elephant—a mythical beast
to the townsfolk—paraded through the marketplace, sweeping away
the throng. Once, drunkards pelted them with rotten fish. More than
a few times they had received vociferous acclaim but scant receipts.
Now they sank into the swamp with nothing to pull them free. For
a moment Bragi considered crying out pee or parsnips, but nothing
would fend off Sir Flop. A play was just a play, his grandmother often
said, and "Tomorrow's another day," but the challenge was surviving the rest of today. Just get to the end, lick your wounds, wake up
tomorrow.

And it might have been merely a flop but for the lines Prince
Helmut added, an adolescent spasm that ended with comic abrupt-
ness in Asta's "*The hairy old boar is tupping the scrofulous bitch.*"

Pandemonium. The giggling Prince Helmut sprang to his feet
clapping madly. Hairy old Regent Boris rose, stumbled about, undecided whether to attack his nephew or the players, at last pummeling
the priest who tried to restrain him. The Queen Mother, unmindful
of *bitch* but stung to the quick by *scrofulous*, flew, all claws, at her
lady-in-waiting. A chorus of screams and curses erupted. Clearly, all
were aware that the hairy old boar was tupping the scrofulous bitch.

The players stood frozen. Bragi ran to the stage, clung to his mother, eyes shut tight. The guards stood ready to fall upon anything that moved, but their training was not in restraint of frenzied nobility. Fish-eye rushed to the players, pushing, pulling them into the chancel behind the rood screen.

"Well, so, yes. You have offended the Queen and the Regent. I regret— Yes. You must go now. Your lives are in danger. This way. Yes."

The rafters rang with panic. The tumult grew. The Queen collapsed. The Priest emitted a litany of squeals. The Regent throttled the chortling Prince, shaking him like a rat, then recoiled, appalled at having touched the anointed flesh. He resumed his assault by tiny mosquito swats at the princely noggin. The guards turned on one another, and the first sword flashed.

Fish-eye led the players through a maze of dark corridors, rousing off-duty guards to aid the escape, directing servants to harness the donkey, load the cart and saddle the horse. Soon they were in flight: Ludd on the mare, Edra and Asta bouncing in the cart, Mik and the boy on a borrowed horse. Ludd held the guide rope leading Yesu, trotting to keep abreast. Three mounted soldiers escorted them into the night.

Ludd or the donkey soon ran out of steam, and the frantic hegira slowed to a walk. They traveled most of the night, stopped finally at a crossroads by a brook. A guard directed them to camp on a hillock, wend left at dawn, and when they came to a village they'd be out of the tiny kingdom. If they made a fire they should keep it low. The soldiers rode off with the borrowed horse.

They pitched camp by the slit of the moon. Asta began a meal of scraps—barley, pork rind, onions, and trenchers of bread a servant had handed them as they rushed away—but went faint and sat by the coals. Bragi huddled beside her, and Edra finished the preparations. They had eaten before the performance, but they needed sustenance.

"Mama?"

"Yes, hon?"

"Did we make money?"

"No," said Mik, unsmiling. As they fled through the corridors he had asked Fish-eye for their fee. "Yes. Well. I regret to say," said the quivering chin as they fled, "that I would need approval for payment, as you did not in fact complete the play." Mik made his duck face for Bragi, though a very bleak duck.

"We got caught in the middle," he explained. "The Prince was mad at his uncle, he wanted to make a stink, and he used us to do it."

"But he was nice." Bragi liked the Prince's kind eyes and long words.

"He was nice, but he screwed us."

"I didn't like the man with the chin," said Bragi.

"Well, he stiffed us on the fee, but he saved our necks."

Bragi was baffled. People were said to be good or bad: his family were good and the pirates were bad, and that was that. But now the nice man betrayed them, the nasty man saved them, and life was an ethical pottage.

Edra, stirring the pot, looked up. "Reminds me of Samos."

"Omigod, Samos," Mik looked up. "I was little."

"Long time ago, we did a Midsummer show. This bigwig—what was his name? But Mik's father, beautiful voice, he played kings, gods, not just the funny stuff, but there he's doing his slimy-old-lecher thing, and this priest yells out *Heresy!* Which made no sense, it wasn't gods or nothing—

"*Heresy!*" Mik imitated the squeal of a drunken pig.

"And all of a sudden it's war: Cristers, Arians, Goo-nostics, and what they called the Paganos, and we were right in the midst. We got out of there fast, caught the first boat out, thinking every breath we'd get caught. We heard there were people killed. Never could figure what we'd done."

She fell silent, stirring the porridge, but Bragi had to ask. "Did you make money then?"

"We survived. That's what counts."

Mik felt his son's eyes on him and raised a bright face. "Shows you the power of stories. People go nuts." He stared into the glowing coals.

A sliver of moon peeked from the clouds. Edra served steaming porridge, and the boy's bafflements faded. The questions would return next day like the fleas they picked off to make room for more, but for now the new moon shone.

—XXI—
Frekka's Trek

It was late into night before they finished late supper. It helped to still the tremor the boy had picked up from Fish-eye's chin. His sleep was scant. He was old enough to worry what might flow from their debacle. Word would spread far and wide that they had insulted nobility or divinity or the patron saint of hairy boars. They would be branded as trouble-makers—surely no fault charged to the mischievous Prince. Prospective hosts would politely decline their service.

From the grownups' night murmurs he knew that every year was harder: the wars, the outlaws, the road conditions, the bedbugs, the clashes of faith and frenzy. If this were the last of the tours, what a blessing: an end to the endless trudge. He could milk the cow, pull weeds, chase chickens, kill Huns, and curl up in his own bed at night. But he was a player now. He got laughs. He felt the joy of the fart dance and rode the flow. He tasted the bitter sweetness of the days, and now he could harness the donkey. He didn't want it to end.

He lay flat on his back, and the dreams flared up like wildfire. No surprise. Fear followed him along on this journey like the moon, sometimes a sliver, sometimes full, always peering over his shoulder to catch him off guard. At times it crawled into his ear the way he fretted that bugs might do. Still, he longed to dream a play that would make them rich. And so he dreamt, despite Gramma's snoring. Most often her snores were a gentle locust chorus, a slow tide rising and receding, but that night she erupted in convulsive binges like Yesu's brays. The boy would startle awake, endure a dozen nasal expostulations, then drift back under the fog. Somehow the dream held fast, the tick's head burrowing deeper.

∼

I knew the story, Frekka's journey, some bedtime fright in my infancy as I was only beginning to know dawn from dusk. The goddess encounters all mortal things, scattered across the worlds, that live by the light of her son. Cypress and olive trees, wolves and sheep, the stuff of the sea, creatures with wings and scales or those dangerous ones with hands and words—all teeming life that springs from seed and the substance of a mother.

Of every creature she asks a promise: no harm to the Shining One. Even the eyeless squirmers deep in unfathomed caverns, even they require the warmth that suffuses the water and sand and stone. *We promise!* they waggle. In the eternal span of one day of my night, the goddess confronts each creature the tide of life spews over the worlds. Every living wiggler pledges love to the God of Light.

My dream comes in frozen images like the weavings in the castle—stark figures, vivid hues, shimmering silk—a dream so sweet, iridescent, yet rife with greater terror than the tortures in the tapestries. My eyes are shut but I see it.

The mother Frekka carries her infant son in one hand like a fragile glowing coal. Any moment a slap of rain might hit and the coal sizzle out, so she holds him close to her breast. Her pace is slow, her feet chafed raw by her sandal straps. Her leathery feet are my grandmother's feet. She plods toward a sawtooth horizon. I hear voices, no eyes.

Promise? Promise? Promise?

I do. I do. I do.

I wake. Gramma is snoring. The night will go on forever. The moon is above, behind, tracking us, eyeing us, cogitating. I scratch an itch and trickle back into the dream.

Frekka reaches high and pulls the clouds from the heavens the way Mama skins a fish. The sky comes clear and the roadway straight. She confronts a great oak clutching the brow of a gulley. *Promise!* she says. A gust of wind echoes, *I do* . . . Another step, another. A wild boar snorts grim rage. *Promise!* the grey-eyed goddess cries. It lowers its glare and grunts a petulant grunt. She passes.

I see them all raising hands and wings and feelers and fronds to greet the sun. The birds, the fleas and creeping things, the elephants a thousand leagues away, old drunkards in gutters, children chasing cats, a torturer doing his job and hoping to finish soon, a little girl lost in her daydream, a scrawny cat poised at a gopher hole, the mighty emperor who rules the whole Earth except the realm of himself—all, all, all. No harm will come to Balthur. I begin to remember the story. I shiver. My grandmother snores. I wake. I dream. All promise—

~

—*Except the Norns.* He woke at the strangled croak of a crotchety Norn or his grandmother's snore. But no, no danger: the Norns had no will of their own. They were only the road that led to your destination, not the road-builder, the hiker, the donkey. They were only the ruts and bounces and bends of the road. You were the road.

Another avalanche from Gramma. The waking boy laughed, then froze. He knew how plays go. Something good happens: they buy the donkey. Then comes the twist: the donkey is dead. There's always the bend in the road. If all creatures make their promise, there would come the bend in the road. The fear crested slowly, a rising tide. There would come the moment when all was secure, except—

The child Bragi could only tremble. The future was being woven from threads of the past. Stories could be lethal. A merry tale of frolicking nymphs might turn with a snarl and bare its fangs. The migrations and conquests, the pilgrim paths, the thirsty drag of the crucifix, the ten years' voyage homeward—each life left its snail trail of glitter and scum.

That was the shadow and substance of his dream. Scenes that might have made for farce: a turtle yawning to swear its solemn vow, the mighty cedar taking a year to nod a simple *Yes,* a school of tadpoles deploying themselves to spell out an affirmative. But too scary for laughs.

It stemmed from some bedtime story his mother told, though he couldn't remember the ending except for its certitude of doom. He struggled to free his feet, but the swamp sucked hard. The instant before he woke to a volley of brays, he stood in the castle before the hideous weavings. To the boy's childish eyes they depicted a perpetual martyrdom of innocence, the betrayal of a promise, the future being born of the thousand dread farces they might chance to play.

—XXII—
Barbarians

"**I** slept!" Edra exclaimed. Bragi woke with the sun in his eyes. He turned on his side and saw a gnarled tree clinging onto a steep downward slope, its branches slicing the morning sky into sausage chunks. Beyond it, a long parched valley and the thatched roofs of a village. He looked around for the horse. The horse had been in his dream, shrunk to the size of a goat. He had thought of the perfect name for the horse, but now he'd forgotten it.

He tried to recall where they were. He tasted the tang of last night's supper, envisioned the ride in the night, heard the raging uncle and merry Prince—so long ago. Every night of his life seemed long ago. His mother moved heavily at the fire, clearing remains of supper. "Where's the horse?" he whimpered.

"The men went to the village."

"What for?"

"Provisions." She knelt beside him and stroked his forehead. Annoying, but there was comfort in the usual things. "Long night," she said, "but we've still got our money pouch. That's what counts."

Gramma appeared from a trip behind the bushes. "Plus, they didn't cut off our ears or burn out our tongues. That was nice of 'em," Her words flashed an edge.

"These days you never know," said Asta, going back to her tasks. "You never know." What was it, wondered the boy, that you never know? And if you never knew it, how would you know that you never know? The sun was too bright in his eyes.

Mother! the Shining One cried to Gray-nag. *Yes!* she replied. Shards of the dream he couldn't be rid of.

Mik and Ludd returned with the nameless horse, sacks of barley and turnips, a wineskin and unsettling news. Their escape had taken them north. No road south except through the petty kingdom they had escaped, risking the wrath of the hairy old boar, otherwise groping through uncharted mountain terrain. A day's travel further north might bring them to an eastbound road connecting with a southern track. At least the road held promise of a midwife in time of need, so their path lay to the north.

"Where's the cats?" asked Bragi.

"We must've lost the cats," his father replied.

"Horse?"

"Right there."

Bragi shut his eyes tight. If he could dream he might fetch up a name, grab it and stick it fast to the horse's butt. Everyone had their job to do and that was his job. But dreams were like cats: they wouldn't come when you called.

He crept out from under the cover and rolled up his mat. Gramma was boiling barley, and they still had honey left. He watched the horse nuzzle Yesu's crested mane and rub her nose on his muzzle. A bristly kiss. What were they thinking? Did horses and donkeys think? He could never stop thinking no matter how hard he tried.

They ate in silence, broke camp and descended into the village where Mik had paid exorbitant prices for supplies. Yet as the cart appeared—with crone, child and gravid mother—the villagers opened their hearts. A throng gathered. A man produced a wineskin and passed it around, a baker a loaf. A twisted old man fed Yesu a carrot, and a stubby priest waggled his fingers in blessing. A tall gawky girl placed her hand on Asta's belly as if it contained a second Christ to make up for losing the first. The troupe grabbed lute and pipes to sing a bright morning song in a dialect close to theirs. Ludd, normally shy, made a wild gesture of thanks and offered a new-minted grin. They finished the music. The hearers voiced their thanks in strange-tongued cheers. Leaving the village, the troupe was in high spirits. So little done to spark such joy.

For the boy the questions swarmed like black flies. Sometimes people were festive, sometimes cruel. How could you tell what was ever to be? How could you know what you never knew? The puzzlements cut like an ax, and your head went splat on the wall.

Mayhap the conundrums lessen as we grow into our years. I can barely fathom the soul of a boy of six, though he grew up to be myself. They called me smart, but I floundered in riddles tat-tatted out by the beaks of the Norns.

Like gray-eyed Frekka, I trod the rutted roads that spider-webbed my world. At times I climbed into the back of the cart, at times might lean on the withered horse or try to match my father stride for stride. I would shake my head and the dreams took wing with a squawk. My other front tooth was loose, and I lost myself in its waggle.

It resembled one of our farces. You hungered for food or a girl or revenge, so you perched your rump on a ramshackle nag and cried *Giddyap!* Far ahead you saw that a bridge was out or a canyon yawned or a monster posed on a rock with its tail afire, but you followed the road, and the road led north.

No side tracks, no forks, barely a curve. Low foothills with patchy pasture for sheep to graze. One day chill, the next sweltering: the heavens were undecided. Days passed in a blur. The villagers had told of an eastbound road a day's journey off, but no such road appeared. Only one thing certain: no choice but north.

Asta was in her seventh month. Her legs and feet were swollen. She often needed to descend to the side of the road and squat to pee. Her face took on a bovine obstinance: *All right, I'm a beast and beasts do what they do.* Countless females—humans, dryads, goddesses, cats—had done the business of birthing, and herself six years before.

Soon she would scream and give birth and the milk would come in. Her mind went to practicalities. Edra would help, but every birth was as different as the babies born, so you needed a midwife who'd seen it all. How could Bragi be shielded from her cries? Who would take her roles if she died? Was there something quirky in that faint insistent heartbeat? A chill in the air. The roadway led north.

The horse went lame. She had always been feeble, but now her foreleg gave out and she could barely walk, much less carry a burden. She stood gazing into the distance, unmindful of the humans milling about her. Mik directed them to go ahead, while he and Ludd fell back to tend to the horse. At length they caught up with the cart and brought it to rest. The father knelt and spoke to his son.

They did the only thing proper, he said. The horse had to be left behind, and a snarling pack of wolves would soon descend to rip out its throat. Better to spare the poor horse. That was the way of it. The boy nodded. One more thing for which he would come to forgive his father. And to forgive himself for never naming her. Better a silly name than to let her stumble anonymous into the void. He tried to hum a tune, spare his mind from aimless blind alleys, but the tune came out in whimpers.

Soon they came to a settlement. Stranger than they'd ever seen: a stockade of tall logs double the height of a man, axed to a point and set in the earth, a sharpened forest encircling the jumble of huts. Barbarians: an ancient word for those half-human creatures beyond the borderlands. From infancy one learned there were men who dressed in the skins of beasts, spoke in gurgles and grunts, worshipped demons, ate babies, drank blood. Now these fiends confronted the donkey cart.

The troupe approached the entry and stopped, awaiting their fate. It was the life they were born to. They had traveled countless roads, confronted glistening blades and narrowed eyes. Facing soldiers, their practice was to send old Edra to meet them. Her face held neither challenge nor fear, nothing to rouse their swords to erection. Her womanhood held a vague threat of witchery, her wit encircled the words they uttered, and her smile was that of their mothers.

The guard who approached was a tall wiry youth. Shaggy blond hair to his shoulders, thin frown, and cheeks that had yet to achieve full bush, though a promising fuzz marked a stalwart jaw. He was barefoot, bare-chested, wearing a bearskin hood and cape, tunic, crude weave leggings, and girded with leather belt and scabbard. He carried a spear his own height. He strutted toward them with a wide stride to add to his bulk.

Edra assessed him with a practiced eye. These striplings could pose danger if they felt challenged to prove their manhood. The tactic was to hold a steady gaze, speak briefly, take long pauses before a reply, and keep a low smile that told them simply, *We pose one another a problem, we both want to solve our problem.*

An exchange of mutually unintelligible blurts, then Edra mimed, with vivid comedic flourish, *Take us to your chief.* Her rendering of *chief* drew on a lifetime of encounters with disgruntled grunts. *Me, you, walk. Deep bow to chief: gigantic height, slab shoulders, brute gaze. He squats, he belches, he frowns, he stretches welcoming hands.*

The crone's lively mime drew reluctant chuckles from the trio of guards, and the troupe was escorted into the compound. They approached the furthest dwelling at the end of a double row of daub-and-wattle huts: a larger cabin of log chinked with clay. Two upright stones framed the door. "They look pregnant," Asta said. Mik posed beside one, sticking out his belly, and Bragi laughed, but the young barbarian frowned. Asta pulled her son closer. Their escort called out at the doorway, and at length they were directed to enter. The door swung open on leather hinges.

The chieftain sat on a three-legged stool, raising his hand in formal greeting. He was young, red-bearded with long sandy hair, wearing a heavy woven cape though otherwise dressed like the guards. His features were fine, almost womanish. His large hazel eyes betokened a mild demeanor in contrast to his headdress: the skull of a snarling bear.

They stood before him with expectant smiles. Bragi saw the others smiling, so he smiled. It was easy to smile when terrified.

"Who do you be?"

Their own language. The chieftain saw their surprise and explained, almost intelligibly, that he had served as a mercenary in the imperial army—which empire he didn't say and probably didn't know. He asked them their destination. Mik explained their dilemma and the chieftain vowed to assist. He invited them to dine and sent the young soldier to fetch stools. Though accustomed to diverse norms, they were startled by his casual grant of equality. Mik and Ludd went out to unhitch Yesu, sending him off to the care of the bearded savages, returning with lute and pipes.

Two servants—most likely slaves—set out the feast. The table was a low slab of wood, supported by stones, with a brazier of coals in the center for warmth. Two gangly boys, adolescents, appeared from an inner door, crowded into the tight confines of the throne room, and stood before the guests looking stern. "Sons," said the chief. "Mother dead." Perhaps the chieftain was older than he looked, or they started breeding young. The boys pulled stools to the table and waited impatiently. Bragi sat up tall in hopes they would notice him.

A supper was served. The wooden bowls were engraved with marks of alien meaning. The servants laid out knives crafted of bronze. The boy recognized the boiled carrots and white bulbs that might be turnips, but no clue to the gray gelatinous lump that filled his bowl. The chief saw the boy's confusion. "You eat." The chief picked up his knife, playfully skewered a carrot, popped it in his mouth. The boy grinned, followed suit and evoked a laugh that warmed his young player's heart. Then he faced the huge gray snot-textured gob.

Its appearance wasn't the worst of it. It stank. He had often smelled rot—dead rats in city sewers, dried squirrels along the road, and once they passed a field where dead felons were left to the dogs—but never had such a fulsome stench wafted up from his supper bowl. A servant edged around the table, filling their large clay mugs with a heavy amber wine. He drank wine, of course, though his mother watered it heavily as she watered her own, but the servant filled his mug to the brim. Would he die if he drank it like that or grow abruptly into a man? The chieftain raised his mug in welcome. All followed suit, and the very first sip wrapped the boy in the sweet smoky hum of bees.

The two sons ate quickly and at the chief's gesture disappeared. Again Bragi faced the slimy lump. His parents' imperative from infancy rang in his ears: *Eat what's set before you.* It was more than parental nagging: you must never risk offending a host's good will. Once he had seen his father as honored guest eat a boiled sheep's eye that stared up in accusation. Bragi dug his knife into the gob of snot.

The first taste of the rotten jelly demanded a swig of the heady wine, a struggle against vomit, then a sudden vast tide of mellowness. He pronged up the sea-stuff ravenously and guzzled radiant honey to wash it down.

End of the feast. Mik and Asta picked up pipes and lute, played a ballad in a style they regarded as *northern.* The boy watched the chieftain's eyes. With the music he seemed to go to a distant land and as it ended was surprised to return. Music had that effect on Yesu. He might be snuffling and snorting, then the music transfixed him, as if unable to tell the boundary between the weeds he nibbled and the squawking raven above. Bragi longed to go to that boundless land.

At length, over the gentle rhythm, they heard a quiet voice. "One two three four five six, one two three four five six . . ." The music broke off. They looked into a shadowed corner and saw the mad-eyed girl staring into the glowing coals. The chief observed their shock. "She come two moons. We feed."

The girl fixed her gaze on Asta, made a tiny two fingered wave as if to ask for music. The lute began again and the pipes joined in. The girl remained crouched in the corner shadows. "One two three four five six . . ." she whispered.

It was late in the night. As the mumbled chant filled the silences, the red-bearded barbarian struggled to speak in a broken tongue to a stupefied Ludd, the tallest male, hence the apparent leader. She came to them two moons before. They saw she was mad, but as a female she had uses. Red-beard had first privilege.

"She come bed. Count one, two, on. I stop." He clasped the befuddled Ludd by the shoulder and stammered out the story. She had stood before him naked, nodding, slapping her thigh on each count. He sat rigid. Then she crouched on all fours as if in childbirth, emitting a bass growl from deep within. Her first words to Red-beard: "Kill brother."

She was mad. Yet for them madness was holy. Like Christ she had traversed the Underworld, like him returned transfigured. She spoke an alien tongue but all could comprehend. Madwoman Rona—it was surely Rona—ran free in the settlement, taking food from any table. She would frolic with children or lurk in shadows. She would defecate in the village common with no one taking notice. She had predicted the players' arrival two days before.

"I kill brother." Red-beard spoke to a terrified Ludd and became more fluent as he drank. Meantime the boy wolfed a third helping of the succulent mucus. His cup emptied, filled, and then the chieftain pushed Ludd aside and spoke directly to the dreamy-eyed child.

"I am Crister," he said. "Hate war. We kill, we kill, never stop kill. Want stop, brother not. Brother want kill, she say kill brother." He sagged lower and chugged a teeming mug of the brew. Bragi saw his eyes go as wild as the mad girl's eyes, then shut tight.

The brother's servants were tortured and a plot revealed. The chieftain went into his brother's hut and brought out his head. He spoke as if it grieved him, the way Mik had spoken of killing the horse, a sadness that had to be done. At last the bear-skulled chieftain waved the music to a close. Rona was gone, resorbed by the shadows.

"Good food," said the groggy Ludd as Red-beard rose from the table.

"May we all find peace," said Asta.

"Is that a bear?" asked Bragi, pointing to the headdress, but no one heard. Might be he hadn't said it. That was the last he knew before the wind bore him to bed.

⁓

That night I smelled dark kelp forests wavering under the wharves and still heard her rhythmic whisper. I wanted to ask her things. *Are you alive? What are you counting? Do you really poop in the common?* I heard her spit and we laughed.

I felt her mad stare. I looked up to her slanted cat eyes and was struck by her age. The raped adolescent had been older than the spitting girl, and now she was older still. She was my mother's age. The mad-eyed girl was a woman. A deeply etched frown between the brows, rough skin, flat lips, cold eyes—she had seen many winters in the days she followed us.

But not one woman. She was many such. A soul may split into many souls, I believe. Each has a trajectory, a dance, a death. In a few moons' time, she was grown up and mad. Each number a day, each day a rape. Perhaps the counting shortened the time she was doomed to stay alive.

❀

Next morning the boy could barely stand, except to stumble out from the hut where they slept and vomit. Before departure his mother made him a nest in the cart. "You'll feel better," she said, "You did fine."

He drowsed, slept till the sun was high, then clambered down from the cart to walk. He recalled little of that supper, only the slimy lump and the heady wine. And Red-beard's bear skull and grief-stricken eyes. And the madwoman's chant.

The barbarians gave them directions east, then south, where they might take passage along the coast. Mid-morning, in the wilderness, they stopped at a puzzling five-way crossroads. No telling direction: the sun was hiding in heavy overcast. After long argument they took a turn to the left.

Next morning, a chilly dawn. More argument, and at last Mik proclaimed in exasperation, "Either we're headed north or the sun's coming up in the west." Either seemed possible.

—XXIII—
A Death

Anything was possible. If the little girl was a woman now, if cats stalked them like wolves, if a goddess talked to a tree, if he dreamt in bright daylight, then why not the sun coming up in the west? Might be the Shining One got drunk and reeled backwards the way Papa did once. Why worry where the sun rose as long as it rose? "If you can't change it," his father always said, "try to survive it." And Gramma would add, "Do what you can and don't do what you can't." Maybe the sky tipped downhill on that side.

The days were overcast. The sun—what they could see through the trees—was a vague blur over the sky. Yet they felt impelled to continue the trudge. Impossible now to get home before the birth but needful at least to find shelter and knowing hands. They had to be on the road. And there were other clues to direction. Check the moss on the trees, but the trees were moss all over. Check spiderwebs, but the spiders were lazy. Check the North Star—it was covered by clouds in the night.

It cleared the third day, and they saw they were turned around. But they had hit a stretch of imperial road, a wide hard-beaten track with stone bridges and tumuli marking intervals, built for armies to march. Travel was swifter, and they agreed they must be coming to a city. In more populous regions, stonework had been dismantled to build castles or churches or other bulwarks against the future, but here the road drew the troupe forward insistently, even as instinct cried that it was wrong, wrong, wrong.

Asta began to recognize landmarks. It must be a road upon which she and her father came south. A tree in the shape of her step-mother Todie. "Funny little belly, the way the trunk bulges out, right there? First time I saw her I thought of that tree. If that's the tree . . ." More signs: a river crossing, an alignment of stones, a reddish rock face that looked like an owl. A new world, a new life coming south, though they carried the wickerwork hamper.

Now they were going north, but the sight of something familiar, however lost in the past, seemed to right the wrong direction. The road must lead somewhere or they wouldn't have built a road.

～

I was as mature as I'd ever be—when in fact my mother was on her deathbed—before I thought to ask why we persisted in the wrong direction. Why not turn around, back to the crossroads and homeward?

"We did. We thought we were going wrong when we were going right, and then right when we saw we were wrong." I couldn't follow. "But I saw a megalith I seemed to recognize," she said. "We couldn't get home before the birth, so I thought I remembered a town." I still didn't understand, but she was fatigued. "I was kind of crazy. If you're crazy enough, then everyone else goes crazy with you."

I didn't ask more. It may have been whatever force that draws us despite our will, the way the night sucks fire upward or the shore draws the tide, or as armies march into battles already lost. Something nameless, untouchable, the curses we carry within our frail wickerwork. Perhaps my childish confusion spread like the plague, leaping shoulder to shoulder like a showman's monkey I saw at a market fair. Perhaps the gods in the basket, like migrating geese, were flying home.

I rarely ventured a word in the days of the northward trek. We were fixed on watching the road one stride ahead, not questioning where it led. The world of adults was baffling to me, more so as I became one. We come at last to accept the incomprehensible, and then we are deemed mature.

~

They stopped by a narrow stream to rest. The boy sat on a rock, his feet dangling amid a swarm of small darting fish that nibbled his toes. His mother, fearful of his silence, came to feel his forehead. She spoke in a low flat voice, as if she never saw him. "That outcrop looks familiar." Beyond it, what?

The journey went forth. She would stare past the tree or rock or river into a younger day, and all felt comfort that she recognized landmarks, though they lay in a wrong direction. They passed an abandoned peasant hut enveloped by vines, window slits empty, roof collapsed. She told of a time on their southward trek when she and her sister had pulled back a leather flap in a vacant hut and found a corpse. Was that the hut?

Bragi walked beside Gramma. She coughed, and he reached to hold her hand. His eyes fell to the feet that in olden days had enraptured the red-nosed merchant. They might be Frekka's feet trudging over the worlds—

Promise! she cried.

No, that dream tried to slip in behind his eyes, but he jerked back his head. The sun beat down cold on the wayward path, and the bushes trembled like Fish-eye's chin. The marker stones stood, scarred granite faces of hardbitten gods. He counted them as they passed, one two three . . .

But the gray-eyed goddess had finished her countings. Balthur stood before her, luminous. She reached to touch him, and her touch told all. She had gathered each *Yes* of the worlds. All living realms shared his light. The breath of the seas, the reaching trees, the sheen of the mountain streams, the gleam in lovers' eyes—all that mothered life. All beings had sworn the oath: neither rock nor fang would strike him down, no wave or tempest's claw. Even the night beasts loved the starlight's glimmer, and that was Balthur. Even the Strange Ones loved him. Nine Realms were united in love.

And yet . . . The boy heard the faint whisper of a long-lost tale and tried to stop counting the marker stones. *And yet . . .*

Old One-eye loomed, empty of head. He strode through the clouds to the face of the mighty wall and conjured a passage through it. The granite closed behind him with a suck like the gulp of a frog. He stood before his queen. Their lips moved with the stupor of runes chiseled into the sky. Bragi read her speech in the air.

Our son will not die. I have walked the Earth. All realms love Balthur. None shall harm him. None.

No matter the dreaming?

No matter. And yet . . .

A chill. In Gramma's stories, he knew that if the child's mother warned, *Look out for the wolf,* you knew there was going to be a wolf. If the mother proclaimed, *Our son shall not die . . .*

The goddess watched the approach of a grinning crone.

Grasping these memories by the tail as they flee, I feel a desperate need to comfort the boy, to tell him, yes, it has always been thus, will always be. The world of dusk is never the same as the world of dawn: the only certainty is change. That's why we play farces. Our clowning is armor against the Norns. And then I see that boy is myself and the armor a tissue of mist.

The weather grew harsh. No inns, few farms to offer shelter, none willing. The trees were the skeletons of monsters. The clouds gnawed the lips of the mountains, and the distant saw-teeth grew into towering crags and bottomless gullies, high peaks and ice. Asta marched heavily. At intervals she rode the donkey cart, but the road grew rutted and the jostling hurt. She squatted more often by the roadside and with a feeble smile reported the baby's healthy kick. Edra walked a measured pace on wobbly knees. She had picked up a nasty cough—nothing to fear, she said—but Bragi saw an odd spasm in her eyes after a fit of the coughing.

She answered his unasked question. "It's called getting old, little boy. Takes my mind off my knees." He didn't like to hear that, though he didn't know why. "There's parts of us give out," she said. "Better maybe if it all went at once. Or maybe not."

Bragi had no idea where they were headed or why. He wasn't sure anyone knew. He heard the covered words his parents spoke, his grandma's cough, queries from Ludd, all blended with the distant howling of wolves through fog. He could barely discern what was said by the others and what was said inside him. Ludd called out that he'd seen the two cats, and Mik made a joke about city cats in the wilderness. The world was no longer what the cats had known.

The mountains' truculence diminished, though the road grew fiercer with crooks and bends as if it were tying a sailors' knot. Middle of nowhere, late afternoon, Yesu balked, let go an apocalyptic "*Hwor-haa!*" then clamped his jaw shut and plodded on.

Edra's persistent cough was a worry to all. She warned Bragi not to get close. "A cough can hop through the air and plop on little boys' heads like pigeon shit," she said. She was joking, he knew, but something was funny. She winced, coughed up phlegm, rubbed her eye, swore at her knees, and kept pace with the donkey cart.

"Don't you be coming down with fever," said Asta. "We need you."

"No, not fever. When I go, I'll go sudden. Maybe just fall in a hole."

A surly "No!" from Bragi.

"She's joking," snapped Asta, and the boy felt childish.

But every question spanned the trudge of another day. He trotted forward. "Papa?"

"Yes. Me. Very likely. In my opinion. What?" He was making a joke, Bragi knew, since he sounded dead serious.

"What if all the people and trees and animals promised they wouldn't hurt you?" He didn't expect a real answer from Papa, but he was the easiest to ask.

"So?" His father didn't grasp the question—fathers never do—but he tried to answer. "So, well, you know the way Yesu balks at crossing a bridge. He never thinks it's safe. But you just look ahead a day at a time. A tree won't fall on you if it can help it—that's no good for the tree—but if a storm comes up, who knows? Does that answer your question?" Mik knew it didn't.

"No."

Yesu balked at a wooden bridge. Mik pulled gently on the lead rope while Ludd banged a stick on the cart, and the beast stepped forward gingerly. Bragi fell back to where his mother rode with her legs dangling over the edge.

"Mama?" The question hung like smoke in his head.

"You feel okay?"

"What if all the people and animals and things all promised they wouldn't hurt you? What about that?"

"Like in the story?" They had passed the pavement, and she flinched at each jounce of the cart. "I wish the road would promise that." His question jarred a memory. Some story from childhood, yes? "Well, hon, you die, but your children go on. Look at us: I'll have a baby, and you'll have a sister or brother, and some day you'll have babies too. It just happens. But it takes a lot of work."

He always got answers to questions he hadn't asked. He hated the way she said *hon*. He was *hon* when she cuddled him as her baby, *Bragi* when she scolded. He preferred *Bragi*.

He rarely spoke with Ludd, who wasn't much of a talker, but the question still itched like bedbugs, so he ran ahead to the bony man as they climbed a steep incline. Ludd kept a steady gait with his hand on Yesu's withers, staring blankly at the beast. Ludd often went blank.

Bragi found words. "What if, say, somebody promised you'd always be safe and you wouldn't get hurt? What if you believed it?"

Ludd was silent. The boy patted Yesu as if to force an answer. At last the bony man spoke in the way he did, barely moving his lips.

"Teo."

"What?"

"In the mines. My friend was named Teo, he told me, named after some king long time ago, name of Teo. King somewhere."

The boy understood that Teo was named after Teo, but that didn't answer his question. Ludd was back in the mines as if he'd never escaped.

"Teo, he was cheerful. Not happy, nobody's happy there, but hopeful, like . . . hope. The way we thought it, the timbers collapse, it buries us, we thought that's good, then we'd be dead. But Teo, he—" The road was straight along the ridge, but the undergrowth was a bristling tangle of snakes. "He was hopeful. *Things'll get better*, he'd say. *They can't afford all their slaves to get killed.* Sometimes he'd make it a joke. *I'm Emperor Teo. I'll proclaim that we're people, then they'll have to treat us nice.* Funny guy." Ludd's eyes followed the donkey's feet. His own feet were huge duck-waddle things that took him any direction, right or wrong. "But he was the one they killed. And I ran off. So I guess he was right: there's hope. Just not for him."

That night they made camp beneath a rock overhang. Not really a cave, just a deep overhang. Bragi imagined bears clawing deep in the rock with chisel claws for a thousand years to escape the storms that struck. No bears now, though maybe the smell of bears.

His grandma would never camp near a cave. "I'm no good with caves," she would say, though she never said why. But she made no objection to the protruding rock. She coughed up phlegm, spat, cursed her knees, felt her way carefully over the rocks, and sat to rest on a ledge at the back of the overhang. It was always her habit to brush away the debris from wherever she aimed to sit—"Don't begrime your queenly bottom!" Mik would shout—but this time she just sat. To Bragi it looked as if she were sitting in a cave. He wanted to ask her his question, but he feared she might answer.

The boy watched Ludd unharness Yesu and lead him down to a clump of mountain grass. The donkey chomped, and Ludd stared into the darkening wood. Suddenly his face contorted into a fierce grimace, he gave out a comical yawp, a laugh or a stab of pain, and pressed his face into the bark of a tree. He must be thinking of his friend. Bragi touched his crucifix and stroked the tiny writhing soul who hung there. The donkey grazed, paying no mind.

Yesu moved to another clump and continued to munch. That was the donkey's answer: keep your mouth full. Go where they lead you and when in doubt stop dead. His comment was the same for all occasions: *Hwor-haa!* After a time, Ludd took his halter and led

him back to the camp. Too much of that kind of grass might cause a
bloat. Ludd's forehead bore grooves from the tree bark.

The bony man tethered Yesu for the night and came to stand
behind Bragi at the fire. He had more to say. He spoke through frozen
lips in that voice that grownups spoke when they didn't want to be
heard. "Main thing, just follow where it goes. It's all jokes."

The evening meal burbled in the pot. As always, Bragi heard the
distant wolves. He smelled a faint odor of skunk—a comfort, since it
might deter the wolves. He leaned over to look in the pot: porridge
with pieces of stuff. The tip of his tongue wobbled his wobbly tooth.

Papa was mending a harness strap, and Bragi heard his mother
go off in the twilight to pee. She had told him she had to do that
whenever his little sister kicked. By day she would squat by the roadside, but at night she sought privacy.

Gramma sat on the ledge in the cave, not really a cave, more like
the back of a mouth. The slanted twilight rays lit her deeply-etched
wrinkles and lent a sheen to the matted white hair. Her eyes glinted
like gems in the setting sun. She cleared her throat as if ready to
speak.

She was the funniest actor of them all. Each had special bits, but
Gramma could just stand there and listen, then react. Like a flash
of lightning the throng saw that someone shared what they knew:
that the world was nuts, that we banged our heads like lunatics, that
we all were madly paddling our leaky boats. They laughed till they
were near to giving up the ghost. *Giving up the ghost* was something
she said a lot.

He smelled the porridge and heard his mother returning from
the bushes. At last he would risk his question: Gramma would know.
He approached, waggling his tooth with his tongue.

"Gramma?"

She coughed and her eyelid twitched. The wolves were silent,
because of the skunk or because they sensed something happening.
She was beautiful in the sunset.

"Gramma, I had a dream . . ." But it wasn't a dream, it was real.
The queen of the gods had spoken words that gouged deep ruts in

the air. He wanted his grandma to say not to worry, nothing to be scared of except his own shadow, she might say. For the first time ever he wanted her to tease him.

"Gramma, I had a dream . . ." He spoke of the Norns and their jowly beaks. He spoke of the bulgy god who threw hammers. He rambled on about One-eye, Grim-grin, and Gray-nag's journey. He felt ashamed of it all. The real worries were Mama having her baby, Gramma's knees, how to keep his loose tooth, though Papa said he would grow another—

He wanted to ask her how to sleep without dreams. How to grow up and find a wife and what to do when you found her. How to make people laugh if they felt mean. He wanted to know how to tell his mother he loved her, and he wanted it to be true.

He could ask her these things. He could ask her now. She was sitting in a cave. She was scared of caves, so her answer would have to be true.

"Gramma?"

"Well—" Her eyes were shut. She took the deepest breath and held it as the cold moon rose. He looked around at the fire, awaiting the call to supper. His tooth came loose. He stared at it nestled in his palm.

"Gramma?"

His grandmother made a sudden snort and a shiver, a deep gasp and shudder that startled him. He looked at her. Her eyes opened wide and went white. Edra was dead.

—XXIV—
Crossing the Bridge

The instant of the gasp, her eyes came open to say *I'm gone*, and she was. She saw him, saw something in the distance, then she died. Bragi was slow in grasping it. He had seen a dead donkey and slaughtered pigs, and corpses from a distance, so death was out there somewhere but not at arm's length. He had seen the spitting girl smeared with gore, but her eyes were alive to him.

"Gramma looks funny," he called.

His mother looked up from the fire. "What?"

"She made a funny noise."

Asta saw the old woman perched on the ledge of rock, head tilted back, mouth wide like a baby bird. She called to Mik, and they rushed to her, touched her, shook her. Mik put his ear to her chest, then stared into her eyes. Asta knelt to hold her trembling son. At last she whispered, "Gramma's dead," but he already knew it. Mik curled against the ancient breasts.

Death, Bragi imagined, was a long slow falling. You were climbing a mountain that grew steeper and steeper with each step, then you couldn't hold on, you pitched over backwards and fell till you smashed on the rocks. Falling asleep and falling sick and falling dead—all fallings.

He had not reached out to stop her plunge. He just awaited her answer to his question, *What if they all promised?* and she had answered: death might come from anywhere. Gramma's cough had worried them, but his father said, when he could speak, that it must have been apoplexia. "Something like that." Her answer to Bragi: if death came to Balthur it would come from an unseen direction.

At dusk Asta ladled out the last of the barley with a bit of salt pork for flavor. "Still have to eat supper, whatever happens," she said. Supplies were meager. Ludd found mushrooms he thought were safe, but none were willing to trust his expertise. In the night the boy heard his father sobbing and his mother humming a song without words.

∽

For many years I thought of my grandmother's death as retribution for not having named the horse. Or for asking a question where death was the only answer. Or I blamed my two-year-old toddler self, who wandered off naked into a market fair—a tumult of sandals and knees and a snarling dog. It was Gramma who found me and jerked me up and hugged me to her. Had my infantile venture drawn us northward and made her sit in the cave?

Why these acts might bring vengeance on Gramma I had no clue, but devils take any excuse to throw eggs at the players. And guilt serves a vital need: it helps us maintain our illusion of control. If we have brought it upon ourselves, it is we who determine our fate. We are not entirely the toys of the Norns.

In decades since, I have cleansed my mind of childish guilt, yet my breath still carries the tang. I had slain countless Huns disguised as roadside weeds. I once squashed a beetle just for the joy of killing. When I played with the spitting girl she showed me a doll she had made from a rag, with a turnip head. She offered it out to me. I held it, took a bite of the head, spat it out and grinned. No malice intended: just something that little boys did. She took the doll, tossed it into the gutter. We played something else.

As I see it now, Edra's death was the opening scene of our last performance.

～

At dawn Mik and Ludd went down to the edge of a glade and took turns digging a hole. The earth was clay and rock, a hard dig, and several times they hit roots and shifted ground. "You go help your father," Asta told Bragi. He went and watched.

"She had a cough," said Ludd.

"Cough wouldn't kill you that fast. Something inside just popped." Mik gave the shovel to Ludd. His voice was drained of feeling. "She used to do this bit where she starts to do one thing, then she does another. Once, I was real little, she played a queen doing five things at once. Big stack of laws to sign, but she has to send off the army, judge a peasant for poaching, tell the king where to find his crown, suddenly goes into labor and they laugh, they laugh—" He took the shovel back and dug doggedly. "This time, no laughs."

The boy tried to help by picking up pine cones and throwing them at a tree. It seemed important to do it. The tree didn't seem to notice.

"She hated caves. *Like somebody's butt hole*, she'd say. But last night she sat there. She must've thought, *Well, it's time.*" He stopped. He couldn't both dig and talk. "She talked about cremation, like they do where Asta grew up. But you have to have the right wood, all that, or else you wind up with a half-baked lady."

He started digging again. He could never resist a joke: if it came to his head he had to burp it out. Again he handed the shovel to Ludd, turned to Bragi, hugged him, explained that Mama was giving Gramma a bath because people wanted to be clean to be buried, whereas donkeys didn't care.

"How do they know they're clean?"

His father seemed not to hear Bragi. "Funny. We had a fight before we left home. Asta said take the shovel, I said no, just one more thing to lug. Back and forth, and then Ma stepped in. *Might need it to bury me*, she said. She was right."

Asta had dressed her as the flashy old bawd, bright spangles, bracelets, red veil across the face—none now to play that role. Mik carried the frail corpse to the ditch, climbed in and laid it down. He placed his fingers to his mother's heart, then climbed out, embraced Asta with his son wrapped dry-eyed around his leg. Ludd shoveled dirt till the hole was full, leaving a gentle mound. They all fetched stones, stacked them over the grave as a cairn to ward off scavengers. "That's the way of it," said Asta to her son. She knew no way to comfort him, so she didn't try.

By midday they descended into a long forsaken valley with a straight narrow road spooling out leagues before them. Travel was faster. Gramma's wobbly knees no longer slowed them and Yesu was less balky at bridges. Perhaps he saw that his masters had started to die. One by one they would gasp and snort and fall into holes till at last he ran free. And they had accepted their misdirection, no longer slowed by doubt. The route lay north. They went north because they were going north.

~

At times I looked about in sudden panic: someone was missing. Then I remembered: yes, someone was missing. Of her death I felt much the same as for the spitting girl. I felt nothing. I felt feelingless. I still knew her teasing, the grab of her hand, saw her gyrating conjurations, heard her masterful lip-farts to the thrust of her backside. She was present to me, but gone.

For some, grief is a cramp that never lets go. Such it was for my father, but I was never up to the task of mourning her. I would start to cry, but the tears were sucked up like ponds in drought. The only pain that seized me was the pain of abandonment. I was the victim. I tried not to blame her for her death, though soon we would need her desperately.

~

Frekka's journey crept into his drowsing head, then fluttered away in wind. His mother had told him the story before he knew any tongue, when his only words were *Mama* and *milk*. She told him the grisliest tales, thinking they left no scars, perhaps to purge her knotted heart. But again the tale came to him like a memory of the future.

His grandma played Frekka for the cats in the play they had never played. Now in his sight she reclaimed the role, freed from her wobbly knees to tread a landscape of dream. The scene had a shimmer to it, a dazzling glare, and the faces rippled like the moon on a lake. He saw her standing majestic, triumphant, firm. The play began. A rotund woman approached, waddling tunefully up the path. Her figure jiggled, her chestnut hair in burgeoning curls, her grin a red slash.

What seek you, woman?

Holy mother, your beauteous son is safe? Have all sworn? Earth, sea, and sky? Things highborn, baseborn, freeborn, newborn, all?

All. Except . . .

Gramma would see the deception, but Gramma was dead and someone else would be wearing the mask. The rotund lady's head nodded side to side like a doll, her voice a squirrel's chitter.

Yes, yes, the gods are such perfect housekeepers. Not like mortals, who always leave one corner unswept, one tuck untucked, so it screws it up for the Norns. Do it perfect, you're caught in their web. But the Queen of Gods, she's made them all swear, every wolf, every bug, every soul, except—

They spoke the words in unison, two ripple-faced foes in a deadly bedtime tale told to a suckling babe—

Except mistletoe.

When the boy was three or four, he had asked his grandma, "What's mistletoe?" He must have asked it because she must have said it. Why, he knew not. A kind of beggar plant, she said, that perched up high in the trees, round clumps that clung to the branches and sucked.

"Is it bad?"

"If you're the tree. Are you a tree?"

"No." He laughed.

"Then you're fine."

Now he heard the grinning lady's exultant squawk, like a jaybird winging away. *Mistletoe!* Old Gray-nag held her breath as the echo resounded and died. Then she spoke with the rigid conviction that springs from doubt. *One sprig of mistletoe. Young, spindly, clutching a high branch of oak. Only mistletoe.*

And what god might take a wisp of mistletoe, twist it into a shaft, a slender delicate shaft, and then, as mortals do, place it where deadliest: in the hands of the blind?

~

Some words are heard before they are spoken. Echoes of homilies, prayers, old farces we've played? The portly lady was Loghi, of course, I could tell by the grin. His words have cozened us from the day the first infant brothers sucked milk from their mother Eve. When I bit the head of the turnip-head doll, Loghi's words were the bite of the turnip. I longed for my grandma to reshape the tale, to shield the Shining One. But we had piled her grave heavy with stone. It held her fast.

~

Flashes of Bragi's waking dream came faster and faster, but never progressing. Frekka's journey, the mistletoe—the story led up to the brink but kept repeating. The Froggies . . . the ham-fisted bride . . . the wall . . . and promises promises promises. The sky was chill. Balthur stared down with merciless light, his blind brother Hod in a shiver beside him. Bragi yearned for the journey to end, not Gramma's way with a snort and a shudder, but with his mother's few simple words: *That's the way of it.* His tongue felt the gap to see if a new tooth was coming.

Mornings there had been frost on the trees and on Yesu's bristly mane. They were breaking camp when the boy saw the figure across the valley, a speck against the chalk ribbon of the road. He imagined he was seeing a dog or a tiny goat moving toward them as slowly as moonrise. It held his eyes as a snake holds the eyes of a new-hatched chick.

To the slow respiration of gods it approached. The landscape appeared to flatten and parch. Where there was oak, there was stone. Green turned gray, grassland was ash, and the sky went as white as a grandmother's eyes. To the boy it appeared that an arid hand was gently stroking the land into death. As the figure came within a league, it morphed to a rider on a mule. He should alert his parents to the rider's approach, but Papa was tending the donkey and

Mama was hearing his sister's murmur. No dream. A mosquito—up early—landed on Bragi's arm. No mosquitoes in dreams. He slapped it, scratched his elbow. "Mama—"

They saw the rider, waited. "Messenger," Asta mumbled.

"Who?" asked Bragi.

"Coming. There."

By noontide the messenger approached with his mule at a walk. As he neared, his odd garb made them wonder. The plumed helmet of Greek warrior in a mosaic the boy had seen, with shoulder gauntlets the shape of wings, long yellow tunic, and bearskin breeches fluffed out like the fuzz of a caterpillar. Boots too big for his skeletal legs. A specter escaped from some lost farce played in the ancient days? He drew up before them.

"The players, yes?" His voice was a soft breaking of wind. He presented a ratty face, protruding front teeth, and an angry lump on his upper lip that gave his mustache a hedgehog bristle. He might be Fish-eye's brother Rat-face. There might be a scatter of rat-faced fish-eyes over the land, all with razor noses and lifeless stares.

Mik nodded warily.

"Honored players . . ."

Rat-face delivered his message. His master, monarch of an unpronounceable realm which had conquered half the known world—the parts of it he knew of—requested their service. Their fame had spread afar. His master knew, the messenger said, that they possessed the faces of ancient gods and might bring them alive.

The bloodless gray countenance, pointy nose, whiskers splayed out in the latest rodent fashion, flat lips— His words oozed falsity, and the troupe listened with apprehension, but they listened. "They'll have food and midwives," Mik whispered to Asta. "We have no choice." Bragi stifled his urge to cry out a warning: it felt safer to stay a child.

They followed the messenger along the blighted road at a steady pace. Far distant, blue mountains, white peaks—a fortification for gods.

∾

This may have been the moment when we crossed a bridge between worlds. In dreams we hear the rush of water beneath and hurry to set our feet on the other bank. We step from the fluster of childhood to senility's embrace with barely a breath between. Why then should we not step into the realm of the gods who lay patiently curled, nose nestled to nose, in our wickerwork? Over the afternoon dark clouds began to gather above us, like the vast throng of cats who gathered to eye the play we never played.

—XXV—
Ragnarok

Through the day's journey the distant blue peaks stood changeless. They stayed distant until so near that they were overwhelming. A wind rose up like mountain breath, driving clouds thick with a murky future scudding across the sky. Yet in the plain the drifts of dust were settled, still as death, inert.

"How does he speak our tongue?" Mik whispered to Asta.

"I speak all tongues," Rat-face called out.

He saw the players' disquiet and, smoothing his bristle of lip, sought to reassure them. His lord was Christian, he said, and therefore rejected the old gods as demons. Yet he honored those false divinities for their services over the aeons, slaying their enemies, bringing conquest and song. The potentate desired the players to present a pageant to celebrate the gods of his fathers and allow them a graceful departure. "He desires that you play the Ragnarok."

A gasp from Asta. "The death of the gods?"

"A curious tale," said Rat-face, brother to Fish-eye, "not unlike our sacred text of the Revelation, envisioning the end of Time. And certainly preordained."

Though cheerful, the envoy's manner did not inspire trust—an odd glimmer in his eye, his nervous fingering of the lump on his lip, the steel glint of his grin. They could only hope for the best, or at least not the worst. One never knew where a story, once begun, might lead. "Could be they'll stop pestering us," said Asta, meaning the gods. "We've shown respect."

"Might we not better play the life of a Christian saint?" Mik asked the envoy. No reply. "The wedding of mighty Teorr? Or perhaps the farce of a husband who buys a dead donkey? We excel at comedy." Not a twitch. But who had told him of the players? Perhaps, like the cats, the envoy was only debris that followed their trek.

By late afternoon they were brought to the hub of the ruler's domain. As with the chieftain's settlement it was primitive, encircled by an earthwork embankment and timber stockade, its crude entrance barred by a wooden gate. "Our hill fort," the bristly envoy announced, though the hill was no more than a modest rise in the plain.

They passed through the gate. Ahead they saw the same daub-and-wattle huts interspersed by a half dozen long houses built of logs. A squad of soldiers passed at a jog-trot. Two old women with besoms swept dust from the dust. A cur chained to a stake snarled at a naked toddler. The stockade sheltered soldiers, servants, craftsmen and their families, with scattered farmsteads beyond. The players saw little of note.

"You wonder at our opulence," said Rat-face.

Mik nodded. "It takes our breath away."

The boy felt his eyes misbehaving. Overhead the murky clouds had cleared away, and the afternoon sky held the sun, the moon and sprinkles of stars. All times of the day were overlaid—brightness to dusk to sunset to night to noon—as liquid as the sea. He heard a burble like porridge at a boil, a crackle like pinecones afire. Lush colors washed the sky and shifted with every breath.

Reality? Delusion? As they came around a squat long house the boy saw the mighty wall. The wall from the bedtime story, the stallion's great stone wall. Topping the height of six men, with blocks of white marble dressed to fit seamlessly, it extended in either direction as far as he could see. Turreted along its rim, armed men in silhouette, it was witness to gods. A massive marble arch framed high oaken doors that cranked open with a grind of winches, clatter of chains and obscenities from the guards, devouring all who entered.

With his next breath he saw architectures for which he had no name: celestial spires, glittering temples, boulevards interwoven with crimson gutters and yellow walls, canals of indigo—an iridescent city whose gilded domes reached up to a dead white sky of sun, moon and stars whiter still. He was seized with dread. He saw that his parents saw it. It was real.

Dumfounded, the players looked about them. "Where are we?" Mik stammered.

"Asgard." Rat-face pronounced the name. The realm of the gods, the stories said, replete with shrines where the gods might worship themselves. The guide turned his leathery face to them with a flash of emerald eyes and led them deeper into the waking dream. Doors opened ahead: oaken doors, bronze doors, portals of silver and gold. Somewhere the donkey and cart were led away. At the end of endless colonnades they caught glimpses at times of the squat log hovels, the women sweeping, the toddler and snarling cur, pigs in mud gutters—contradictory realities folded into one another like the sighted and sightless brothers. The visions flared and dimmed like fireflies, overwhelmed by the glaring whiteness.

They were silent as they traversed the spiderweb avenues of divinity. They came at last to a massive bronze door inset with fiery jewels, adorned with deep-hewn faces and gouged by runes. Unseen hands swung it open. At their guide's commanding gesture they entered the throat of a giant—a marbled hall whose walls were alive with myriad blurs. Now the adults followed Rat-face as if there were nothing surprising about the doors or the walls or the emerald eyes. He should ask Gramma, but Gramma was gone.

At the far end of the hall—a day's journey on hands and knees—a gaunt figure sat enthroned on a high-backed chair. His face was in shadow, his bald head glowed in the torchlight. A low growl filled the vastness—distant thunder, the movement of layers of rock, or a monstrous grumbling gut. A sweaty stench seeped from the marble walls, an odor of heroes dying and dead. An albino raven flitted above them an instant and vanished.

Then a shiver. The boy beheld Old One-eye, his black socket wide, his good eye, like Ludd's, slanted away from his nose—to see the past catching up or avoid the onrushing future? Bragi stared straight ahead as long faces moved at the blur-edge of sight. He was starting to grow accustomed to astonishment.

"Pause here," said Rat-face. He approached the throne—close now—and spoke in low rasps. The potentate gave a nasal grunt. The boy caught the glint of an eye. The envoy nodded, returned to the group, and ushered them out of the presence. Unseen hands shut the door.

"Just as well we didn't attract his notice," Asta whispered to Mik. Bragi recalled the day they butchered the pig last autumn. The pig was unblinking until it felt the knife.

They stepped into an antechamber where Rat-face explained arrangements, smiling benignly. They would play in a field outside the walls with spectators seated on the earthen slant. A wooden frame hung with leather had been erected as backdrop and painted in oxblood with sacred runes, which would surely assure success. The populace from the city, from leagues around, from all the Nine Realms, would assemble to view the pageant.

"How many?"

"Vast numbers."

"Will they hear?"

"Cannot gods be heard?"

"But gods— We're not gods. We're simple players. We play to amuse."

"Your viewers will be amused. By royal decree."

A pregnant pause and the envoy spoke further. He felt compelled to tell them that the field on which they would play was the killing field. Felons, captives, beasts brought to slaughter, all met their fate on that field. No killing in Asgard, but at a convenient distance. "This affords you great honor," the envoy said, "as you play on sacred grounds."

Mik could hardly afford to object, yet the prospect was unpromising. "But gods—"

"We desire to die."

Rat-face tilted his head in a meditative pose. His face dissolved by slow degrees. The grin held steady, and now he showed the features of the leathery mask of Loghi: long jaw, razor nose, the gemstone eyes. The players faced a god. For a breath, and then the boy saw it was only illusion. He was seeing Loghi in all things, the figures, the stones, the clouds. His parents showed no alarm.

"To die?" Mik whispered.

From here, my liege, my tale rides a tide of improbability. I write only as I recall it. I was six and was told I had a vivid imagination.

How to imagine a world snuffing out its own existence? Could it be that the gods truly desired to die? Mayhap they longed for sympathy, that they might be worshipped more fervently if dead. Mayhap it made for a better story, a tale that would make lots of money. Mayhap a stratagem to confuse their foes or any excuse for a party or perpetual weariness unto death. Mayhap they were moved by the same primordial force that moves a sow to eat her litter.

This I could not comprehend, though in later years it came clearer. The gods had grown fat on fear. Whatever their powers, none sufficed. The apples of youth, impregnable walls, the merciless hammer killing and killing, all the promises—nothing sufficed to halt the capering specter of doom. Only in death could they be secure.

I could hear the clatter-beak Norns in a tale my mother told before I was old enough to hear it. We might have striven harder to avoid our fate, but it would come. However we altered our journey's route, yet it would come. Plant a seed, it sprouts. The seed makes the olive, the turnip, the baby sister—mayhap the deed? The tales always ended with somebody dead.

The envoy's words were absurd. He was claiming godhood, yet mortals could no more believe it than if he had claimed to be a donkey. Bragi longed for his father to make it into a joke. Those were the lines of a lout who bought a dead donkey, who squandered three wishes, who entrusted his fate to a fart dance. But Mik was mute in the face of omnipotent madness.

Asta raised her voice. "Honored sir, you should be aware: our masks are not those of the Norse gods. They were my father's legacy, but their origin was surely to the south. Some lost Roman who wandered beyond his—"

"They will serve." The sole imperative, Rat-face said, was that Balthur the Shining One should die. The All-father could no longer suffer night horrors regarding his son. He must be spared the agony, even at the ultimate cost. "There are many variants to the tale. You may play it as you will. We shall gather at daybreak."

Mik stammered. "But would it not be . . . sacrilege?"

Rat-face repressed a smirk at his simple innocence. "You have too much respect for the gods. True, we shaped humans as slaves to worship us. Noble achievement! Creatures who roll their imbecile eyes, croak out madness, teach their children to lie, to lie, to lie, and believe each ludicrous pig-squeal. To praise the gods is to pour sweet syrup on rotten meat." His sweeping gesture made his helm plumage waggle. "You see, I have spoken sacrilege. No consequence. You must trust."

He led them outside the walls to view the playing field of low stubble baked by drought. "Better for discus throwing," Mik muttered to Asta. A waist-high platform six paces wide was backed by a leather screen with huge scrawls of dry clotted blood: a magical invocation, they surmised.

"Nice view," said Ludd with faint cheer.

Bragi was years older now, though still only six, and he understood: failure was certain. The field was impossible for a stage. The viewers, under coercion, would watch with murderous eyes. Few words would be heard in the open air, and no farce routines could work to fill out the time. They would be playing tragedy.

They stood silent with downcast eyes. They were not asked to agree: it was assumed. No escape from Sir Flop, and how could they trust Rat-face's glint-eyed assurances? Yet the boy had often seen his parents in the depths of despair—never for more than an eye-blink. A challenge indeed, but they had played Teorr's wedding to Sir Paddo's delight, and a story was only a story. They would trust to the masks and depend on the gods to play out the death of the gods. On that they might rely. Edra's frequent comment: the gods were never known for their common sense.

Rat-face proposed a generous fee, assured them the service of midwives if needed, and promised safe passage thereafter. He escorted them to sleeping quarters. They passed through the vast vaulted chamber, lost sight of the high marble walls, and around the corner of a towering temple they found themselves entering a humble long house. They were shown bunks along one wall where they might find repose. A dozen or so dim figures stood staring. Rat-face disappeared.

Two wall torches tickled the darkness. The troupe were offered food and sat to be served by an elderly bearded slave whose eyes were clouded like Edra's. The dinner was hearty: a pungent meat, boiled roots of a testy plant, and great drinking horns of beer. Despite their anxiety—or because of it—they were jovial as they feasted. Whenever one of them tried to bend the talk to the morrow—what would they do for the play? how should they prepare?—someone interrupted. Mik would make the snuffles of a boar, Asta would sing a ballad, or Ludd would twist his face into wormy squiggles, his specialty when all else failed.

The smoky long house sheltered twenty or thirty souls, and a half dozen were clustered at the fire pit in the center. They viewed the strangers with dull suspicion, resisting intrusion into the boredom of their lives. At first the little band's merriment attracted hostility, but soon curiosity. One burly soldier laughed at Ludd's grimace, and Mik picked up the cue, reaching out playfully to strangle the bony wall-eye into myriad grotesqueries. The soldier raised his drinking horn to toast them, splashed beer into his face, and all boundaries dissolved in laughter.

Bragi knew that these humble figures were gods. As below, so above: the gods had their ranks. These were the flunkies: the scullery gods, stable-boy gods, soldier gods, handymen, gardeners, char-women, janitors, blacksmiths, all required to make life livable to their masters. Being a god didn't mean you were anything special. It only meant you were stuck there forever.

The players had no speech in common with their comrades, so they talked by signs. The absence of words brought a closer bond-ing, even as they hooted and hissed and laughed and flung epithets, and at times the clamor subsided to silence and the silence brought simple kinship.

More figures appeared in the long house. From time to time someone would launch into a merry tale—of love, of heroics, or of gelding pigs—and all would listen raptly, whether or not they remotely grasped the words. The tales—proclaimed with eloquent gesticulations—became more personal. Mik told of the death of his mother. Ludd spoke of having lied, having led his friends northward, not wanting to lose the life he'd found in laughter. Again Mik made as if to strangle him, and the merriment rose to mountainous heights. Only Asta was silent, her eyes half closed, awaiting nativity.

Bragi drank too much beer. As mirth became hysteria and the torches flared up in a jig he tried to stay awake, but sleep rolled over him the way a sow might roll on her litter. Vaguely he heard two watchmen arrive to quell the song and the shouting, and then, before the sun had risen, before the tribe gathered, before the wicker trunk opened and the masks were tied in place, the boy saw his own distant eyes widen to view the Apocalypse.

◞◟

Apocalypse. In my churchly schooling I was told the word signi-fied revelation, enlightenment, scales falling from the eyes, keen sight through clouded glass, and at last the luminous vision of almighty God. But its prologue was four dread horsemen bearing pestilence, war, famine and death—though readings might differ.

All change brings about the death of the old. For the better, one hopes, though the outcome is never assured. The murderous Saul, at a stroke of lightning, was converted into the sainted Paul, but he might well have risen more fiendish. As I sat my wife's deathwatch

I witnessed an apocalypse: a destruction and revelation, but I saw it not as the end of history but as a daily act, as common as each day's urinations, shared with donkeys and cats, males, females, nobility and clergy, all. Each day a death, each day rebirth.

I will not wager the fate of my soul on the narrative that follows. It may have been only the consequence of too much beer. Or a fabrication in my subsequent forty years, a whim to round out the story and end it with a bang. It may be delusion wrought by the Prince of Darkness or the glimpse of a play that would make us money. Still, at the time, it was real.

—XXVI—
Nativity

Dawn. Behind the makeshift tiring-house the players donned their masks. Bragi wore the mask of the singer of songs, though he had never sung a whole song and possibly never would. At the outset they knew that Mik would play Wadan, Asta Frekka, Ludd a tall gawky Loghi, and Bragi would stand as the songless songster. Other roles would have to be played by cats or crows.

They had not rehearsed. "Just play what comes," said Mik. Nothing more to be said. His mother, distracted, left open the wickerwork hamper. The boy saw the other faces nested within, heard their heartbeat, felt them beginning to breathe, awaiting their cue. Amidst thickening clouds the sun rose like a seabird, stopped at its height. Suddenly noon. The time was now.

The players stepped into view, but Bragi held back for a final peek. The throng spread up the embankment, across the fields, over the plain as far as he could see. Their faces were every color, every age, commingled like seeds in the wind. A graybeard with infantile eyes. Men set to kill or caress. Women plumped up with the juice of life or crouching like beaten dogs. Children already wrinkled, senile, scarred. Soldiers with shrunken hearts and tearful eyes, blind beggars clearing their throats, whores seeking trade without hoping to find it.

The choppy red-bearded sailor, the gimpy barmaid, the one-armed warrior, the albino priest, bearskin barbarians, blood-eyed pirates, legions of cats, old Sir Paddo clapping, his gaunt wife with hands to her heart. Fish-eye and Rat-face, a weeping Prince Helmut, and a mean little boy that Bragi once punched in the nose for reasons he couldn't recall. It might be the entire realm of mortals gathered to witness a singular entertainment: the death of Light.

Not only mortals. Bragi saw the flunky gods from the night before. He saw throngs of Froggies, Dwarves, the Wood Elves and Mountain Elves, the myriad many-eyed multi-pronged creatures who curled in the shadows. Nine Realms gathered in stark silence. He caught a sharp breath. On the rise where the city had been—no city now—he saw the tree.

A lone sapling, barely the height of a six-year-old, it shook in the breeze, its leaves like delicate shivering hands. Then the tree began to age. Over a sluggish trek of time the boy saw it thicken, stretch upward, and with a prodigious lurch its fingers pierced the sky, clutching at clouds. All gaped. Its bark bore scars deeper than Gramma's memory. Its trunk swelled the width of a mountain range. Its leaves were huge flat palmates, long ovals, silvery green, red, yellowed, some in the shape of birds. Bragi heard the wind speak the name he knew from a dream. *Yggdrasill.* The World Tree loomed above the stupefied multitude.

The terrified Ludd, masked as Grim-grin, stood at the edge of the stage. The apprentice was now protagonist. He heard himself whisper. He couldn't understand it. He whispered louder. "Unmaker," he heard himself say. "That's me."

The boy stumbled onto the stage. The throng was too vast for speech, so the players played in extravagantly precise gestures that drew viewers into comprehension. They spoke only in whispers, cuing each other to play an elegant pantomime dance to the mountains beyond. Of a sudden their voices burst forth in a song of praise to the fiery god in the sky—

—As Balthur emerged from the clouds, face brighter than human eyes could bear. Asta's Frekka mimed the mother's joy in her son's immortality as other masked phantoms emerged from the glare to cluster beneath the God of Light, toasting his health with the heady liquor of bees. All realms cheered him—gods, mortals and beasties, elves and bugbears, all. The players spoke in stage whispers to cue the action—

Shine, my son, we are past the dreams. We dance.

I'm tossing a blackberry at you, love. Tell me if you feel it.

I'll whack you with an apple!

The merriment was as infectious as the laughter of yesternight. The players were past caring who their fellows were, the gathering masks who swarmed the stage. They had simply to play the story to its end. A throng of gods danced in a widening arc under the blaze of Balthur. Playfully they tossed up pebbles, berries, trinkets at him to herald his immunity. Their antic missiles bounced off harmlessly— the tickle of rain as it spattered the sun.

The phantoms danced in sedate celebration as the sky around the fiery Balthur began to dim. They showered him with heavier missiles: a stone, a thighbone, the horn of a bull. The god was struck by a blade that melted and a spear that flew to splinters. And now a clownish Teorr heaved his mighty hammer. Upward, upward, splitting the clouds, it glanced off with a resonant *ping*.

My son has conquered death!

Asta pronounced the line in a voice that trumpeted over the hills, and merriment swept the multitude. The boy in the mask of Bragi saw blind Hod, brother to Light, at the edge of the make-believe. A tall bony Loghi approached him. Under the tumult the boy could hear words.

Why not join the sport? Honor your brother? Celebrate Light?

No eyes.

The Grinner thumped the blind god's chest. *Share our joy.* He brought forth a bow. *Bend this bow.* He notched an arrow. *Send forth a dart of harmless mistletoe.*

Blind Hod raised the bow. Loghi steadied his aim. The dart was released. A mistletoe shaft twirled its spiral into the Sun God's heart. Balthur began his plummet.

~

I heard a hurricane gasp from the throng, and at that breath my mother's water broke. A cramp curled her forward, then she forced herself up to queenly stature. What happened could not be happening. Some future day, when the Christian god despaired of his whim, the stars might fall and the world go dark, but not before harvest, not before next market fair, not before my sister came free.

~

A beardless youth hurtled onto the stage crying, "Balthur! Balthur!" Loghi's voice seeped through his razor grin—

No longer here. I would sing his praise, but alas, he's belly-up.

A woman, convulsed with rage, stumbled free of the throng. "Have you no soul?" she cried. Loghi's words slithered out—

I do. The soul of your world. You, ruled by madmen? You, violators of children? Are your bowels evil for reducing your food to excrement?

Bragi pulled to get free of his mask, but it clung like the dogs who bite onto the noses of bears. He looked about for a leg to wrap onto. Humankind brayed like a vast herd of donkeys and scattered like panicky chickens. The sky filled with squawks. A woman slapped her child. A bullish soldier tore open his armor, ripped flesh, splintered ribs, seized his heart and threw it throbbing onto the beaten ground. Clouds raced over the sky, swallowing birds the way birds swallowed flies.

Balthur's fall spanned a world of waiting. Not until midafternoon did the cheek of the God of Light strike earth. Frekka sank to her knees. The boy heard a scream. His mother was screaming. No, his mother was playing the mother of Balthur seeing her son struck dead. End of the play, and they'd start up the music, take a bow, eat dinner, drink beer, and sleep what Gramma called the sleep of the dead. But his mother was screaming for real.

She lay on her back, fumbling at her mask in the throes of birthing the baby. The water had broken the moment the shaft found its mark, and her pangs spanned the hours of the Shining One's fall. Her cries were the whine of a dog, the snort of a sow, a raptor's screech. She clawed at her dress as if to get naked, to be only a cat bearing kittens or a cow in a hidden thicket. Mik shoved to get to her, but the mob was thick. The boy couldn't move his feet. He began singing a song of nonsensical words, yelping it out in sobs.

The fallen Balthur lay on his face, a guttering candle, flickering. A black swirl ascended the western sky, rushing over the hills, a swarm of black flies coalescing into the hooded specter of Hel. A hand pressed the hills into silence. The specter spoke in the voices of all she had ever consumed, a discordant chorus of dead—

I come for the god snuffed out.

Balthur's corpse sagged in the clasp of Loghi's daughter. One-eye rose in his royal pavilion—a maskless One-eye whose sockets ran blood—and begged for his son—

Balthur belongs to the Living Realms. From his face all souls take blessing. All will die in darkness.

Then I shall feed profusely.

Even Hel will starve without the living to feed her.

The drone of the flies subsided. For a moment she tried to fathom the death of death, and then her voices rose—

I may spare him if tears in a flood sweep him free. If a single creature holds back grief, then I must have him.

A keening swept upward. From the realm of the Mortals, they cried. From the realm of the Strange Ones, they cried. From the realm of the Wood Elves, River Elves, deep realm of the Dwarves, all cried for Balthur. From the realm of the Gods— All turned to Loghi.

Loghi wept.

〜

My vigilant liege, you rightly question why the villainous trickster should weep? Was it not he who seeded the madness, fed the panic, tipped the gods over the brink? Should he not erupt in derisive laughter, claiming sole title: Unmaker?

Yet great villains are inconstant. In the silence, Loghi—or Ludd playing Loghi—raised his hand to his mask and peeled off his grin. He wore another face: a storm of rage. He peeled it off: the face was red-nosed, ludicrous, deformed. He peeled it off, peeled off another, peeled more, and his last face was eggshell, unborn.

It was this eyeless face that wept. Mayhap in memory of the child he had been, ten thousand years foregone. Of the salt womb that spewed him out. Of the spit of his copulations, male to female, female to male, human to horse. Mayhap he wept in remembrance of Light.

~

The corpse hung limp in the grasp of Hel. The hills swarmed with uncounted souls weeping out a flood that Balthur might be restored. All creatures wept, even the eyeless herbs whose tears were sap or slime, except only—

Rona.

Bragi saw her. An ancient female—dark-skinned, near-naked, leathery skeleton and withered dugs draped in a threadbare shawl— stepped out from the afternoon. Her eyes were tiny sparks in deep sockets, her mouth a fierce grimace. Her fingers made an endless counting and counting and counting. Her voice was the delicate trill of a reed—

Oh I'd weep if I could. I've did it a lot. My son, one son, another, all gone. Sorry, but my son died in six thirty-two, three four five, and he died in ten sixty-six, seventeen sixty-three, four five six. Same thing, eighteen fourteen, sixty-one, nineteen fifteen, lot of 'em then, I'm sorry, I am. One two three, and he died in nineteen forty-four, fifty-one, two thousand three and four and five and six, O Christ! And he keeps on dying, dying, he just won't stop, the sorry bastard, he won't!

She choked out a grunt and spat, hawked sputum and spat, spat again, then pulled her rags about her.

So all my tears are gone. Got no more. Can't cry. I don't wish death on another soul, but I'm all emptied out. No memories left. No flagon of grief from the grief store. Sorry. Nothing. Never.

Balthur melted into Hel's embrace, faded into the hum of flies. The sky held a grayness reflecting the heat of the multitude.

The rest of the play was brief: Loghi fled, he flew, he swam. The raging gods wove a net, he was caught, nailed to a rock, and above him a viper's venom drooled down to burn his face into a scream. Ludd was lost in the Loghi mask, but now he scrambled, frantic to flee. The boy had to laugh: even in terror the bony man was all elbows and prancing knees as he scuttled away to the hills, clinging to words he knew as a boy. "Fresh fish! Eels, herring, sturgeon! Big fish, little fish, bluefish, blackfish, yellowfish! Fish! Fish! Fish!"

In the fragments of light across the turbulent field, the boy saw his mother. She struggled to hold to her goddess role, crying out lines in a tongue not spoken since girlhood. Mik knelt beside her, stroking her as he struggled to rip away the mask fused into his face.

The pains came sharper. She fell, stretching lengthwise, arching her back, then folding into a wad, struggling up to her elbows and knees, squatting, then seized by a spasm, curling onto her face. She writhed to expel this demon who tore at her vitals, clawing to be set free. The tide rolled in.

Earth pitched into epileptic jerks like a rat in the jaws of a mastiff. Humans fled over the barren field driven by merciless wind, pursued by the raging wolf Fenris cracking their bones in his jaws. Ham-fist grasped the great serpent Jormungand and killed it, killed it again, killed it limp as a snot-rag and still it would not die. Its spittle sprayed his piggish eyes and he fell in the dirt, blubbering.

The boy saw dying gods sprouting up from the earth. He saw the scab-covered sky sucking chill from the rocks. He saw the multitude flailing blindly, running in circles, raising their pleading hands. Teorr's unmastered hammer went rampant, killing without aim. *Crack of rocks, gush of blood. Day of ax, day of wolf, day of sleet, day of steel—*

The Norns cackled in merriment, converged around the writhing woman as if the contractions were sucking them dry. A rift split the plain, sinkholes gaped, and myriads fell into the void, squeaking like tiny birds. Stars exploded in cities, fires outracing the wind, the world scorched bare by a massive updraft of rage. Old One-eye howled out his joy: nothing more to fear.

～

Did I see what I saw or did I imagine it? If the sun were gone from the sky, how could I see? It was all babble, frog belch, clack of beaks, guttural hoots. I tried to tear open my eyes, though I knew it was only a play. Did I see it or only imagine?

Years before, as I slipped into sleep, my mother had told me the tale of the Ragnarok, a story vaguely remembered from a time when all was a blur, a story that never existed except in the chant of her voice. A voice now shrieking, howling, braying in birth—

—And not until now did I feel how deeply the claws raked my face. I carry the marks. No mirror would show it. Not until now, as I write it, do I feel the scarring, impalement, the dance in midair. I was only six, but older than many already dead.

⁓

To the boy all moved in stupor. The Earth tipped aslant and he clung to whatever held fast lest he plunge to the stars. His heartbeat slowed to the pace of winter. Raptors circled and floated down, alighted on random cadavers. A trumpet sounded long and high, and dead warriors drifted over the crest of the hills like clouds streaming red at sunset. A dazed goddess staggered about in a swirl of dust offering apples.

The mother crouched panting. In labor with Bragi she had known the hardest work she had ever done, but the task was plain. She had never been so sure of her craftsmanship. Billions of women had done it and now was her time. Wolves howling for blood were a minor distraction and could wait their turn: she had work to do. But this labor was otherwise. Her girl was a maenad ripping the gates of birth. The tide surged again.

The boy watched the playing out of the play. Stories change at each telling, and he might have changed its course. He might have reached out to touch the spitting girl, taken her hand, cradled her turnip doll. He might have kissed his father's hand when he buried Gramma. He might have named the horse. He might have loved his mother. He might still sing to his sister as she crowned.

But he knew the story had sprung from elemental fear: fear borne by the howls of wolves, suffusing the Shining One's dreams, fear that built the wall and secured the armaments, that spurred the killing and killing and killing. A fear that wrung all the tears that an ancient mother could cry. They had carried the fear in their hamper. It enlivened their wildest farces: the curse of facing mortality.

The boy turned from the chaos to the tree. Yggdrasill's limbs were above the clouds, its rugged trunk blotting the peaks. Midway up, etched against rutted bark, he saw a figure—naked, blood-streaked, dangling from one arm held by a spike through the wrist. From limitless distance, the boy saw the eyes of the dangling man: one eye ablaze, the other black as a shithole. From the barren socket a flutter of wings, and a dazzling white bird took the sky. The boy stroked the tiny worm on his crucifix. To seek wisdom, his mother said, they nailed themselves to trees.

From the core of the tree a glow emerged. It cast a brilliance over the surly murk of the sky. The radiance was flame. The tree was afire. A great wind swirled about it lifting an echo across the Realms, Wadan's last murmured words to his son: *Live . . . Breathe . . . Be . . . Survive . . . Endure . . .* Words in an alien tongue.

It must be the end of the play. Bragi's mask widened its lips to sing an unknown song, but he heard the wails of a newborn. His sister was singing it for him.

—XXVII—
Homeward

Stories continue past their ends, however we try to restrain them. As I approach the last words of this narrative, my liege, allow me to pile a stone cairn atop the grave of this tale, lest scavengers devour it.

At dawn, there was dawn. The death of the God of Light did not forestall the sunrise upon the cares of the day. I unsnarled my blanket, stretched on my sleeping mat, narrowed my lids and faced the morning sky. Open field. No city, no stage on the slope of the hill, no legions of dead, only Yesu, still hitched to the cart, grazing a parched patch of grass. I saw no wickerwork casket, no costume duffels or cookware. It had flown or was filched in the night.

My father stood checking the money pouch beneath his belt, but no one came forth from the arid plain to pay the promised fee. We gathered our gear without a word. The gods were gone. I sat alone in the morning chill—

—With the troupe's new player nursing at Asta's breast. Later I knew that my mother came near bleeding to death, but the screams that had pierced me were all in my head: she was a Northman's child.

My fledgling sister was frail but ravenous for life, fiercely sucking the milk of a future. Haunted by our nameless dead horse, I was driven to name my sister before she died, though she had no intention of doing so. My parents rejected the names I proposed and named her Maria, perhaps to curry the favor of monks who might give us lodging on our journey homeward. They worshipped a goddess Maria, my father told me. No matter: my sister always had her own secret name that none of us ever knew. I called her Kitty, and when she was older I called her Kat.

We ate some leftover bread, packed up, found a road and followed it. None sought to plumb yesterday's substance or interrogate its aftermath. A world died, a world was born: it happens every day. No divine interventions, eruptions or mistletoe twigs are needed to wipe out the past. The past is past. It may die with a blast of thunder that shatters mountains or with a granny's soft gasp. It may gouge its curse in our bones or purge us clean. Though masked as a god of song I had been unaware that birth and death sing in harmony.

There were only my father, my mother, my turnip-doll sister and I. Ludd had disappeared. For many years I surmised that he had fallen into a sinkhole or gone back to selling fish. Then I spoke to a trader who made the long trek from the north-of-the-north to civilized lands, and he told of a famous bard: a tall bony man who could make the silliest faces, who sang of the ancient gods, who told tales of three wishes, dead donkeys, tales of Apocalypse, and more. The trader described him unmistakably: the funniest, loneliest man alive.

Our sole imperative was to survive the journey home. There were days of hunger and cold when there seemed no end to the trek, unless the end to which all roads lead. There were nights I heard my father mumbling low curses, my mother crying to die, and times when I wanted to smother my yowling sister. But always came the next day's dawn, and we rose to do our business, eat our fare, harness the donkey and move onward. No thought to direction, only to moving onward.

Our money ran out. Mik found odd jobs on farmsteads, or in villages on market days he and Asta would play the pipes and tambour or lute, and some gave them coins. Busking, he called it, though she said, "They give us money for pretending not to be beggars."

And once we encountered a robber, but he was so weak from hunger that my father readily beat him up. I got in a few kicks, and then Mama yelled to stop it. Mik took his knife away. "No offense, friend, but you'd do better as a beggar than a robber." We gave him some bread and dried fish.

At a port town, our provisions thin, we had to sell Yesu. "We need the money," Mama told me in that cold *Northmen-don't-cry* voice, her only tool of survival. I couldn't help it: I hid myself in a public latrine and wept. She got a good price for the creature and the cart.

Of course I loved her—tried to, at least—but she never lost her sharpness. Mayhap an inheritance from her father, the raider of coastlines, or mayhap from being sucked dry by her brood and the work of the day. Several times on the journey home she came near death, kept alive only, I believe, by the need to nourish my sister. I loved to see Kitty suckle, but I never again heard my parents, Mik and Asta, snuffling in the night.

Some days to the south, stopping for provisions, we heard a report of our last performance. It was said on good authority that a petty lord had summoned magicians who conjured a great working, an earthquake birthing demons, erasing his hilltop hamlet. "Good luck we missed it," said Mik to the publican who told of it. The tale had made passage between the worlds.

In this time I grieved for my grandmother Edra more acutely than when she died. So much had transpired, and I wanted to hear what she thought of it all, but she spoke not a word. One day it occurred to me, as I ate a dried fig, that she never would. I longed to hear the tease in her voice and feel the sinewy stroke of her hand. At a dawn of frost-covered trees I thought of her saying once, "Look at the trees!" I stood looking at trees.

The last two moons of our journey home were by water. The stream, we were told, would widen toward the south and surge to the sea. Mik secured us riverboat passage by working crew, Asta in the galley, and we came at last to a coastal town sprawling over a scatter of islands. There we found passage on a slow barge, and along with Mik they took me on as a cabin boy, though I was far too young. Even in coastal waters the captain got seasick whenever he wasn't drunk, so my task was mostly to clean up the captain.

Our last stage of homecoming, from the coast to our village, was arduous. We begged rides from farmers with wagons of hay or loads of manure. We might sit all day at the side of the road, waiting in vain, or hike onward when Mama could manage. We were thankful for minimal gear. Perhaps the wickerwork casket was stolen, fated to carry its curse to other towns, other tribes, other centuries. Or perhaps it was burnt to ash.

On our arrival home our neighbors swarmed about us, eager for news. My father was skilled in telling the most toothsome lies to feed the peasants' deep hunger—which they themselves would deny—to know the world that lay beyond. I was spared the hair-ruffles of *How he's grown!* by their wonderment at the baby. Until then, while I liked her, I had never seen her utility.

The neighbor entrusted to tend our produce and livestock had died in a brief epidemic, so the farm was replete with brambles, and our hut was rife with wild pigs. Mik drove them out, killing two with an ax, and we hosted a sumptuous feast in our stinking hovel. We were told of births and weddings and murders, and the Cristers among us reported sure signs that the Second Coming was nigh, as it had been for years beyond count.

Nothing for us at home except the stink. I knew without being told that our touring was at an end. My grandmother gone, two children to feed, and hostile rumors in our wake, we faced a bleak future. Our bit of land was a freehold, so Papa sold it, and with our gleanings we took passage to the great city. The sun seemed amenable to rising in the east, so we left at dawn.

For myself, it was another journey to bafflement. The city was a vast pottage of every race and tongue and faith, though of course Yesu Christ was the god of the day. We found humble lodging, a single room above a baker's shop. Asta took in laundry when she was able and gave lessons on the lute. Mik scored a job scooping horseshit out of the street. I practiced my pee and parsnips lines just in case, and when older worked in a tile factory.

The moons passed. Papa did day labor and pickup work as a scribe, sometimes played his pipes in taverns, and then by accident found a new calling. One night, at the drinkery where he played, he saw a novel entertainment. A screen of white linen a double arm's length in width was illumined by candles behind. Rapid taps of a woodblock, and a tiny fat man appeared—a tiny fat man's shadow— dancing on the screen, shouting in some odd tongue from the rivers of the East. When the second figure danced on, a tiny cursing female, there was no mistaking it: a loving husband and wife in a screaming fit, the ancient font of comedy. There followed a soldier, a priest, a whore, two snarling dogs and a monstrous devil with glowing eyes. No one understood a word or needed to: the laughter was tumultuous.

And in my father the urge, the obsession, the lust to tell stories was unstoppable. It would need only hands and candles and spirit, and shadows were easily carried from inn to inn. He accosted the shadow-master—an old Turkik coot who spoke only a dozen words of our tongue—and managed to say what he wanted. Returning home he announced that, though in his mid-fifties, he was now apprentice to shadowplay.

One pays for a knowledge of craft. The old Turk's price was steep, and Mik took on heavy labor to make ends meet. But he learned quickly and soon became partner to Belgistos, the old man's unpronounceable name. At times I helped with shows, but for me they held little appeal. I had tasted the sweet fear of stepping before the multitude and squeaking out my lines. With a screen between myself and the mob, I missed that savory terror.

For my sister it was otherwise. From the time she grew past a toddler she was at the shows. They would dress her as a boy so as not to cause discord. About her tenth year, when the old man at last succumbed to being old, she began to perform in the shadow plays—a girl playing a boy playing merchants and drunkards and whores and vultures and demons. But that would be her tale, not mine.

I see her rarely. When you send me to the city on business, three days' journey, I visit her. We speak little—our kinship best felt in silent presence—though once, at the time we buried our father, she was oddly talkative. "Storytelling is a heartbeat," she said. "Bards tell stories, soldiers tell stories, and men tell lies to their wives. We players are only the echoes. I play the shadows of shadows." My father was speaking through her, pronouncing his epitaph.

My parents died eight and nine years ago, of natural causes. I believe they lived good lives and knew it at the end. My father Mikolaus Mikopolous suffered great pain, but you could barely see it. He was a fountain of jokes, and when he became unable to speak he would make his *who-farted* face, his *befuddled-duck* face, his *crosseyed-saint* face, and we couldn't help but laugh. In his last breath he launched into a stream of gibberish from a dozen wild farces he'd played, went into a fit of coughing, and stopped being alive.

My mother Asta Gerdsdatter grew faint soon after and withered away. In her last days she would rub at the scar on her thumb, the senseless blood oath she had sought to obey. She stands before me when I reprove myself for a failing, but also in those rare times when I feel gratitude for the simple breath of life.

I thought I had spent all my tears at the death of my wife and infant daughter, yet I cried three days for each of my parents, and then, as the ancient mother said in the play, all my tears were gone.

Over the years I have had thoughts of Rona—the little spitting girl, the raped adolescent, the prophetess, the crone without tears—and what our lives might have been if not for what our lives were. Had the myriad sons she mourned sprung from the six who gored her? Was her spittle a prophecy? Might all have been otherwise if I had embraced her turnip-head doll? Our lives appear so accidental. Of the cats who tracked us, I have only the slightest clue.

For myself, you know the rest. Though I had no prospect of a formal education, God moves in mysterious ways, favoring me by sending a plague that decimated the city. I once heard a priest call the fever—with its buboes, its shits and its madness—a friend to the poor. Perhaps he was right. The priesthood required replenishment, so despite my lowly origins I was admitted to the cathedral school, with the further aid of my father's friend, a bibulous deacon.

I had to become Christian, of course—no great matter, as I still wore my tiny crucifix. There I befriended your son—may he rest forever in peace—and before taking vows I left to enter your service. I became a husband, a widower and the lifelong disciple of grief. I do write lyrics and little plays, sending them to my sister Kat, yet in the few rude lines I spoke at the age of six, I feel I gave my ultimate gift to the world: a few bursts of laughter in distant climes.

My childhood odyssey opened a chamber in my heart where I go to be lonely, and I carry it with me like the cursed casket of masks. Happiness was never my ambition, though I surely have more than my share of quotidian pleasures. You have been a model of patience when I wallow in melancholy. My grandmother had the right idea— "Just stay alive!"—and I shall dutifully follow her precept as long as I may.

Much ended then. My life as a player. My sightedness. And oddly my fear. Perhaps the Revelation described in sacred text charts the journey from devastation to the ultimate acceptance of loss. Only then can we see a light of renewal. Not that my losses—which neither wall nor hammer nor promise could rebuff—have sharpened my sight, but they dissolve the cataracts of fear. I still feel shivers as I hear the howls of wolves, but I choose to believe they sing.

Should I die in your service, O my gracious Theodoric the Stout, I would ask that my epitaph might be, if priests will permit the vernacular, the words that made me legend: *I need parsnips.*

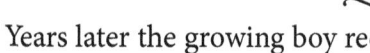

Years later the growing boy recalled the dawn that followed the downfall, debacle, the unmaking of all existence. Over the forty years since that singular day—the birth of his sister, death of his childhood, major weather event—he recalled the dawn. They awoke on a hillside, a quiet over the land except for the newborn's nicker and mewl. Perhaps the workings of great magicians brought them through the night and cleared the valley below. It was barren: no sign of a road, no corpses or chasms or walls. Something ended that left no trace. That was the way of it, his mother would say. Or his grandma. Or all the generations.

"I just need to cry," said Asta. Nursing the baby she cried a while, then blew her nose on her fingers, flicked it off, said, "All right, I'm done with that." The boy saw her sad many times thereafter, but he never saw her cry. She picked a small twig from the ground. His father touched it.

"What's that?"

"Yggdrasill? What's left?"

"Plant it."

She stuck it in the ground where she sat, raked dirt with her fingers to set it firm. Two pairs of green eyes watched from among the rocks, two twitching tails. "Wish we could sit here and watch it grow," said Asta, "The cats must be hereabouts. They'll have something to climb."

—Afterword—

If any fans of historical fiction have ventured to read this, a few explanations are due.

For reference, our setting has been the beginning of the 7th Century, commencing in the Grecian Peloponnese, up the eastern coast of Italy and points north, then south to Constantinople. But as the narrator explains, the circumstances are kept vague, in keeping with the dim knowledge of his six-year-old self. In this muddled era of Late Antiquity, our sense is that few adults could be sure what was happening about them. Vast changes were under way, but no one was watching the TV news. Today, despite our electronic gizmos, we may be equally clueless what's happening about us.

~

We confess to various historical anomalies: those for whom it's important will find them, so we need not point them out, except to confess to shoving a few centuries this way and that. Our excuse is that it's a book of fiction. And we've chosen to avoid the history-speak of many genre novels, though a few archaic terms may have crept in, as our cat slips into the closet at times. We've assumed that our colloquialisms have equivalents in their speech. The ancients didn't say *okay*, but they surely said something that filled the same function. And we felt compelled to write it all in English rather than Greek or Norse.

But one major historical leap-frog requires elucidation. Any Intro to Theatre course will tell you that, with the advent of political Christianity, the theatre died out and was only reinvented in liturgical drama hundreds of years later, with popular theatre growing out of religious pageant plays. Claiming between us a Stanford Ph.D. in theatre history, we're aware that proposing a 7th Century touring troupe flies in the face of textbooks.

Yet ancient theatre consisted not only of the Greek festivals but also a popular tradition, attested, to a degree, in the mimes of Herondas and fragments from the Oxyrhynchus excavations. Did all the comic actors shift to herding goats, or did they keep making bucks by getting laughs? In the genesis of commedia dell'arte, did amateurs performing in annual mystery plays somehow reinvent the art of comedy, or did they draw on centuries of craft?

Our premise, of course, is not to claim proof. It's fiction.

∽

Our characters' journey is heavily based on our family's ten years (and more) of heavy touring throughout the United States. There's a great difference, of course, between traveling via donkey cart or in a Dodge Maxi-van, as well as in our repertory, yet many episodes have roots in our experience. The positive aspects of writing it as fiction were (a) that we didn't have to travel those miles again and (b) that we could imagine stuff we didn't have to perform.

The story draws, in its dream fantasies, on a play we created with Shotgun Players (Berkeley CA) based on Norse myth. We're indebted to some of the actors for elements of characterization. And we've changed the names ("Thor" to "Teorr") as a means of distancing from standard preconceptions.

Bragi is a composite of our son, our daughter, and the six-year-olds we have known and been—and yet even more of the geezers we are—asking again the questions we haven't yet answered in our decades of working together. We wonder who has the answers, or, as in Bragi's memory of the hydra story, if answering one will result in multiple questions sprouting up with needle teeth.

∽

Overall, the story leads to a question: what is the Ragnarok in Norse myth, the Apocalypse in Christian tradition, or whatever we face today? We don't aspire to the sweep of science fiction, so our own view is based on a very personal interpretation of Christian myth: that the catastrophes of Armageddon are like Buddhism's bardos: stages of soul passage in the face of mortality. It's not historical prediction: the world ends neither with a bang nor a whimper. But it ends for each of us, each time we're forced to radical change and each time we give birth, grow, and die.

~

We met and mated as raw undergraduates, and have worked in collaboration for 60 years. After five years of university teaching, we opted for independent theatre work, co-founding Milwaukee's Theatre X and in 1974 The Independent Eye. We both write and act; he directs and designs; she has been composer, accountant, and solver of conundrums.

Our scripts have been staged by over forty professional theatres, as well as in Canada, Israel and South Africa, and we have produced resident seasons in Milwaukee, Chicago, Lancaster PA, and Philadelphia, as well as three radio series for public radio stations across the US. But the heart of our work has been touring, with thousands of performances and every sort of host in 38 states—a way of keeping works evolving in long-term repertory and a means of encountering a vast array of humans.

In recent years, we have turned to fiction. Our short stories have appeared in *The Moth*, *The Storyteller*, *Printers Row Journal*, and other publications. Through our own WordWorkers Press, we have published four novels, two anthologies of our plays, and a memoir. We write a weekly blog at www.DamnedFool.com, and our theatre work is archived at www.IndependentEye.org.

Our expectation is that we'll work till we croak.

Lightning Source UK Ltd.
Milton Keynes UK
UKHW020640010221
378044UK00014B/1547